UNIVERSITY TALES

www.penguin.co.uk

Also by Jack Sheffield

The Teacher Series

Teacher, Teacher!
Mister Teacher
Dear Teacher
Village Teacher
Please Sir!
Educating Jack
School's Out!
Silent Night
Star Teacher
Happiest Days
Starting Over
Changing Times
Back to School
School Days
Last Day of School

Short Story

An Angel Called Harold

UNIVERSITY TALES

1988/89

Jack Sheffield

bantam

TRANSWORLD PUBLISHERS
Penguin Random House, One Embassy Gardens,
8 Viaduct Gardens, London SW11 7BW
www.penguin.co.uk

Transworld is part of the Penguin Random House group of companies
whose addresses can be found at global.penguinrandomhouse.com

First published in Great Britain in 2023 by Bantam
an imprint of Transworld Publishers

A CIP catalogue record for this book
is available from the British Library.

ISBN 9781787635548

Typeset in 11/15pt Zapf Calligraphic 801 BT by Jouve (UK), Milton Keynes.
Printed and bound in Great Britain by Clays Ltd, Elcograf S.p.A.

The authorized representative in the EEA is Penguin Random House Ireland,
Morrison Chambers, 32 Nassau Street, Dublin D02 YH68.

Penguin Random House is committed to a sustainable future
for our business, our readers and our planet. This book is made
from Forest Stewardship Council® certified paper.

For Elisabeth

Contents

Acknowledgements

In the late eighties I moved from my headship into higher education. It gave me the opportunity to teach again and encourage the next generation of teachers. I remember this time in my life well and have recounted it through the eyes of my new hero character, Tom Frith.

It was a wrench to leave behind my *Teacher* series of fifteen novels but refreshing to have this new impetus to my writing. *University Tales* became the new project and for that I have to thank my editor at Penguin Random House, the ever-patient Imogen Nelson. Although we are generations apart, she has definitely tuned in to my sense of humour!

I have been fortunate over the years to have the support of the excellent team at Transworld led by Larry Finlay. Special thanks must go to Viv Thompson who puts up with the fact I am a frustrated copy-editor at heart. Her cheerful and understanding correspondence keeps me grounded and, along with Richenda Todd, she continues to improve my novels.

There is a terrific literary agent out there who usually phones me when he is walking his dog. I refer to Phil Patterson of Marjacq Scripts. It was a partnership that began with a chicken and lettuce sandwich at the Winchester Writers' Conference in 2006. Bribery was never this cheap! In return he promised to read my first novel, *Teacher, Teacher*, and we've never looked back since. If you're interested in Airfix Modelling Kits circa 1980 he's the man for you.

My main supporter is, of course, my wife, Elisabeth. Her patience is remarkable. The discussions we have about developing plots while enjoying her latest culinary creation are always eventful. Writing novels is a way of life for me now. With the support I have around me, may it long continue.

There are a host of wonderful booksellers and events managers out there. Particular thanks must go to Nikki at Waterstones Milton Keynes, Laura at Waterstones York, Kirsty at Waterstones Alton and Sam at Waterstones Basingstoke.

Finally, if you've borrowed this book from your local library, keep in mind they are the cornerstone of a cultured society. The eight-year-old Jack who visited Compton Road Library in Leeds began a journey that is now well travelled.

Prologue

'Welcome back, Dr Frith.' The plump, balding man behind the reception counter looked up at the tall, broad-shouldered lecturer and grinned. The badge on the lapel of his blue blazer read: 'Peter Perkins. Head Porter. University of Eboracum'. 'So . . . you got the job.'

Tom Frith put down his leather satchel and smiled. 'Hello again. Yes, it all happened quickly in the end. After my interview with Professor Oakenshott I moved on from my deputy headship to take up this post. It's a one-year temporary lectureship in the Faculty of Education.'

The porter nodded knowingly. 'That's because Dr Pierpont retired. You'll be taking over from him. Just what we need. Bit of young blood to liven up the place.' He turned and selected a key from the line of hooks behind him. 'You've got Room Seven. Sharing with Mr Llewellyn. Go through the quad to the door labelled "Cloisters". Then upstairs and you can't miss it. Here's your key.'

'Many thanks and, please, call me Tom.'

'Thanks, Tom.' They shook hands. 'I just answer to Perkins,' he added simply.

Tom slipped the key into his pocket. 'Thanks, Perkins.'

The friendly porter watched him walk away. After thirty years he had seen it all. The eager newcomer in the baggy oatmeal cord suit looked so young. *Good luck,* he thought. *Poor sod, you'll need it.*

Tom walked through an imposing Victorian archway and down a flight of Yorkshire stone steps. Then he stopped and looked in awe at the sight before him. Lit up in the early-morning sunshine was an ancient, enclosed quadrangle frozen in time. Its centrepiece was a beautifully manicured lawn bordered by a path of worn cobblestones. Around him on all sides were high walls of weathered brick studded with sash windows and topped with a steep roof of grey slate tiles. This was the site of the original college, now over 150 years old. On the far side of the quadrangle another much larger archway led to the buildings of the twentieth century: lecture halls of glass and steel alongside tall pebble-dashed blocks for student accommodation.

However, on this early-autumn morning in the city of York the university campus was quiet. The arrival of the students was still a week away and the world of academia was silent. It was Monday, 5 September 1988, and for Tom Frith, a thirty-two-year-old bachelor, an eventful year of dreams and disasters stretched out before him.

Chapter One

Blue-Sky Thinking

Tom opened the door marked 'Cloisters' just as a tall, slim woman came out. She had long blonde hair, blue eyes, and wore a yellow summer dress with a halter neck and canvas flats on her feet. 'Hello, can I help?' she asked with a smile.

'I'm looking for Room Seven.'

She looked at Tom with interest. 'You must be the new tutor.'

'Yes. Pleased to meet you. I'm Tom.'

They shook hands. 'Inger,' she said.

'Inger?'

'Inger Larson.' She smiled. 'Norwegian parents.'

'Ah . . . lovely name,' said Tom a little lamely. 'Are you in the Education Faculty?'

'Yes, I teach Music. What about you?'

'English and Primary Education. It's a one-year secondment.'

For a moment Inger studied this handsome newcomer with his long wavy brown hair, craggy features and slightly dishevelled appearance. 'I guess you're here for the faculty meeting.'

'Yes, I was told ten o'clock.'

'Well . . . I'll probably see you there.' She glanced at her wristwatch. 'I'm meeting a colleague so must fly.' She pointed to a wrought-iron staircase. 'Top of the stairs, then down the corridor to the end. You'll be sharing with Owen. If I see him I'll say you're here.'

'Thanks,' said Tom. 'Pleased to have met you.'

'Likewise,' she said.

He watched her stride confidently across the quad, sunburned and glowing with health. With the image of this attractive and dynamic woman on his mind, he climbed the stairs.

On the door of Room 7 a cardboard label had been inserted into a metal slot. It read 'O. Llewellyn'.

Tom knocked and waited for a reply. There was none so he walked in and looked around. It was a cosy yet functional study. In the centre of the room was a circular wooden coffee table surrounded by four threadbare armchairs and, in front of the dormer window, two wooden desks butted up against each other. There were two bookcases: one was empty and the other was filled with ring binders, assorted books and an old leather rugby ball. On the mantelpiece above a cast-iron fireplace stood a single photograph in a glass frame. Tom peered closely. It was a rugby team of fierce-looking men. The words 'Clwb Rygbi Y Tymbl' had been added in black pen across the grey sky.

'You must be Tom,' said a voice with a lilting Welsh accent. 'I'm Owen.' A stocky thirty-something with a mass of curly black hair and an unshaven face, dressed casually in jeans and a T-shirt, stood in the doorway. 'Inger said you had come up.' He nodded towards the photograph. 'My old rugby team,' he said with pride. 'The village of Tumble in Carmarthenshire.'

'Tumble?' queried Tom.

'Near Llanelli in South Wales.'

They shook hands. Owen had a grip like a vice. At five feet eight he was six inches shorter than Tom but he looked superbly fit.

'Pleased to meet you, Owen,' said Tom. 'What brought you here?'

'My wife, Sue – a Yorkshirewoman from Skipton. She's a PE teacher like me.' He looked Tom up and down. 'So . . . what's your story?'

'I was a primary school deputy head in Harrogate. I spotted a one-year lectureship advertised for English and Primary Education, and it was something I'd always wanted to do. I thought I'd give it a try.'

Owen nodded. 'Well, best of luck. As you can see, we're sharing, so make yourself at home. You've got a desk, a bookcase and a couple of drawers in the filing cabinet. If you need anything just ask.'

Tom began to empty his satchel and placed on the bookcase copies of *Candida* by George Bernard Shaw, the *Complete Works of Shakespeare, Poets of the First World War* and a huge tome entitled *Twentieth-Century American Literature.* They looked lonely but it was a start. Then he put his satchel on the empty desk and stared out of the latticed windows. Below him, the quadrangle was no longer empty. Two figures had appeared. 'There's the guy who interviewed me,' said Tom.

Professor Henry Oakenshott, a white-haired man with stooped shoulders, was hurrying after a short, stout woman with a severe black fringe and the scowling demeanour of a preoccupied Rottweiler.

Owen joined Tom at the window and gave a wry smile. 'That's *the* Wallop,' he muttered ominously. The definite article added emphasis in the same way as *the* Tower of London or *the* Brandenburg Gate. This was clearly a formidable woman. 'Or, to be more precise,' added Owen, 'Edna Wallop, the Deputy Head of Faculty. Poor Henry doesn't get a word in.'

Tom frowned. 'Guess I'll be meeting her soon.'

'Yes,' said Owen, 'at the faculty meeting, but we can grab a coffee before then. Come on, let's go down to the common room.' He opened the door and pointed to the label. 'Add your name here, Tom.' He grinned. 'Shows you belong.'

Tom took out a Berol marker from his pocket and wrote 'T. Frith' under Owen's name. It wasn't the right moment to prefix it with 'Dr'.

On the other side of the quad was the staff common room, a large space with a woodblock floor, high ceiling and arched leaded windows. Behind a long counter two ladies were serving tea, coffee and fruit juice, and Tom and Owen went over to join the queue.

Tom looked around at the sudden flurry of activity as members of the faculty appeared from all sides. Many were in groups catching up on holiday news while others were checking the wooden pigeonholes for their mail. Seating had been lined up in the centre of the room in a rough semicircle and facing a desk behind which three chairs had been arranged.

He and Owen lined up behind a pencil-thin woman in a leotard and a baggy cardigan. She had spiky red hair and was standing in a haze of cigarette smoke.

'Hi, Zeb,' said Owen. 'How was your summer?'

She took the cigarette from her lips and flashed an engaging smile. 'Brilliant. Went to Ibiza. Met an Italian guy. He taught me how to snorkel.'

'And what did you teach him?' asked Owen.

She gave him a dig in the ribs. 'Cheeky bugger. Anyway, who's your friend?'

'This is Tom. He's here for a year's secondment in Primary Education and English Literature.'

She stood back as if judging livestock. 'I approve,' she said with a wicked smile. 'Hi, Tom.'

They shook hands. 'What do you lecture in?' he asked.

'Dance and Drama. Call in some time. Tall, hunky men are always welcome. We do all kinds of creative stuff.'

Owen rolled his eyes and tugged Tom's sleeve. 'Come on. The meeting will be starting soon.'

They collected mugs of coffee, a couple of custard creams and found two seats at the end of the second row.

'So that's Zeb,' said Tom with a smile.

'Yes,' said Owen. 'Elizabeth Peacock, prefers Zeb.'

'Quite a character,' said Tom.

'Definitely. Brilliant teacher. Smokes like a chimney. Something of a man-eater. Spreads it around, you might say.'

Tom raised his eyebrows and said nothing.

Owen sat back and sipped his coffee while Tom looked around at his new colleagues and counted them. There were thirty-six. All of them were subject specialists, but also involved in teacher training. He spotted Inger Larson drinking orange juice and deep in conversation with a skeletally thin man on the back row. He wore blue jeans, a black waistcoat over a crisp white shirt and a colourful bow tie. His long grey hair had been tied back in a ponytail.

Yet another distinctive character, thought Tom.

Suddenly the hubbub of conversation died: Edna Wallop had entered. She was followed by an ashen-faced Henry Oakenshott and a skinny young man who looked like an extra from *Miami Vice*. His sky-blue linen suit had huge padded shoulders and he carried a mobile phone the size of a house brick.

'Yuppy,' murmured Owen quietly.

Edna put a folder on the table, surveyed the faces in front of her and walked over to Tom. Above the heavy jowls and behind her black-framed spectacles were a pair of piercing grey eyes. 'Frith, isn't it?' she said. 'The new temp.'

Tom stood up. 'Yes, pleased to meet you.'

She didn't offer to shake hands. 'I'm Dr Wallop. Henry told me he had roped you in for a year.'

'That's right. He mentioned helping out with placements for teaching practice.'

She frowned and nodded towards the tall, angular man sitting next to Inger. 'You'll need to speak to Victor about that.'

'Victor?'

'Victor Grammaticus, our ponytailed professor.' It was said with more than a hint of disdain. She sighed deeply. 'Anyway, we'll talk later.'

She walked back to the table, surveyed the sea of faces and waited for absolute silence. 'Good morning,' she said, 'and welcome back. I'll be meeting with all the team leaders during the week but this morning we need to progress the new timetable. It's part of our rebranding process to ensure we stay ahead of our competitors.' There were muffled groans from the back row.

Undeterred, Edna continued, 'I should like to introduce Mr Gary Duff of Duff Solutions in Leeds. Mr Duff is the CEO of a dynamic IT company that has made significant strides in recent years.' Edna surveyed the nonplussed faces before her and moved on quickly. 'You will recall filling in a timetable questionnaire at the end of last term and this data has been transferred to Mr Duff's unique IT program, Omnino Perfectus.'

In the back row Victor Grammaticus smiled and whispered to Inger, '*Omnino perfectus* . . . absolutely perfect.'

Edna paused and frowned at the man she had described as *our ponytailed professor*. 'This will revolutionize those laborious hours spent by Victor,' she added pointedly.

Owen nudged Tom. 'Professor Victor Grammaticus,' he whispered. 'Great guy. Teaches mathematics.'

There were a few forlorn glances towards the huge noticeboard at the back of the room. The previous term's timetable was still there, neat, precise and colour-coded on large sheets of squared paper. Tom guessed it must have been a labour of love for Victor. This was followed by a few discontented grumbles and a shaking of heads. Edna seemed to pick up the mood and pushed on with the demeanour of a recalcitrant wrecking ball, moving smoothly into business-speak.

'So, people, it's time to start thinking outside the box and take things to the next level. I'm pushing the envelope here, colleagues.'

Owen shook his head in despair. 'Here we go again,' he whispered. 'She hasn't been the same since she went on an American management course.'

Edna was now on a roll. 'With this in mind we're buying in efficiency-enhancing software to rationalize our teaching timetable.' She looked at the spotty-faced IT wizard with the slicked-back hair. 'So it gives me great pleasure to welcome Mr Duff. He's a top man in IT whose work is in accordance with our blue-sky thinking.'

Blue-sky thinking, thought Tom. *Interesting*.

She sat down and all eyes turned to the strange young man with the confident smile who stood up and waved as if he had just won an Oscar.

'Hi, everybody. I'll keep this short. I'm Gary but I answer to Gazza.' He paused for effect while his audience looked bemused. 'Dr Wallop here was looking for a package of solutions so we synergized together.'

A few sniggers rose from the back row.

'Duff Solutions is at the cutting edge of technology and, while your timetable is complex, we rationalized it effectively using my adaptation of the COBOL programming language.' He held up a sheaf of paper. 'I have here individual timetables for faculty members so please collect yours before leaving.' He fanned them out on the table. 'It may be 1988 but this is twenty-first-century innovation. So take a breath, people, it's time to eat a reality sandwich.'

He sat down quickly and his padded shoulders followed close behind.

There was a stunned silence while Edna stood up. 'Thank you, Mr Duff.' She scanned the room, again apparently sensing the apathy.

Victor Grammaticus had raised his hand.

'Yes?' said Edna curtly.

'You mentioned this computer program had been *bought in*,' asked Victor in measured tones. 'How much is it costing?'

'As one would expect, the going rate for this level of technical support,' said Edna. 'It's comfortably within our budget,' she added with a hint of menace. 'Fortunately, Mr Duff has bought into our philosophy and his work empowers us all to demonstrate our corporate values.'

It was clear to Edna that the audience was becoming restless and it was time to close the meeting. 'Anyway, we'll touch base later and, when the new term begins, we'll hit the ground running.' With that she hurried away, leaving Gazza at the table. Henry Oakenshott followed her, looking as though a little more life had been squeezed out of him.

Owen and Tom collected their spreadsheets emblazoned with the Duff Solutions logo and sat down to study them. The first line of Tom's timetable read: 'Monday 9.00–10.00 a.m. Primary One. Main Hall.'

Owen looked from his sheet to Tom's. 'This can't be right. I'm in the gymnasium at the same time as you.'

Tom was confused. 'Gymnasium?'

'Yes, the main hall is our biggest space. It's our gymnasium. I use it for PE.' A thought struck him. 'It's also the dance studio. Let's check with Zeb.'

They found her on a bench in the quad. She had just

opened a new packet of twenty John Player Superkings, distinctive cigarettes that were ten centimetres long.

'Hey, Zeb,' said Owen. 'Have you checked your timetable?'

'Yes, it's fine.' She lit up her cigarette.

Owen looked thoughtful. 'When you filled in the timetable questionnaire did you call the main hall a dance studio?'

'Yes, of course. I've always called it that.'

'It's just that I called it the gymnasium.'

'I know that,' said Zeb, 'and the Primary tutors call it the main hall. So what?'

'Compare your timetable with mine.'

Moments later the penny dropped. 'This guy has made a balls-up,' said Owen. 'Because he doesn't know the building he's assumed your studio and my gymnasium are different rooms.'

'Bloody hell!' said Zeb. 'There'll be chaos when the students turn up if it's not sorted. Let's collar the little tosser now.'

Back in the common room, Gazza was sitting behind the table looking relaxed. Life had been good to him. After completing a BA in Mathematics at Essex University he had gone to work for the tailor Hepworths in Leeds. When the early days of new technology hit the high street, the manager had sent him on a two-week course to learn the computer programming language COBOL.

A year later, after inheriting a substantial sum following the death of his father, he'd formed his own company. It was when he had encouraged a local garage owner to computerize his accounts that Gazza realized the world lay at his feet. After sending a postcard to local businesses and colleges he was delighted to receive an immediate response from Dr Edna Wallop of Eboracum University. They had hit it off immediately. They also spoke the same language. Both were disciples of *blue-sky thinking*.

Tom and Owen followed a determined Zeb back into the common room. Owen tugged Tom's sleeve. 'This should be fun,' he said.

Zeb didn't take prisoners. 'Gazza, there's a problem,' she said and tossed the copy of her timetable on to the table.

Gary Duff looked up in alarm. 'Pardon?'

'The main hall is triple booked on Monday morning.'

The first flicker of concern appeared on Gary's face. 'Impossible,' he said. 'My program is foolproof.'

Zeb turned to Tom and Owen. 'Give me your timetables, guys.' She spread them out. 'Gazza . . . Look at the first session on Monday.'

Gary wasn't used to being told what to do. After all, he was the CEO of Duff Solutions, and his staff – namely Nigel, a teenager with severe acne – never questioned his authority.

'So . . . what's your problem?' he asked with as much disdain as he could muster.

Owen leaned forward. 'I think it's *your* problem, boyo.'

Gary looked up nervously at the fierce Welshman. 'I used the data given to me by Dr Wallop. So what could go wrong?'

Zeb leaned over the table and tapped the lists with a red-varnished fingernail. 'COBOL is fine if you use it correctly.

You've obviously made a fundamental error by not using a precise drop-down list in the original questionnaire . . . hence the chaotic outcome. The only blue-sky thinking going on at the moment is your suit!'

Realization dawned on the face of the would-be entrepreneur. His world of Common Business-Oriented Language had crumbled around him and he picked up his mobile phone and stumbled away to report to Edna Wallop. It was a meeting that could be heard across the quadrangle and minutes later Duff Solutions went into voluntary liquidation. By lunchtime Edna had gone cap in hand to Victor and asked him to do the new term's timetable and Tom had begun to appreciate the fractured politics of his new academic world.

On Thursday, Tom was packing his satchel to go home when there was a knock on the door and Henry Oakenshott appeared. 'Excuse me for barging in, Thomas, but I wanted to know how you were settling in.'

'Oh, hello,' said Tom, surprised. 'Do sit down.'

'Thank you but it's only a brief visit.'

He was breathing heavily and Tom presumed the climb up the stairs had been demanding. Tom stood up.

Henry was holding a book in his hand and he put it on Tom's desk. 'I always give a small gift to our newcomers and Tolkien is a wonderful read.' It was a copy of *The Fellowship of the Ring*.

'That's very thoughtful,' said Tom. 'I love books and I shall certainly enjoy this one. Thank you so much. It's a really kind gesture and very much appreciated.'

Henry gave a gentle smile. 'That's good,' he said, 'and

I'm pleased you've made a good start.' He turned to leave, but stopped in the doorway and looked back. 'I remember my first week,' he said quietly. 'It was a time I shall never forget. A new world stretched out in front of me. I do hope you enjoy your time here at Eboracum.'

He closed the door after him, leaving Tom to reflect on his gift and his kindness.

It was Friday afternoon before the revised timetable was complete and Tom stood back to admire the veritable kaleidoscope of coloured squares, each one directing a group of students to the correct room at the right time. The task had been laborious but satisfying.

Owen, Tom, Zeb and Inger had volunteered to help Victor with the mammoth cross-referencing. As Victor had said at the outset, 'If it's not done properly the students will suffer and this is *their* time. We have to give them the best experience we can offer.' Victor reported to Edna that it had been completed but received no thanks.

'I think we ought to celebrate,' said Victor. So they followed him through the streets of York to the Black Swan, a wattle-and-daub pub that had been a popular meeting place since the fifteenth century. Victor ordered three pints of Theakston's Best Bitter, a gin and tonic and an orange juice and they took their drinks to a table in the far corner of the beer garden. The sun was shining and the sky was as blue as a starling's egg.

'Well done, everybody,' said Victor. He raised his glass and pointed to the heavens. 'This is my kind of *blue-sky thinking*.'

Everyone laughed and Tom thought how good it was to relax.

Victor leaned over to him, casting a kindly eye on the newcomer. 'Busy first week for you, Tom. I really appreciated your help.'

'I enjoyed it,' said Tom. 'Learned a lot and I can plan my lectures with a bit more confidence.'

'Don't be disheartened by the episode with Edna. We're used to it now.'

'Yes, I was concerned. In fact, she said she would have a word with me but it's not happened.'

Victor nodded sagely. 'That's not unusual. You need to understand that over time Edna has become the *de facto* leader and now her word is law.'

'How did it get to this?'

'Henry is a lovely man but a bit of a fossil; he's still living in the 1950s. I've been here for twenty years. He was a fine Head of Faculty until Edna arrived. Things went downhill after that.'

'That's sad.'

'In Edna's case the title Deputy Head of Faculty is merely an oxymoron. She has none of the qualities of leadership. She is the Deputy Head of *words*, not of *lectureship*.' He sighed, supped deeply on his beer and shook his head. 'Her failure to motivate this team is a great sadness.' He nodded towards Owen, Zeb and Inger, who were engrossed in relaxed conversation. 'There are talented individuals here but their skills are being wasted. Such is her legacy.'

'I was puzzled by her language in the meeting,' said Tom. 'All this stuff about *rebranding* and *pushing the envelope*.'

Victor smiled. 'Edna revels in overblown rhetoric but her words were more hyperbolic than usual. She takes hubris a little too far, I think. Her excessive self-confidence will one day be her downfall. If it was a Greek tragedy it would lead to her nemesis. You can only defy the gods for so long.'

Tom relaxed as the conversation ebbed and flowed. Zeb was waxing lyrical about the Liberal Democrats. Back in March the Social Democratic Party and the Liberals had formed a new party. 'It's the future,' she declared. 'At last a moderate middle ground instead of the Toffs versus the Socialists.'

'Waste of time,' said Owen, a staunch Labour voter.

'Now, now,' said Inger. 'Our conversations about politics always end in arguments.'

'I agree,' said Victor. 'In the meantime, we can celebrate doing our bit for the new intake of students.'

'Freshers' Week should be interesting,' said Zeb. 'The students are all into acid tents, rave music and Ecstasy.'

'Not for me,' said Owen.

'Nor me,' added Inger.

'Different world to my primary school,' said Tom.

Zeb puffed on her cigarette and leaned forward. 'Guys. Look around you. It's 1967 all over again . . . the Second Summer of Love.' She stood up. 'Come on, Inger, our round.'

Owen saw Tom watching Inger as she walked away. 'If you're wondering,' he said with a mischievous smile, 'she's thirty and single.'

'Really?' said Tom, intrigued.

Owen spoke quietly: 'Interesting background. Father was a Norwegian economist. Mother an Olympic skier back in the fifties.'

Later on, Zeb moved to sit next to Tom. 'Hope it goes well

for you next week, Tom. I saw on the noticeboard you're First-Year Tutor.'

'Yes, Henry said I needed to take over the role from Dr Pierpont.'

'It's straightforward enough,' said Zeb. 'They come to you if they have a problem. Usually just a few eighteen-year-olds missing the comforts of home. Nothing too demanding.'

At six o'clock they left the pub and walked back towards the university car park. Zeb set off to walk to her flat in the city centre and Owen climbed on to his bicycle to ride to his house on the Hull Road. Victor unlocked his Rover 200 and drove off to the home he shared with his partner in Easingwold. Tom stopped next to his 1980 hatchback Ford Escort. It was parked alongside Inger's bright red Mini.

'So where do you live, Tom?' she asked.

'In Haxby. I'm renting a cottage. How about you?'

'I rent as well. My flat is on the Knavesmire opposite the racecourse. Ground floor, thankfully.' She gave a whimsical smile. 'I have a baby grand piano. It would have been tough to carry it up a flight of stairs.'

Tom watched her drive away. It occurred to him that he had missed out on the *summer of love* but, as he set off for home himself, past the chocolate factory, he could not help wondering what the autumn might bring. He also reflected on his first week. The faculty meeting had been a strange experience and the misguided Gazza had received his just desserts. Latin had been one of Tom's A Levels and, like Victor, he had known that *Omnino Perfectus* meant *absolutely perfect*. Well, not in Gazza's case.

Then he thought of Inger Larson. On his car radio, Phil Collins was singing 'Groovy Kind Of Love' and he smiled and hummed along.

Meanwhile, Inger was intrigued by the arrival of Tom. There was something engaging about him. The fact he appeared to be an innocent in the complex world of higher education made him even more appealing. But when she parked outside her apartment she sighed deeply. She carried a secret that could never be revealed.

Chapter Two

Innocence and Experience

It was 9.00 a.m. on Friday, 23 September, and Tom had survived his first week of teaching. The timetable had gone to plan and his lectures had been well received. However, although it had been a successful beginning, a day of contrasts was in store . . . in more ways than one.

'Good morning, everybody,' he said and scanned the faces before him. He was meeting his Primary One group again. There were fifteen students and he felt he had already begun to get to know them well. It was a mixed bunch. There were five men and ten women. All were fresh from sixth form apart from three women in their mid to late twenties, labelled so-called 'mature students'. One of them, Ellie MacBride, was also a Main English student and a member of his first-year English group.

The session was entitled 'Classroom Organization' and Tom was well prepared. He had set up a carousel slide projector showing children's activities from his primary school. There were images of strategies to support mixed-ability teaching and practical approaches to classroom management. Twelve of the students were soon busy making notes and there was a lively exchange of questions and answers. Tom was concerned to note three young men in the back row who looked as though they were about to fall asleep. On Monday Amir Surami, Dan Milburn and Brian Stocks had been full of energy. Today they looked like death warmed up.

A bell rang at ten o'clock. 'Thanks, everybody,' said Tom. 'Have a good weekend and I'll see you at nine on Monday when we'll be discussing your first school placements.' The students filed out of the room with the three forlorn men bringing up the rear.

'Amir, Dan, Brian,' said Tom. 'Hang on a minute.' They paused, dropped their duffel bags and leaned against the wall. It looked like an identity parade. 'How are things?' As First-Year Tutor the welfare of students was part of his remit. To date no one had knocked on his door.

Amir was from Leeds, Dan's home was in Newcastle and Brian was from West Sussex. It was a union of north and south.

Dan and Brian looked towards Amir, who appeared to be the leader.

'Bit mixed,' muttered Amir.

'When's your next session?' asked Tom.

'Eleven,' said Amir. 'History with Dr Peters.'

Tom made a quick decision. Their main subject was History. 'In that case, call round to my study after coffee and before you go to your lecture. I'll see you just after ten thirty.'

They all nodded as if life had lost its meaning and trooped out.

*

In the common room Tom collected a mug of coffee and an unexpected slice of flapjack and went to sit next to Owen, who had spent twenty pence on a *Daily Mirror*. He was scanning the headline 'Fergie's Hideaway Down Under'. Apparently, Sarah Ferguson, the Duchess of York, had decided to visit her sister, Jane Makim, in the Australian outback in Wilga Warrina rather than return home to baby Princess Beatrice.

'Royalty!' muttered Owen. 'I'd get rid of the lot of them.' He flicked through the pages shaking his head. Under another headline, 'Judge Kicks Out His AIDS Son', a magistrate revealed he had already handed out twenty thousand pounds to his son who had caught AIDS from a dirty drug needle.

'Difficult times,' said Owen. 'This AIDS business seems to be gathering momentum.' However, his demeanour improved when he read that Neil Kinnock had been re-elected as leader of the Labour Party. He folded up his paper, slipped it into his sports bag and supped the last of his coffee. 'So, almost there, Tom. Your first week teaching. How's it gone?'

'Fine, although I've finally got some first-year customers coming to see me with a problem.'

'Probably just homesick,' said the unsympathetic Welshman.

'Maybe,' said Tom as he wondered if it was safe to break his teeth on the rock-hard flapjack.

'Take it easy with that,' said Owen. 'I think Wimpey use it to build their foundations.'

Tom looked cautiously at the dense chunk of rolled oats.

'Mavis behind the counter brings it out occasionally. I've

heard her husband eats it but the poor guy won't have a choice.' The tough Welshman looked at her in awe. 'I wouldn't take her on at arm wrestling.'

Tom studied the imposing figure of Mavis Shuttlebottom and the effortless ease with which she lifted the giant teapot. She had the physique of a Bulgarian weightlifter. For a moment Tom saw her glance in his direction and he lifted the flapjack into the air with a cheery smile and pretended to take a bite. Mavis responded with a muscular wave and a thumbs up.

Owen got up to leave. 'By the way, Sue and I are going to the pub for a bite to eat straight after work. It would be good to meet up. Why not join us?'

'Thanks. I've no plans. Where are you going?'

'The Keystones at Monk Bar. Chicken in a basket and a pint.'

'Sounds good. I'll see you there.'

On his way out Tom discreetly dropped the flapjack in a bin and headed across the quad to the Cloisters door.

At 10.25 a.m. he arrived at his study and was surprised to see Amir, Dan and Brian standing in the corridor. 'You're prompt,' he said with an encouraging smile. 'That was a quick coffee break.'

'We didn't have a coffee,' said Amir sadly.

Puzzled, Tom ushered them in and gestured to the chairs. 'Well, there's time for one now.' He filled the kettle, switched it on, selected three reasonably clean mugs from the cupboard and spooned in some Nescafé. He was aware of sudden interest from the students.

As he waited for the kettle to boil Tom sat down and

faced the listless threesome. 'So, there's clearly a problem. Tell me what it is and I'll do my best to help.'

Again Dan and Brian, still behaving like nervous teenagers, looked to Amir for leadership. 'Well . . . it's *porridge*,' he said with gravitas.

The kettle boiled and Tom jumped up while he processed this unexpected declaration. As he poured the boiling water into the mugs he asked, 'Did you say *porridge*?'

'Yes,' they responded in unison.

Tom put the mugs on a small wooden tray, added a couple of teaspoons along with a bag of sugar and a bottle of milk from the fridge.

The three young men fell on the coffee as if it had just been discovered.

As they began to slurp it down Tom asked quietly, 'I thought you said *porridge*.'

Amir put down his mug. 'Yes. You see, that's all we've got . . . or rather *had*. We ran out last night.'

'Are we still talking about porridge?' asked Tom.

There were fevered nods.

'That's all we've had to eat,' said Amir.

Dan chipped in: 'We haven't got any money.'

'I daren't ring my mother,' muttered Brian.

'What about your grant?' asked Tom.

'It's not turned up,' said Amir. 'We're broke and there's no porridge left.'

'I've nothing in the bank,' said Brian.

'And I'm desperate,' said Dan.

There was a packet of chocolate digestives in the cupboard. Tom ripped open the packet, scattered the biscuits on a plate and set it down on the coffee table. 'Help yourselves,' he said.

The three young men did not need asking twice and began to devour the unexpected feast.

Tom glanced at his watch. 'You need to get off to your History lecture. Take a few biscuits for later.'

They gathered them up, undeterred by the prospect of melting chocolate in their pockets.

'What lectures have you got this afternoon?' asked Tom.

'Only History of Education at three with Professor Oakenshott,' said Amir.

'Fine,' said Tom. 'Come back here immediately after this morning's lecture and we'll decide what to do next.'

In the bursar's office, Frank Bottomley, a rotund, cheerful man in a creased three-piece suit, was sitting behind his desk. 'Ah . . . it's young Dr Frith,' he said with a smile. 'How are you getting on?'

'Fine, thanks. Sorry to trouble you but I have three starving students with a problem. Their grants haven't turned up.'

'Oh dear,' Frank said with a careless wave of the hand. 'It happens from time to time. I've already had half a dozen knocking on my door. Some of these local authorities are a bit lethargic. So . . . who are we talking about?'

Tom scribbled down the three names. 'All Year One students in my Primary Education group.'

The bursar gave a beatific smile. 'No problem, Tom. We have a contingency fund for this sort of thing. I can arrange for an immediate interim payment of fifty pounds per student, which should tide them over. Tell them to call in this afternoon.'

'Excellent,' said Tom. 'Many thanks. They will be so grateful. They've been living on porridge for the past week.'

'I love porridge,' Frank said and patted his tummy. 'Particularly with a spoonful of golden syrup. Perfect on a cold morning. I was brought up on it.'

With a vivid image of the bursar's perfect winter warmer in his mind, Tom set off for his next lecture with his first-year English group: he would be proffering an insight into the classic poetry of William Blake's *Songs of Innocence and of Experience*. He walked through the quad and towards the archway that led to the English Faculty's lecture rooms in the south block. Suddenly Edna Wallop appeared by his side.

'So, you've almost survived your first week, I see,' she said abruptly.

'Yes, thanks. I've enjoyed it.'

She feigned surprise. 'Really? I've found life in this faculty too demanding for actual *enjoyment*.'

'The timetable is working well,' said Tom guardedly.

Edna muttered something under her breath and then gave him a stare. 'It's not rocket science.'

It certainly was to Gazza, thought Tom. He was beginning to dislike this bombastic woman who appeared to constantly demean the efforts of others. 'I thought you would be pleased,' he added pointedly.

Edna was seemingly well drilled in dealing with young upstarts and the enthusiastic Dr Frith clearly fell into this category. She gave him another hard stare. 'Let's be clear,' she said. 'According to Henry, you *appear* to have core competence.'

Tom did not appreciate the word *appear*. He had worked hard for his academic achievements. Born in Grassington in the Yorkshire Dales, he'd left God's Own Country at the age of four when he moved to Kesgrave village on the eastern edge of Ipswich. His father had secured a post office job there. Tom had spent his early years at Woodbridge School and gone on to achieve A Levels in History, Latin and Maths. He had always wanted to teach and attended the teacher-training college in York before moving on to Leeds University and securing his PhD in the School of Education. It had been a long hard slog but a journey well travelled: teaching the eager children in his Harrogate primary school had been the perfect reward.

'I intend to give this appointment my best, Dr Wallop,' said Tom firmly.

Edna was clearly used to having the last word. 'Do bear in mind that from the get-go the university demands one hundred and ten per cent.'

As she strutted away Tom reflected that, while her charisma bypass had proved successful, her grasp of percentages left much to be desired.

William Blake was one of Tom's favourite poets and soon the eighteen students in English One were furiously making notes prior to their first assignment.

Finally, in a lively question-and-answer session, Ellie MacBride raised her hand. 'Tom, what did you mean when you said that *Songs of Innocence and of Experience* were intended by Blake to show the two contrary states of the human soul?'

Tom had already realized this slim twenty-seven-year-old

with the long black hair and South Yorkshire accent was a bright woman and eager to learn. He considered his response. 'Good question, Ellie. According to Blake, these states co-exist. They're necessary to human existence, as can be seen in the poems that contrast the lamb and the tiger. So, for example, innocence is about fertility and joy.'

Ellie nodded knowingly. 'And *experience* is about being selfish and cold-hearted.' She said it with feeling.

'Exactly,' said Tom, and Ellie gave a sad smile.

The bell in the corridor rang. 'OK, well done, everybody. I'll see you when you hand in your assignments. Have a good weekend.' And they all ambled away.

Tom and the three hungry students set off for a welcome lunch shortly after midday. As they walked out of the university a watery sunlight filtered through the wind-torn clouds and cast a tapestry of flickering shadows on the medieval streets of York. Soon the west towers of the Minster came into view. Here was the jewel in Yorkshire's crown and Tom hoped these young men would grow to appreciate this magnificent building, the largest medieval cathedral in Britain.

As they walked up Petergate he did not notice the parliament of rooks above their heads that stared down at them with beady eyes. Their relentless gaze was a harbinger of uncertain times ahead but Tom remained blissfully unaware. All that was on his mind at that moment was quelling the hunger pains of these downtrodden students.

In the cafe, Tom ordered the traditional Yorkshire fish, chips and mushy peas plus a huge pot of tea and generously thick slices of bread and butter . . . A Friday feast for the impecunious trio.

Thirty minutes later, appetites satisfied, they set off back to university for their meeting with the bursar and Tom was left feeling the inner glow of the Good Samaritan.

Climbing the stairs to his study Tom met Inger on her way down. He pressed back against the wall to let her past. A hint of Dior perfume hung in the air and for a moment her long blonde hair caressed his shoulder. They were standing on the same step. She was wearing tight blue jeans, a white collarless blouse and a baggy green cord jacket.

'Hi, Tom, how's the first week teaching gone?'

'OK, I think.' He felt a little tongue-tied standing so close to this beautiful woman. 'What about you?'

'We've begun work towards our first concert of the year.'

'Sounds good,' said Tom.

'It's on the eighteenth of next month in the music room. I've got some great singers. You should come.'

'I'd love to. Do you need any help?'

She smiled. 'Can you sing?'

He paused before replying. He didn't think his rendition of 'Blowin' In The Wind' on his guitar qualified. 'I was thinking more of behind the scenes.'

'That's kind. Yes, any support would be gratefully received.'

It seemed their brief conversation was at an end but Tom wanted it to last a little longer. 'Just a thought . . . I'm meeting Owen and his wife for a drink and a pub meal on my way home. Would you like to join us?'

There was a moment's hesitation. 'Sorry. I have another commitment.'

'Fine,' he murmured. 'Another time maybe.'

'Have a good weekend,' she said and skipped down the stairs.

He watched her open the door to the quad and stride past the flower border. Slanting rays of autumnal sunshine lit up the chrysanthemums, bronze, amber and scarlet. It was an uplifting sight but he couldn't banish a touch of sadness as Inger walked away.

When Tom headed towards Monk Bar, one of the four great gateways of York, he spotted two racing bicycles chained together outside the Keystones pub. Owen and his wife were already there. Sue, an athletic, diminutive thirty-year-old in a figure-hugging tracksuit, jumped up when he walked in.

'Hi, Tom. Pleased to meet you. Owen said you're a great study partner. Hope you will feel the same way about him as the term progresses.'

'Good to meet you, Sue.' They shook hands. 'Actually, he's been really helpful. I can now recite the Welsh rugby team by heart. So . . . what are you having?'

'Thanks. Pint for me,' said Owen, 'and a lime and lemonade for the 1980 Yorkshire Women's Sprint Champion.'

'Impressive,' said Tom.

Owen lowered his voice and gave Sue a secret smile. 'Yes, soft drinks only from now on . . . especially in her condition.'

Tom looked puzzled.

'It's no secret, Tom,' said Sue. 'I'm pregnant. It's just been confirmed.'

'Congratulations. It's a celebration then.'

Sue was shaking her head at Owen in mock despair as Tom walked to the bar.

Soon they clinked glasses and relaxed. While they were eating their basket meal the television above the bar was burbling away. On the BBC *News* Sue Lawley was telling the nation that Margaret Thatcher had apologized for the drunken rampages of hooligans in Spain; Lady Diana had visited air traffic control at Gatwick Airport, and Edwina Currie had told pensioners who couldn't afford to heat their homes to wrap up warm for the winter.

'Guess what, Tom?' said Sue. 'We're getting a new telly. I'll be dragging him to Curry's tomorrow.'

'What's it like?'

'Top of the range,' said Sue with enthusiasm. 'A fourteen-inch colour portable with full teletext service for up-to-the-minute news.'

'And a remote control from your armchair,' added Owen.

'The future's here today,' said Tom. 'That's the latest technology.'

'You'll have to come round the next time Wales are thrashing England at rugby,' said Owen with a grin.

Sue frowned but the meal continued with gentle banter and Tom enjoyed their company. He was a little deflated when they left.

A few minutes later he drained his glass and returned it to the bar. As he walked to the door he glanced through the window and stopped, transfixed. In the distance, walking up Lord Mayor's Walk and alongside the ancient city wall, was the distinctive figure of Inger Larson. Close to her was a tall, fair-haired man. They looked relaxed and he had his arm around her shoulder.

Tom gave a philosophical shrug. He recalled reading once that true love stories never have endings but in his case it had never got started. On impulse he decided to drown his sorrows. He returned to one of the bar stools and ordered another pint. There was no hurry to get home.

Suddenly he smelled cheap perfume. Two women appeared and sat on either side of him.

'Hi, Dr Frith,' said a lively voice. On the stool to his right was Kath Featherstone, a student in his Primary One group.

'Oh, hello,' said Tom guardedly.

'Can we join you as you're off duty?' To his left was Mo Greenwood, another of the so-called 'mature' students.

Tom did a quick double take. The two women were wearing T-shirts and skin-tight jeans that looked as though they had been sprayed on. Neither was wearing a bra.

'I'm sorry but I was just leaving.' He had been caught off guard. This was a different experience to a swift half on the way home after teaching his class of primary children.

Meanwhile Ellie MacBride had placed a tray of three vodka and tonics on a table in the far corner where a group of Year Three men from the rugby team were downing pints. She walked towards Tom in a determined manner. 'Leave Dr Frith alone, you two. Use some common sense.' She tugged them away. 'Your drinks are over there.'

'Sorry, sir,' said Kath and Mo coyly and brushed seductively past him.

A minute later Ellie came to sit on the stool next to Tom. She was wearing a sweatshirt and jeans and placed her glass on the counter. Then she stared into the mirror behind the bar. 'Sorry about that, Tom. They're both a bit giddy tonight. They don't mean any harm. Just enjoying their freedom.'

Tom looked into the mirror and returned her gaze.

Finally, he turned towards her. He couldn't deny that he found her intriguing. 'Freedom?' he said quietly.

She sipped her drink, pushed back her long hair and looked up at him. 'Yes. Off the leash at last, you might say.'

'Really?'

She nodded. 'Their husbands were both miners at the Cortonwood Colliery in South Yorkshire. When Thatcher closed the pits everything fell to pieces. It's a tough life with a drunken, abusive partner. Both married at eighteen, then divorced a couple of years ago.'

Tom frowned. 'I didn't know that.'

'Getting accepted here was a big step for them. I met them at interview and we bonded. It was a turning point in their lives.' She looked down at her drink. 'Mine too.'

'So what's your story, Ellie?' asked Tom.

There was a long pause. 'I think that's for another day.' She stood up. 'In the meantime, I'll leave you in peace. It looked as though you wanted some private space when we walked in and not to be propositioned by two noisy women out for a good time.'

'You're different to them,' said Tom.

Ellie looked thoughtful. 'Maybe, but you will have gathered we're the oldies in the group surrounded by teenagers.'

'And you bring life experience to the sessions,' said Tom.

'Very true.' She gave him a direct stare. 'Bit like today's lecture, Tom . . . *experience* surrounded by *innocence*.' She picked up her glass and walked away.

It was late when Tom eventually parked his car outside his cottage and searched for his key. As he stood in the doorway he reflected on the day. It had been one of contrasting emotions: pleasure at supporting hungry students; annoyance when confronted by Edna Wallop; curiosity at the elusive conundrum that was Inger Larson. There had been other women in his life, but there was something about the blonde Norwegian that particularly intrigued him.

He was also realizing that there were students with different needs, different backgrounds, different experiences. It was his job to turn them into teachers and a long road lay ahead for them.

Above him on this autumn night the stars, like far-off fireflies, held steadfast in the firmament while scarlet backlit clouds drifted towards an endless horizon. Suddenly a shooting star burst across the heavens with a spear of white light and he smiled and thought of Ellie MacBride.

Chapter Three

Changing Lives

At the beginning of October Tom Frith looked out on a morning of autumn mists and amber hues as he parked his car outside Hutton-le-Dale Primary School. The season was changing. In the hedgerows busy spiders were making their intricate webs, robins and wrens were claiming their territory and russet leaves were falling from the trees like countryside confetti. He could sense anticipation in the air. Tom's fifteen Primary One students were having their first taste of teaching during an introductory one-week school placement. This morning he was due to see four of the group before he returned to teach his English Two group at one o'clock. It was Tom's first school practice visit and an eventful day was in store.

He collected his satchel and paused to look at the scene before him. The distant fields of corn stubble framed the pretty school building of weathered Yorkshire stone, and as he walked through the school gate, he followed a few mothers holding on to their five-year-old children. A tiny grey-haired bespectacled lady was standing in the entrance porch welcoming each child with a friendly smile. First impressions were positive as the bell in the tower rang to announce the beginning of the school day.

'Good morning, I'm Tom Frith from the university, here to check on Mr Stocks and Mrs Featherstone.'

'Hello, Mr Frith. Welcome to Hutton-le-Dale. I was expecting you. I'm Mrs Doughty, the headteacher.'

'Thank you for your support,' said Tom. 'I'm hoping this week will give them a feel of what's in store.'

Her eyes twinkled. 'Ah, yes . . . *what's in store*? Who can tell? Every day is different.' She looked up at Tom quizzically. 'And what's your background, Mr Frith?'

'I was a deputy head in a primary school last term. I'm at the university on secondment.'

'Excellent,' said Mrs Doughty. 'Someone with recent practical experience. That makes a pleasant change. Do come in.'

Tom followed her into the school office, feeling reassured. If this was how school visits always began, life would be perfect.

'So, what's your opinion of our students, Mrs Doughty?'

'Well, there's a long way to go but they both appear comfortable in the classroom and I've put them with my two most experienced teachers.'

'That's very kind.' Tom was anxious to make good use of his time in the school. 'So . . . is it convenient to see them now?'

Mrs Doughty smiled. 'Of course. Follow me.'

The corridor was filled with vibrant displays of the children's artwork and writing. There were colourful leaf patterns, paintings of trees and fields and a selection of autumn poems.

'This is wonderful,' said Tom. 'Inspirational work.'

Mrs Doughty beamed. 'Thank you. I have a talented staff. They always endeavour to present the children's efforts in the best possible way.'

The visit turned out to be a positive experience for Tom. Both students were working alongside teachers and supporting group activities. Brian Stocks was in a class of nine-year-olds and listening to children reading in the Book Corner. It was a safe, secure start.

Down the corridor in the top infant class of mainly six-year-olds Kath Featherstone looked confident. The lively twenty-eight-year-old who had approached Tom with seductive innuendoes in the Keystones pub was a world away from the professional, smartly dressed woman in the classroom. There was a clear determination about her approach as she moved from group to group supporting an early writing activity. The fact she had two children of her own aged eight and six obviously gave her an inner confidence regarding the needs of these young children.

Reassured, Tom caught up with them at morning break. 'Well done. You're in a really good school and you can learn a lot here. How do you feel?'

'I'm enjoying it,' said Brian. 'I wasn't sure when I arrived but my teacher has given me clear instructions.'

'It's what I want to do with my life,' said Kath with a determined air.

Tom smiled. 'It shows.'

He thanked the class teachers and called into Mrs Doughty's office. 'Will you be able to join us for morning coffee?' she asked.

It was tempting but for Tom time was short and it was over ten miles to the next school.

'Sorry, another time. I have to get to Blunt Common by eleven.'

There was a flicker of recognition from Mrs Doughty. 'Yes, I know the school. I hope it goes well for you.' She didn't elaborate but Tom sensed a hint of caution in her words.

As Tom drove towards the old mining village of Blunt Common he soon realized it was no longer a thriving community. The mine had closed, unemployment was high and an air of malaise seemed to cover the slate-grey rooftops. A few of the shops on the high street had been boarded up, there was litter in the gutter and an overwhelming sense of decay everywhere. It was as if the village had lost its soul.

Tom spotted the school at the end of the high street but there was no car park, just a tall wire fence, a tarmac playground and a huge Victorian building that had seen better days. He pulled up in a side street near the school, picked up his carbon-copy notepad and got out. Across the road two long-haired scruffy youths were sitting in the gutter. They were smoking roll-up cigarettes and drinking beer from a can. One wore a leather biker's jacket, the other a Guns N' Roses T-shirt.

'Oy, mister!' shouted Leather Jacket.

Tom looked up cautiously. 'Yes?'

'Give us fifty pence an' we'll look after yer car.'

Tom shook his head. 'No, thanks.'

'Lot o' cars get damaged round 'ere,' declared Guns N' Roses.

'Don't need any minders for my car,' said Tom with a determined stare.

'Ah wouldn't be too sure 'bout that,' shouted Leather Jacket.

Tom was annoyed and came up with what he thought was an apt riposte. 'My dog will take care of it.'

'Did y'say a dog?' asked Guns N' Roses.

'Yes,' said Tom, feeling he had finally got the upper hand. 'A *fierce* dog.'

He turned to walk away.

'Is yer dog good at puttin' out fires?' shouted Leather Jacket.

Tom got the message. He stopped in his tracks and decided to make an orderly retreat. He climbed back in his car and drove off to accompanying laughter and V-signs. After a few turns through the estate he pulled up outside the local greengrocer's in a more civilized area. He looked around cautiously and concluded this was as safe as anywhere. He locked his car and set off for the school entrance.

A cheerful secretary took Tom down a dark corridor to the headteacher's office. She tapped on the door and gestured for Tom to walk in. A huge, bluff, red-faced Yorkshireman stood up. 'Welcome to Blunt Common,' he said with a bone-crushing handshake. 'I'm Keith Battersby.'

'Thank you, Mr Battersby. Pleased to meet you,' said Tom. 'I'm here to see the two students.'

'You're new,' he said.

'Yes, I was a deputy in a primary school last year. I've got a secondment to the university for this year.'

Mr Battersby looked reassured. 'That's good. You'll know what you're looking for.' He glanced out of the window. 'Where's your car?'

'Outside the greengrocer's.'

'Best place,' the headteacher said.

'It didn't seem safe round the back of the school.'

There was a nod of understanding. 'Wise decision.'

Beyond the wire netting Tom caught sight of Leather Jacket and Guns N' Roses slouching away into the distance. 'In fact, those two threatened to set it on fire.'

Keith Battersby sighed. 'Sadly, no surprises there. The Dewhirst brothers are a bad lot.' He looked out of the window at the rows of council houses, crumbling red brick and graffiti and shook his head. 'Tough area, lots of vandalism. They eat nails and spit rust around here.'

'I get the message,' said Tom. 'Anyway, I'm really grateful to you for giving our students this opportunity. It will be useful first-hand experience.'

The headmaster smiled. 'They'll certainly get that. Demanding place to cut your teeth but if they survive here they'll do well.'

'So . . . any early impressions?'

Keith Battersby looked thoughtful. 'They're a contrasting pair, no mistake. The young lad is a bit wet round the ears but he'll only get better. The woman is a different kettle of fish. Definitely one for the future. She's made of strong stuff.'

'That's good to hear. If I could spend a bit of time in each classroom and see them in action that would be really helpful.'

He glanced at the timetable on the wall. 'We've thrown Mr Surami in at the deep end. He's in Miss Phillips's class doing a geography lesson. Miss MacBride will be teaching at half eleven. She's in the deputy's classroom helping Mr Ecclestone with a maths project.'

*

Amir Surami glanced up nervously when the door opened. Tom gave him an encouraging smile and then sat on a chair at the side of the class and opened his notebook. The young man was standing in front of a map of Great Britain.

'What's the capital of England?' he asked.

Nine-year-old Tony Hardcastle, a ruddy-faced boy at the back of the classroom, put up his hand.

'Yes?' said Amir, clearly delighted to have had an immediate response.

'E,' said Tony.

'Pardon?'

'E, sir. T'letter E.'

'Ah, yes, good try,' said Amir. 'I meant, what is the capital *city*? It's the biggest in England. You can drive there or go on the train.'

Another nine-year-old, Chardonnay Backhouse, raised her hand.

'Yes?' said Amir hopefully.

''Ull, sir.'

'Hull?'

'Yes, sir. My grandad took me on t'train. 'E says 'Ull is bes' place on earth. There's nowt better.'

'No, this place is a really big city down south.'

'Leeds, sir,' shouted out a confident Barry Earnshaw. 'That's down south.'

'Good try but no, it's not Leeds,' said Amir. He seemed to relax for a moment. 'In fact . . . that's where I live.'

An excited Siobhan Duckworth raised her hand. 'Sir . . . sir . . . my sister Chantelle lives in Leeds.'

'Really?' said a bemused Amir. This lesson wasn't going as he had planned.

'Are y'married, sir?' yelled Melody Shenbanjo, obviously a girl who told it how it was.

Tom was surprised there was no reaction from the severe-looking Miss Phillips, the class teacher, who was marking books at the back of the class. She glanced across at Tom but didn't intervene. There was no clue as to what she was thinking.

Meanwhile Amir shook his head.

'Well, 'ave y'gorra girlfriend, sir?' asked a persistent Siobhan.

'No, I haven't but that's not what I'm asking,' said Amir. 'So . . . what is the capital city of England?'

'If you 'ad a girlfriend, sir, would y'tek 'er t'London?' asked Siobhan.

Amir's eyes lit up. 'Yes. London! Well done.'

'My sister Chantelle is lookin' fer a boyfriend, sir.'

'Is she?' Amir had begun to flounder and looked in desperation in the direction of the class teacher. However, Miss Phillips had folded her arms while wearing a sphinx-like expression. Tom assumed that in her opinion Amir was being introduced to the school of hard knocks and she was leaving him to sink or swim.

By the time Tom got up to leave, Amir had gradually managed to get the children back on track. They were filling in the names of cities on a photocopied map of Great Britain. He had a quiet word with the young student and thanked the unhelpful Miss Phillips through gritted teeth.

At eleven thirty, Tom walked out to the tarmac playground where Ellie MacBride, in a smart grey business suit, white blouse and flat shoes, was assisting the deputy head with his class of ten- and eleven-year-olds. The children were in small groups measuring the height of the school building using a click wheel, a clinometer and sheets of squared paper on clipboards. It was clear that Ellie's organization was excellent. All the pupils were on task while Mr Ecclestone was nodding in approval. Tom noticed she challenged the most-able while providing the least-able with appropriate guidance. She looked very much at home in this environment.

Shortly before the lunchtime bell the children filed back into school behind their teacher. Tom walked beside Ellie and they stopped on the playground.

'Excellent lesson, Ellie. Well done.'

'Thanks, Tom.'

'How do you feel it's going?'

She considered her response. 'I'm working alongside an experienced teacher. Discipline is good. I took his advice and started firmly. It's a poor area but these are great kids, willing to learn.'

'Who made all the clinometers?' he asked.

'I did. Burned the midnight oil.' She gave that infectious grin Tom was beginning to know so well. 'Mr Ecclestone was seriously impressed.'

'And so am I,' said Tom.

'Thanks. I'm enjoying it.'

Tom looked at his watch. 'I have a lecture at one so must dash. I'll thank the head before I go. In the meantime, keep up the good work.' As he turned to leave she laid a hand on his arm.

'Tom . . . I'm just doing what you told us to do.'

'And what's that?'

She smiled and gave him a meaningful look. 'To change lives one day at a time.'

After speaking to the head, Tom retrieved his car and, switching on the radio, drove back to York. Whitney Houston was singing 'One Moment In Time', the official song of the 1988 Olympics. He was lost in thought as the miles sped by. It had been that sort of morning and the song seemed appropriate.

It was twelve forty when he arrived back at the university and he hurried upstairs to his study. After collecting his lecture notes and buying a sandwich from the canteen he found an empty bench in the quadrangle. He sat there skimming through his summary of the novels of Scott Fitzgerald for his American Literature session when he heard a familiar voice.

'Hi, Tom. Are you free later this afternoon?'

He looked up. It was Inger Larson. 'Oh, hello, Inger,' he mumbled through a mouthful of breadcrumbs.

'We've got a concert rehearsal at five. Only half an hour. Just voices and strings. It's in the music room if you're free. Richard from the Science Faculty is looking after sound and lighting. I was hoping you could give him a hand.'

'Yes, of course. I'll be there.'

'Thanks. See you later,' and she hurried off. Once again, Tom wondered why this woman had such an impact on him.

His lecture went well. Tom had selected *The Great Gatsby* and *Tender is the Night*, two keystones of modernist fiction, for the group discussion about the American poet and short story writer F. Scott Fitzgerald. The themes of money and class, ambition and loss dominated the session and Tom was pleased with the positive interaction.

At afternoon break he caught up with Owen back in their study. The energetic Welshman was about to leave, clutching a clipboard and a stopwatch. 'Hi, Tom. Like ships that pass in the night. How did this morning's visits go?'

'Mixed,' said Tom. 'Saw a couple of very contrasting schools. The students were fine but it made me think about the quality of experience they're getting.'

'Luck of the draw,' said Owen.

'I'm helping Inger later with the concert.'

'They're always special,' he said. 'What are you doing?'

'Working on sound and lighting with a science guy, Richard.'

Owen grinned. 'Brilliant scientist. Complete nerd. Pity about his unfortunate surname.'

'What's that?'

'Head!'

'Head?'

'Yes, Richard Head. His parents must have had a warped sense of humour. Poor sod went through school being called "Dickhead".'

Chuckling to himself, the outspoken Welshman hurried off.

Shortly before five o'clock Tom broke off from marking some early assignments and looked out of the window. Henry Oakenshott was walking slowly around the quadrangle. His gaunt and cadaverous face was grey. Tom felt saddened to see this kindly academic in such a poor state. The Head of Faculty was clearly a very ill man.

Tom tidied his desk and set off for the rehearsal. It was

his first visit to the spacious music room. Instruments were everywhere; a tiered stage dominated one corner where Inger was gathering members of her choir. Tom paused next to a serious-looking young woman gripping a cello and four students tuning up violins.

A short skinny man in a shapeless Aran sweater and with a rust-brown goatee beard tapped him on the shoulder. 'You must be Tom,' he said. 'I'm Richard. Inger said you're assisting with sound and lights.'

'Oh, hello,' said Tom. Immediately he felt an empathy for this nerdy little scientist. 'Yes, I offered to help out. Inger said to come along.'

'Have you done this sort of stuff before?' Richard asked while wiping his black horn-rimmed spectacles on the sleeve of his sweater.

'Only at my primary school.' Tom looked around. 'All this is much more high-tech by the look of it.'

Richard gave a sympathetic smile. He had two huge front teeth that made him look like an expectant rabbit. 'Don't worry. I've done this lots of times so just follow my lead. I'll be back in a moment. There's a microphone check I have to do first.'

Tom walked to the back of the hall. Inger was deep in conversation with her choir and the tuning up of instruments created a discordant hum of sound. At that moment the door opened and a tall man in his late twenties walked in carrying a violin case. He swept back his long fair hair, waved to Inger, took off his denim jacket and sat down. After snapping open the catches of his case he took out a magnificent violin and proceeded to pluck the strings with practised ease.

Tom recognized him at once. It was the man who had accompanied Inger up Lord Mayor's Walk with an arm draped over her shoulder. They had looked relaxed together. He watched him with a mixture of surprise and envy.

At that moment Richard reappeared. He looked preoccupied. 'Tom, let me show you the console speakers. We need to check audio feedback.'

Tom felt as though he was back at school in a physics lesson as Richard swept him along with the science of sound systems. Fortunately, he was a quick learner.

'It would be helpful if you could handle this, Tom, as there's a tricky bit in the middle of the concert where we've got subdued lighting on the choir and a spotlight on the first violin.' Richard nodded towards the tall man who was practising a dramatic *spiccato* with his bow bouncing on the strings.

So he's first violin, thought Tom. *I can't compete with that.*

Inger spotted the two of them and came over. 'Thanks, Tom. I see you've met Richard.' She gave him a flashing smile and Richard seemed to go weak at the knees.

'We've made a good start,' said Tom. 'Richard is clearly an expert.'

Inger smiled again. 'Well, one of his published works is entitled *The Concept of Sound in Western Modernity*. Essential reading for us ordinary mortals.'

Tom wasn't sure if she was teasing the geeky professor.

She glanced up at the clock and called out, 'Let's begin, everybody.'

There was a buzz of activity as everyone settled in their places.

Tom went to stand next to Richard by the sound console. On it was a programme sheet with the heading: 'Concerto for Violin and Orchestra in D Major, Op. 61. Ludwig van Beethoven (1770–1827)'. It was covered with Richard's jottings and timings.

Inger tapped her baton on her music stand and gestured towards the blond Adonis. 'Good news, everybody. We have some unexpected assistance today. This is Andreas and he has kindly agreed to join us for the concert as first violin. Andreas plays in the Oslo Philharmonic and will be in England until the end of the month.'

Andreas shrugged his shoulders and gave Inger a wide-eyed smile. Minutes later he was playing with exhuberance and swagger while Tom marvelled at his precision and tempo. This man was clearly a hugely talented violinist.

It was a busy half-hour for Tom and he followed Richard's lead as the intense scientist scribbled further indecipherable notes in the margin of the programme.

At the conclusion of the rehearsal Richard collected his sheet of notes. 'Just a few queries for Inger,' he said and they walked over to join her. Next to her Andreas was putting away his violin.

'Thanks, you two,' said Inger.

'That went well,' said Richard. 'No problems and Tom was a great help.'

'Excellent,' said Inger. 'Andreas, this is Tom, a newcomer to the faculty. He's helping with the concert.'

Andreas smiled. 'Pleased to meet you, Tom. Thank you for your assistance.'

'It's a pleasure,' said Tom with an appreciative glance at Inger – which Andreas noticed but said nothing.

'For the past five years Andreas has been a member of

the Oslo Philharmonic,' said Inger. 'They're in-between concerts and he's taking a break.'

'With my girlfriend,' added Andreas with a winning smile.

Tom's heart sank.

'Of course,' said Inger quickly, 'but the concert comes first.' She gave him a determined stare. '*Det er riktig?*'

'*Ja, søster,*' replied Andreas with mock sheepishness.

Later on, Tom was helping Richard stack the amplifiers. 'What was all the Norwegian chat?'

'Inger was just saying that it was right that the concert came first.'

'I see . . . and what did he say?'

'He simply agreed.'

It was shortly after ten o'clock when Tom settled down in his armchair with a glass of beer and turned on the television. On the news the Labour Party Conference in Blackpool rumbled on but his mind was elsewhere. He switched over to *Miami Vice* where Don Johnson as Sonny Crockett was tracking down a drug dealer. As usual he was wearing a suit that required a government health warning. Tom shook his head and switched off. As he sipped his beer he reflected on the changes in his life. Finally, he came to a decision.

He would ask Inger Larson an important question.

Chapter Four

An Echo of Memories

It was early morning as Tom drove towards York. Each day the temperature had dropped and an autumn mist covered the distant countryside with a mantle of silence. Tom stared out through the windscreen at an eerie world, featureless and blurred. Around him the hedgerows were covered with the fine lace of spiders' webs and dead leaves swirled in an eddying breeze. When he arrived at the university the rays of a pale sun were creeping over the sleeping city. It had been a journey of shadows but he smiled with anticipation as he parked his car. Today was Tuesday, 18 October, the day of the concert, and Inger Larson was on his mind.

Owen and Victor were in the faculty common room when Tom walked in to check his mail. Owen was shaking his head in dismay as he scanned his *Daily Mirror.* 'Great shame about John Smith,' he said.

Earlier in the month the Scottish Labour MP and Shadow Chancellor, John Smith, had suffered a heart attack in Edinburgh. A heavy smoker and a lover of rich food, his lifestyle had finally caught up with him. After three days in intensive care, and now a prolonged stay in hospital, it was uncertain when he would return to parliament.

Victor gave his usual considered response. 'He could have become one of the great Labour prime ministers.'

'Too true,' said Owen.

'What about Neil Kinnock?' asked Tom.

Owen looked thoughtful. 'We could do worse than having a Welshman in Number Ten. It's just that sometimes he goes over the top in his speeches.'

'Lacks gravitas,' said Victor. 'Which reminds me . . . Edna has called an impromptu faculty meeting this afternoon at four thirty p.m.'

'What's it for?' asked Owen.

'Probably another of her quixotic projects,' said Victor.

Tom shook his head. 'Inger won't be pleased. We were supposed to meet at five in the music room to prepare for tonight's concert.'

'I'll have a word with Henry,' said Victor. 'He attends all the concerts. Maybe he can persuade Edna to move the meeting to later in the week.'

'I passed him in the car park,' said Tom, 'and he looked really ill.'

There was no doubt that these days the Head of Faculty appeared to be a broken man.

'And the Wallop is no help,' said Owen. He glanced up at the clock on the wall. 'Anyway, must get on. I've got Primary Two in the gym.'

Tom walked across the quad and climbed the metal stairs to the Cloisters corridor just as Inger emerged from her study.

She was clutching a large folder of music manuscript plus a heavy box of concert programmes.

'Morning,' said Tom. 'Can I help?'

She gave a tired smile. 'Thanks, Tom. I'm going down to the music room. Maybe you could take the programmes. They weigh a ton.'

'Fine,' he said and hefted the box under his arm.

As they walked around the quad Tom glanced at Inger. He sensed her anxiety despite the determination in her stride. A week had passed since he had asked her if she would like to join him for a drink after work. He recalled that moment of hesitation followed by a tiny shake of her head. It seemed she was too busy with preparations for the concert. They had stood there beneath the beech trees outside the university entrance while leaves, gold and yellow, drifted down at their feet. There had been a brief silence until Tom gave a gentle smile and said quietly, 'Another time perhaps.'

When they reached the music room Tom put down the box. Everything appeared organized. Richard had been in earlier and arranged all the chairs for the orchestra and the audience. 'By the way,' said Tom, 'I've heard that Edna's called a meeting for four thirty this afternoon.'

Inger frowned. 'Damn! The stupid woman! She knows it's the evening of the concert.'

'I think Victor is trying to get it postponed.'

Inger sighed. 'Let's hope so. I'm not changing our five o'clock rehearsal. We need a final run-through.' She scanned the rows of chairs. 'It's likely to be a full house.'

Tom shared her concern. 'Even Edna must realize this is important.'

'Maybe.' She shook her head. 'I guess these things are sent to try us.'

Tom glanced down at his wristwatch. 'Sorry, Inger, but I have to go. Students will be waiting.'

She nodded. 'Thanks, Tom. Catch you later.'

Tom walked to the doorway and paused. When he looked back Inger was sitting deep in thought. She had bowed her head and clenched her hands as if in prayer. At that moment he felt helpless. He wanted to make her problems go away.

'Inger,' he called out. She glanced up. He was silhouetted in the doorway. 'Do remember, I'm here if you need me.'

As he closed the door he didn't see the sudden look of alarm on Inger's face. For an instant there had been fear in her eyes.

I'm here if you need me. Those words had once been said by another and she could never forget. Once again they crashed across her consciousness. She remained motionless, like a pale angel in the cavernous space of the music room.

She was still sitting there when Andreas walked in carrying his violin case. He smiled at his sister. 'I need to practise,' he said and walked towards the seats on the stage. As he took out his violin, he considered her demeanour. 'You look concerned. Don't worry. Your concerts are always a success.'

'Thanks.' She gave a deep sigh. 'It's just that life can be difficult sometimes.'

He put down his violin and walked over to sit down beside her. 'Tell me about it,' he said quietly.

'It was something Tom said.'

'I've just passed him. He seems a nice guy. Richard told me he's a good teacher.'

'Yes, a kind man, I think,' replied Inger.

'So what did he say?'

'Something that brought back an unhappy memory. It was unintentional. Just made me feel a little sad.'

It was clear to Andreas that once again the equilibrium of her life was out of kilter and a shroud of sadness had settled upon her. It happened occasionally. He leaned closer and held her hand. 'Tell me,' he said gently.

She gave Andreas a wan smile but shook her head. Then she suddenly stood up and tugged his hand. 'Come on, little brother. Let's practise.'

An hour later, Andreas packed up his violin, kissed his sister on the cheek and left her checking the programme. As he walked out she saw a different silhouette in the doorway. It brought back a certain memory and she shivered at the thought.

She had met Kai Pedersen in Oslo after a concert and they had dated a couple of times. However, she had been thinking of ending their brief relationship when he had stopped in the doorway of a bar, looked back and said, *I'm here if you need me.*

It had sounded sincere and a week later she had agreed to meet him again.

At the time she was on the rebound, following a brief fling with a driller on the Oseberg oil field. The field, named after a famous Viking ship, had transformed Norway's oil and gas industry, and Bjørn Olsen had been very excited to work there. Unfortunately, he'd insisted on telling her so, repeatedly, and she had soon tired of his banal stories. The relationship ended quickly. Then Kai Pedersen came into her life.

He was a smart, intelligent engineer and for the last three years he had worked on Norway's Atlanterhavsveien, the Atlantic Ocean Road. It was a remarkable project. Over five miles long and built on several small islands, it was connected by causeways, viaducts and eight bridges. Kai had driven her to see the largest of them, the Storseisundet Bridge, and then it had happened.

Inger had been visiting her parents in the tiny village of Langøy and was enjoying her day out with the tall, suave engineer. On the way back from the bridge he pulled into a wooded area. They kissed, gently at first, until he became more insistent. '*Jeg vil ha deg nå,*' he whispered in her ear. 'I want you now,' he repeated, this time in English. Inger would never forget the change in this man. What happened next was both brutal and savage.

It was a secret she could never share, even with her brother, who would have sought retribution. Since the attack she had tried to move on, even though there were moments during the still of the night when she relived the terror of that day. She dedicated her life to music, finding inner peace in the quietude of harmony. It had also become her armour against unwanted attention. Two years had passed since that day but the echo of her memories still seared her soul.

At lunchtime the dining room was full when Tom walked in. It was a vast new building that could house hundreds of students and he joined the queue at the stainless-steel counter. Today's choices were on a large blackboard, including vegetable risotto, burger and chips, and egg salad.

It was a sign of the times that the preparation of food had been contracted out at huge expense. The university's governing body had announced that they were educators and had no intention of taking on auxiliary services such as meals. Tom selected the risotto and joined Owen and Zeb at a table in an alcove at the far end of the room where lecturers tended to gather.

Zeb had finished her salad and lit up a cigarette while she flicked through the pages of Owen's newspaper. The headline read: 'FERGIE – Do you really know what you're doing? Two more weeks away from baby Bea.' The Duchess of York was enjoying a fun-filled tour of Tasmania on her twenty-ninth birthday.

'So much for a mother's love,' muttered Zeb. She skipped past the article concerning the Liverpool soccer star Jan Mølby who had been jailed for three months after driving at 100 mph in a 30-mph area and turned to the agony aunt column. Marjorie Proops was offering advice to a confused man under the heading 'Should he pay for lessons in love?'

'Poor sod,' she muttered. 'I could soon put him right.'

Owen put down his knife and fork and pushed away his plate. 'I heard from Victor that Edna wouldn't change the time of the meeting.'

'Bloody woman!' muttered Zeb.

'Does anyone know what it's about?' asked Tom.

Owen shook his head. 'No idea.'

Tom frowned. 'Inger looked a bit tense this morning. Her final rehearsal is at five and it's important it goes to plan.'

'Whatever the Wallop has in store for us,' said Owen, 'it had better be good.'

'Not a chance,' said Zeb. She got up to leave. 'Hell will freeze over first.'

Tom and Owen watched her skip around the tables and head for her dance studio. 'Sadly, she's right,' said Owen.

At 4.30 p.m. the common room was crowded. When Tom walked in he sat down next to Owen and Zeb. He spotted Inger in the back row deep in conversation with Victor. She was looking anxious. There were murmurs of discontent as Edna appeared, clearly in a bullish mood. It was noticeable that Henry wasn't present.

She faced a disgruntled group of faculty members and didn't hold back. 'Good afternoon, everybody. I'll keep this short. Henry apologizes for his absence. He's not himself today.' She surveyed the room and gave a curt nod towards Victor. 'I'm also aware of tonight's concert, which sadly I'm not able to attend owing to a prior commitment. In the meantime, you'll be pleased to hear we have a one-item agenda.' She scanned the room. 'I've called this meeting to enable each one of you to complete a test . . . but first I have a question.' She paused for dramatic effect. 'What's our USP, people? Think hard. What's the unique selling point of our faculty?'

Everyone presumed it was rhetorical except the introspective Richard Head who raised his hand.

She frowned. 'Yes?'

To everyone's surprise he stood up and gestured to the assembly. 'Edna, it's in front of you,' he said simply.

'You always were obtuse,' she said with a shake of her head.

'It's *people*,' said Richard determinedly. 'It's us. We're the USP.'

'Explain,' said Edna curtly.

'Look around. We're an eclectic group of tutors with different skills. As a group we are greater than the individual parts. Together we're a team that produces high-quality courses in a wide variety of disciplines.'

There were appreciative nods of agreement around the room.

Edna smiled. 'In that case you will not mind completing a simple test. You may be aware that the Myers–Briggs Type Indicator is one of the most popular personality tests in the world. At my recent conference in London led by the American management guru Alphin Kruger it was confirmed that it has a ninety per cent accuracy rating. The data will provide me with an accurate profile of your ability to make decisions.'

Victor raised his hand.

'Yes?' said Edna with a scowl.

'I'm aware of the test,' said Victor. 'It's used in industry.' It was his turn to stand. 'For colleagues who aren't familiar, it's simply a questionnaire that assigns four categories, namely: thinking or feeling, introversion or extroversion, sensing or intuition and judging or perceiving.' He paused and then looked keenly at Edna. 'So I have to ask . . . is it relevant to us and, more important, how will you use the findings if we agree to comply?'

'If!' exclaimed Edna. 'There's no *if*, Victor. This is a requirement. It will go towards the efficiency of our faculty. I want us to go the whole nine yards on this one.'

There was a communal groan.

'May I ask what was Henry's opinion?' asked Victor.

'Henry is not here,' said Edna bluntly. She pointed to a pile of pale blue A4 sheets on the table. 'So I want everybody to take a questionnaire before you leave and deliver it to the office by the end of the week.' She stood up and surveyed the discontented faces before her. 'That's it, people. Time to move on.'

Zeb leaned over to Tom and Owen. 'Can't take much more of this. This woman is insufferable and, sadly, these days Henry is no more than her lapdog. What you've just witnessed is the start of the unravelling of the faculty. It's going to be chaos. I'll be looking for a new job,' she muttered and stormed out.

'She's really upset,' said Tom.

'I'll speak to her,' said Owen. 'I've not seen her like this before.'

Tom saw Inger hurrying out with Victor and Richard. 'Anyway, must go. It's rehearsal time,' said Tom.

'I'll be there tonight with Sue,' said Owen. 'Maybe a pint afterwards? You'll have earned it if you're working with Richard.' He grinned. 'Remember to open the door for him.'

Tom looked puzzled.

'Just a thing he has,' said Owen. 'He doesn't touch doorknobs. Afraid of picking up germs.'

'Really?'

Owen nodded. 'Yes. Richard's a great guy. Just a bit quirky. Victor explained it to me. He said that Freud referred to it as obsessional neurosis but apparently nowadays we call it obsessive compulsive disorder.'

Tom reflected that he was learning a lot in this new world of higher education. His primary school in Harrogate seemed a long way off these days. He picked up a questionnaire and hurried out.

At five o'clock the music room hummed with activity. Inger had selected a few extracts from the programme and took the musicians and choir through their paces. At last, she nodded in appreciation. It had been a successful rehearsal and by 5.45 p.m. all was ready. 'Back here in an hour, everybody,' she called out.

Meanwhile the intense Richard made a final check of the sound system and then stood back and removed his spectacles. He cleaned them on the sleeve of his Greenpeace sweatshirt and relaxed. Everything was now in order in his organized life. He glanced at his watch. 'Come on, Tom. Let's get some well-earned refreshment.'

'Sounds good,' said Tom. 'In the refectory?'

Richard shook his head. 'No, my local.'

Soon they were ambling through the ancient streets of York. Richard paused outside a video-rental shop. There was a huge poster advertising the opportunity to rent the film *ET*. Six years ago the extra-terrestrial film had been a smash hit and soon it could be enjoyed in your own home. 'I'll be renting this one, Tom. I'm a big fan.'

Tom was learning much about the likeable yet quirky academic. Even so, he was puzzled by the lanyard that Richard wore around his neck from which hung a printed card behind a Perspex label. It stated his name, address, blood group and the fact he was allergic to penicillin. What Tom did not know was that many years ago Richard had been a scout leader and the motto 'Be Prepared' was at the core of his organized soul.

As they walked up Goodramgate, Tom was fascinated by its unique architecture. He'd learned that the first floor of the medieval jettied houses hung over the ground floor for the disposal of waste in times long ago. Richard led the way into the Cross Keys, a snug Victorian pub, where they were greeted by a burly barman.

'Usual, Richard?' he asked.

'Thanks, Stanley.'

The barman looked enquiringly at Tom.

'Same for me please,' said Tom and was reassured when two pints of Tetley's bitter were placed on the bar. They found a quiet corner and for half an hour Tom was treated to an insight into the science of sound and how electrical signals transmit through the auditory nerve to the brain.

On their way back to the university they spotted Edna Wallop standing outside reception. She was deep in conversation with a huge man in an ill-fitting suit. His Bobby Charlton comb-over to hide his bald patch looked vaguely ridiculous.

'Who's that?' asked Tom.

'Cedric Bullock, a local businessman and one of the governors. They're thick as thieves, those two.'

As they walked past, Edna gave Tom and Richard a hard stare and then muttered something to her companion. He responded with a frown.

By seven o'clock all the seats in the music room were taken. Inger was dressed in a smart black dress with a pale blue silk scarf around her neck. She picked up her baton and turned to face the audience. 'Good evening, everybody, and thank you for supporting our concert.' She gestured towards the orchestra. 'We are blessed with a new crop of talented first years and I know they are looking forward to the experience. You will see from your programme that we are beginning with a famous piece by Wolfgang Amadeus Mozart. Like Beethoven, it has been said he was God's gift to humanity. Please note that it features a solo by our first violin, my brother Andreas, who is on a brief sabbatical from the Oslo Philharmonic. So please sit back and enjoy Mozart's Concerto Number Three. Composed in 1755, it is generally regarded as the most popular of his five violin concertos. Often described as an interpretation of art and soul, we should like to share it with you tonight.'

Richard dimmed the lights and the concert began.

'Brother?' whispered Tom. 'But he said he'd come over to spend time with his girlfriend.'

'That's right,' said Richard. 'He and his girlfriend, Annika, go everywhere together.'

'Annika?' repeated Tom as the penny dropped.

Towards the end of the piece Tom noticed a slight disturbance at the back of the room. In the darkness, Victor was leading Henry towards the door. The moment passed quickly. Meanwhile, Richard turned the spotlight on Inger. The next piece was a piano solo by one of Inger's students. Tom was spellbound as Inger conducted Rachmaninoff's Piano Concerto No. 3 with the confidence she only displayed when she was immersed in her music. Finally, the applause rang out loud and long.

The evening was a triumph and when the lights came up at the end Inger was surrounded by colleagues and their partners expressing their appreciation. Tom was helping

Richard stack the speakers at the side of the hall when he saw a tall, graceful young woman standing next to Andreas. She had high cheekbones and long auburn hair. Richard spotted Tom's interest. 'That's Annika,' he said.

Tom could see the attraction for Andreas.

As the crowd dwindled away into the darkness Tom managed a brief word with Inger. She was with Andreas packing up her music while Annika had gone to collect their coats.

'Thank you,' he said. 'That was a wonderful experience. Loved your Rachmaninoff and the Mozart.' He glanced at Andreas. 'Brilliant solo. You're clearly as talented as your sister.'

'Thanks, Tom,' said Andreas.

'We all appreciated your help,' said Inger. 'I'm just so relieved it went well.'

Suddenly Richard appeared. 'Tom, I need a hand with the music console if you've got a moment?'

As Tom and Richard walked away Andreas smiled at Inger. 'I like your new colleague.' Inger nodded knowingly: she guessed where this was going. 'I could invite him to join us for a drink,' he said with a mischievous smile. 'Annika has a bottle of *akvavit* and tonight is a celebration.' Andreas knew Inger had a liking for the traditional Scandinavian flavoured spirit.

'*Oppfør deg, lillebror,*' said Inger with a stare and dug him in the ribs. 'Behave, little brother,' she repeated.

'Fine,' he said and gave her a hug. It was good to see his sister relaxed at last. He picked up his violin case and put his arm around her shoulder. 'So . . . just the three of us then.'

*

From across the room Tom watched them leave arm in arm. As they walked out into the night he wished he could have joined them.

The following morning Tom was eating his breakfast cereal and watching BBC *Breakfast Time*. John Stapleton was reporting that Sir James Black had discovered a life-saving heart drug when the telephone rang. It was Owen.

'Tom, I have some bad news.' There was a pause. 'It's Henry. He was rushed into hospital late last night.'

'Oh no!'

'Victor rang a few minutes ago. He's letting everyone know. He was with him after the concert when it happened.'

There was silence as if the words were hard to find.

'Owen. Are you still there?'

There was a deep sigh. 'Tom, it's really bad news . . . Henry died at three o'clock this morning.'

Chapter Five

Books and Dust

A month had passed since the death of Henry Oakenshott. The funeral had taken place at the end of October and Victor had delivered a moving eulogy. It had been a sombre group of tutors and students who paid their final respects. Since then life had moved on and the season was changing. It was the time of the dying of the light and a cloak of mist shrouded the frozen land. Winter was coming.

'Bloody cold,' said Owen. 'Maybe we should get some curtains.'

It was 8.30 a.m. on Friday, 18 November, and Owen was standing by the study window, staring out at the quadrangle below. Spiders' webs, like strings of winter pearls, decorated the windowpanes. The grass sparkled with frost and the cobbled pathways had been salted. Students, some of them huddled in hand-me-down duffel coats and wrapped in long thick scarves, hurried towards the refectory for a bacon sandwich and a mug of hot tea before lectures began at nine o'clock.

'Curtains . . . good idea,' said Tom. He was sitting in one of the armchairs engrossed in a book.

Owen was curious. 'What are you reading?'

'*Lord of the Rings*. It's brilliant. This is the first one, *The Fellowship of the Ring*.'

'The first one?'

'It's a trilogy, the classic by Tolkien.'

Owen sat back at his desk. 'This is a classic too,' and held up a copy of an old hardback, *Physical Education in England since 1800*. 'I'm doing some history stuff this morning with Year Three.'

Tom got up, opened his novel to the title page and placed it in front of Owen. 'Read that,' he said quietly.

Owen stared at the dedication, written in neat cursive handwriting. 'Ah,' he murmured with understanding.

It read:

To Frodo from Gandalf.
Enjoy your journey, Tom.
With best wishes,
Henry Oakenshott, September 1988

Owen nodded and handed it back to Tom. 'That's special.'

'It was an unexpected gift at the end of my first week. I remember how supportive he was.'

'A lovely man,' said Owen. 'Shame the Wallop made life hell for him. I think he gave up in the end.'

'I'll treasure this,' said Tom. He placed the book back on the coffee table and glanced at his wristwatch. 'Anyway, must go. I've got Primary One first session.'

'By the way,' said Owen, 'Victor asked for some help to

clear Henry's study tonight. Come along if you can. Perkins is bringing some cardboard boxes.'

'Fine,' said Tom. 'Glad to help.'

'It's like Aladdin's cave,' said Owen. 'There're hundreds of books. Victor said he had no family and his wife died ten years ago. Sad really.'

'I'll miss him,' said Tom. He grabbed his coat and scarf from the hook behind the door. 'Catch you later.'

'Lunchtime,' said Owen.

Tom gave him a thumbs up as he pulled on his coat and picked up his satchel. 'See you then.'

Once outside, his breath steaming, Tom walked across the frozen cobbles to his first tutorial of the day. He had no idea what lay in store. It was only later he would learn that Fate moves in mysterious ways.

At morning coffee time Tom was sitting with some of his Primary One group in the refectory following their tutorial. He had found it was a good opportunity to catch up with his students in an informal setting. They were enjoying hot drinks and discussing the news of the day.

Brian Stocks was grumbling because British Rail had announced a 21 per cent increase in the cost of long-distance season tickets. 'More expensive to get home,' he complained. He lived in the pretty village of West Chiltington in West Sussex and the South Downs seemed a long way off on this freezing North Yorkshire morning. Meanwhile, and much to the disgust of the women close by, Dan Milburn and Amir Surami were showing great interest in a picture of Miss Iceland who had won last night's Miss World contest.

Ellie MacBride was flicking through the pages of her

Guardian newspaper. 'Look at this, Tom,' she said. There was a photograph of Princess Diana presenting prizes at Barnardo's Champion Children awards. 'Imagine being married to Charlie-boy. I wouldn't wish that on my worst enemy.' Meanwhile Prince Charles was making different headlines after describing modern architecture as huge, blank and impersonal.

However, it was another relationship which had come to an end that caught Ellie's attention and she shook her head in dismay. The marriage of forty-one-year-old Elton John to his wife, Renate Blauel, had ended with a £5 million pay-out. 'All he wanted was a son, but he can't go on living a lie.'

Tom nodded in agreement. 'Different lives,' he said quietly.

Ellie looked up, her green eyes like mirrors of an experienced past. 'Exactly,' she said with determination.

It was then that her friend Kath Featherstone stood up and tapped a spoon on the table. 'Come on. Move yourselves. Time to go.'

Everyone except Tom got up to leave. 'What's happening?' he asked.

'Children in Need,' said Ellie. 'We're raising money on behalf of the Students' Union.'

'That's great,' said Tom. 'What are you doing?'

She grinned. 'You'll see.'

There was half an hour before afternoon lectures and Tom and Owen set off for the warmth of the faculty common room. In a far corner was an annexe, a cosy space with armchairs and a television set. A cluster of lecturers were there, including Inger, Zeb and Victor. They were enjoying mugs of hot tea and watching the BBC *News*. Tom and Owen sat down beside them.

'Good timing, guys,' said Zeb. 'Mr Brylcreem is on.'

Education Secretary Kenneth Baker had recently announced that he intended to introduce national testing with more emphasis on grammar. Tom's world was experiencing a seismic shift. Teacher training was changing. The National Curriculum was gathering momentum and copious ring binders had begun to circulate with prescribed topics for the various stages of education.

'Tough on the new graduates,' said Owen.

Zeb frowned. 'Never mind the poor students; there's even talk of *us* being assessed. God knows how they will do that.'

'Where will it all end?' mused Inger.

'Imagine what's in front of our students,' said Victor.

The mood changed suddenly as the next item was introduced. Edwina Currie had launched her 'Keep Warm, Keep Well' drive with a recommendation for a liberty bodice for women and silk long johns for men.

A few lively conversations sprang up around the room.

'Actually,' said Owen, 'I'm not embarrassed to admit that I wear long johns under my tracksuit on days like this. Makes sense. Mind you, not bloody *silk* ones!' he added as an afterthought. 'And anyway . . . what's a liberty bodice? I thought they went out fifty years ago.'

'Well, I've got one somewhere,' said Zeb. 'I bought it after seeing *The Bitch* at the cinema. Joan Collins was wearing one. She looked amazing.'

At that moment a group of students passed by the window. They were dressed as scantily clad nurses and doctors with a sign offering kisses for ten pence. Two of them carried bright yellow buckets with 'Children in Need' scrawled on the side. In spite of the bitter weather, they were doing a roaring trade.

'Hey, Zeb,' said Owen with a grin. 'Go and get that sexy underwear on. You'll make a fortune. Loads more than this lot.'

Zeb got up to leave. 'Get lost, you Welsh degenerate . . . and in any case you couldn't afford me.'

There was laughter as everyone filed out.

Moments later they were surrounded by eager students in the quad. Everyone tossed coins into the bucket but politely refused the offer of a kiss. Suddenly Ellie MacBride was facing Tom. 'Only ten pence, sir,' she said coyly.

Tom took a fifty-pence piece from his pocket and held it up. She took it from him and dropped it in the bucket. 'Tom, for that you get much more than a kiss.'

He smiled. 'Thanks . . . but I don't pay for kisses.'

As she walked away to catch up with the gaggle of students, she stopped and called back to him, 'Perhaps you don't need to.'

Tom watched her as she followed the others to the students' common room. Those without afternoon lectures could always be found there watching the latest episode of *Neighbours* with Kylie Minogue as Charlene and Jason Donovan as Scott. For these eighties students it was compulsive viewing.

Before they disappeared from view, Ellie turned and waved to Tom.

Yet another brief encounter, thought Tom and each one more intriguing than the last. Her remark had been light-hearted but, still, it had made him feel rather uncomfortable.

*

Tom was well prepared for his afternoon session with his English Three group. A module on the war poets had been included during the first semester and they were studying the poetry of Rupert Brooke, Wilfred Owen and Siegfried Sassoon. Tom was describing how Wilfred Owen had tried to tell the truth about the physical and mental trauma of war in his poems 'Anthem for Doomed Youth' and 'Dulce et Decorum Est' when there was an interruption. With a clatter of heavy footsteps, Edna Wallop walked in.

As was her style, she completely ignored the students and strutted to the front of the room. There was a new taciturnity about her these days, a churlish indifference to her colleagues. Newly installed as the Acting Head of Faculty she was even dressing differently. Her two-piece tweed suit sported *Dynasty* shoulder pads that made her resemble a Bond villain. Obviously an attempt at stylish elegance, it merely looked over-elaborate and pretentious.

She looked up at Tom with unblinking steel-grey eyes. There was no preamble. 'I need a word after your lecture. I'll be in my study.' Without waiting for an acknowledgement, she walked out.

Tom tried to gather his thoughts. 'Now . . . where were we?'

'The pain of war,' a helpful voice from the back called out.

'Ah yes,' mumbled Tom. *And how appropriate,* he thought.

Tom arrived at Edna's office and tapped on the door.

'Come,' issued a strident voice.

He walked in and was surprised by the untidiness. Papers were scattered on the floor, her desk was a sea of reminder notes and a jumble of books teetered on the coffee table. It was a large room with two windows. One looked out on to the quad while the other gave a view of the entrance to the university. There was an all-pervading smell of tobacco: propped against the desk lamp was a pack of Castella cigars.

She was studying a pale blue sheet of A4. Finally, she looked up. 'I wanted to see you because the test results are in.'

For a moment Tom assumed she was talking about the students.

'I was interested in your responses to the Myers–Briggs Type Indicator,' continued Edna.

'Really?'

'Yes,' said Edna. 'You came out under T for Thinker.'

'Interesting,' murmured Tom.

'It would appear that you use logic, fairness and honesty in your work.'

'That's good to hear,' said Tom, still unsure where this was going.

'You'll gather I'm a great fan of this process.'

Tom decided to play devil's advocate. 'And what about you, Dr Wallop? What was your result?'

To Tom's surprise she grinned like a Cheshire cat. 'E for Extrovert, of course. I have a gift for multi-tasking. It would appear I possess a flexible and liberating framework for understanding individual differences and strengths.' She leaned back contentedly. 'Although I was aware of that *before* the test.'

There was a pause while Edna shuffled other papers on her desk.

'Well . . . thank you,' said Tom. 'I presume you're giving colleagues their results. I'm sure they will be appreciative.' It was difficult to keep the sarcasm from his voice.

She frowned. 'Of course not. For every action there's a reaction. That's what I want from you.'

'I see,' said Tom . . . but he didn't.

'It occurred to me that you are in an ideal position to provide me with vital information.'

'Am I?'

She leaned forward and her gaze was piercing. Tom realized the denouement had arrived. 'Yes, and if you do this task well I may well review your *temporary* lectureship. Later this year there could be the offer of a *full-time* position.' She pushed back her chair and waited for a reaction.

'What exactly is it you want, Dr Wallop?'

Her eyes narrowed. 'I want you to observe Victor very carefully. He can be troublesome at times. Occasionally he's too clever for his own good. Next semester I shall be introducing new initiatives. Undoubtedly he will oppose them. I want to know what he's thinking. Do I make myself clear?'

'Crystal,' said Tom, perhaps a little flippantly. The penny had dropped. Edna wanted an informer.

'So, Tom, what do you say?'

It was the first time she had called him Tom.

He stood there, trying to think how to frame his reply.

'I know this may come as a surprise,' she said, 'but let's drop it in the pool and see if it makes a splash.'

Again there was a long silence.

'Well? What have you got to say?' She began to sound agitated. 'This could be advantageous to you in your career. Opportunities like this don't come round very often.'

'As you said, Dr Wallop. Apparently, I'm a *thinker*.'

'Yes, you are, but I want you to listen up.' She stared up at him. 'You may be thinking this is a big ask.'

'It certainly is,' said Tom. He knew his next response could determine his future career.

'So . . . what do you say?' asked Edna with a predator's smile.

Tom walked to the door, opened it and said, 'Dr Wallop . . . my answer is no.'

Edna gave him a look that would have turned most men into pillars of salt. A tirade of expletives followed him as he closed the door behind him and walked with a measured tread back to his study.

Tom was ashen-faced by the time he reached the Cloisters corridor and leaned back against his study door, his mind racing. Finally, he walked in and sat in one of the armchairs, head in his hands. He felt his career was hanging by a thread. A few minutes had passed when there was a tap on the door.

It was Inger. 'Sorry, Tom. I'm looking for Owen. I've had to rearrange a piano lesson so I'll be late for tonight's clear-out of Henry's study.'

He gave her a blank look. His mind was elsewhere.

'Tom . . . what is it?'

'Sorry, Inger.' He leaned back. 'It's complicated.'

She closed the door behind her. 'Can I help?'

He shook his head. 'Thanks anyway but not this time. I've just had a difficult meeting with Edna. The result is my days here are probably numbered.'

She sat down. 'What happened?'

He sighed, bowed his head and ran his fingers through his long hair. 'She made me an offer and I refused.'

'Would you like to talk about it?'

'Thanks. Perhaps later. I need some time to think.'

She looked at her watch. 'Do you have another lecture this afternoon?'

'No, just a couple of tutorials later on.'

She stood up. 'Fine. Talk to Owen if you feel able. I'll see you later.'

Moments later Inger was striding across the quad towards the music room. Tom was clearly in distress and she wanted to help. She knew deep down he was a good man and it was sad to see him in such a state. Above all she knew that, at times like this, life could be a fickle companion.

Tom completed his tutorials and stared out of the study window at the darkness beyond. He decided to pack his car with the latest box of assignments before setting off for Henry's study to assist with the book-sorting. In the quad under one of the lamps that led to the reception area, a large figure approached him. It was Cedric Bullock, the governor who had been in conversation with Edna earlier in the day.

'Hello, Dr Frith,' he said. 'Good to meet you at last. My name's Bullock. I'm on the governing body.'

'Good afternoon, Mr Bullock.'

'I'm glad I've caught you, a word to the wise you might say.' His voice and manner were condescending in the extreme.

Tom said nothing. He had taken an instant dislike to this man.

'I've been in conversation with Dr Wallop this afternoon.' He moved closer, a bloated figure in the lamplight. 'She mentioned she had spoken to you. That's right, isn't it?'

'It is,' said Tom quietly. He was wondering what might come next.

'It occurred to me that you might want to consider carefully your support for Dr Wallop in whatever she asks of you.'

Tom remained silent.

'I believe she has mentioned to you the criteria upon which your continued employment in this university depends.'

Tom sighed and shook his head. 'I'm well aware of it,' he replied testily. 'I hope that you understand this as well as Dr Wallop. My integrity is more important than my employment here.'

Cedric Bullock looked shocked. 'Of course, but . . .'

The sentence remained unfinished as Tom turned on his heel and walked away.

It was just after five o'clock when Tom entered Henry's study. He took in the scene as motes of dust hovered in the lamplight. Victor, Owen and Zeb were already there, sifting through a compendium of books the like of which he could barely imagine. Richard Head and Perkins the Porter were stacking boxes under the bay window.

'Thanks for coming, Tom,' said Victor. 'We're sorting them into different piles. Richard and Perkins are boxing those that could go into the university library. If there's any that would help your course put them in a box and label it. Also there may be a few you would like for yourself. The rest will be going to the charity shop.'

'OK,' said Tom. 'I'll start with this bookcase.' He looked in amazement at the literary riches before him. They were covered in a layer of dust. Among the collected works of Shakespeare was a veritable Athenaeum of classics. Soon he was filling boxes with the works of Charles Dickens, Jane Austen, Virginia Woolf, Lewis Carroll, C. S. Lewis, Emily Brontë and Jonathan Swift. The list was endless.

Owen had picked up half a dozen weighty tomes and showed them to Victor. 'These could definitely go in the college library,' he said. 'Perfect for the History of Education module.' He moved on to sorting through a collection of books on the windowsill. Next to the poems of Ted Hughes were some novels by J. R. R. Tolkien. He blew the dust off *The Two Towers* and *The Return of the King*. 'Hey, Tom!' he called out. 'Here's the rest of your trilogy. You ought to have these. Henry would have wanted you to read them.'

'Thanks,' said Tom and he put the novels in his satchel.

'This takes me back,' said Victor. He had blown a cobweb off an old copy of a magazine entitled *ROSLA: The Raising of the School Leaving Age* and he held it up.

Zeb smiled. 'ROSLA . . . I remember it well. Otherwise known as *Return of Slouchers, Layabouts and Arseholes*.'

'You always did have a gentle turn of phrase,' said Victor.

Zeb stopped to look around her. 'Just trying to break through the mood of melancholy in the room . . . but yes, sorry, everybody. It's just that looking around here is breaking my heart.'

'You're right,' said Victor. 'Henry left us too soon. The problem is that ageing doesn't come alone.'

There was silence. Even the old clock on the wall with its faded Roman numerals had stopped ticking, the battery long since expired.

'It's so sad,' said Zeb. 'All that's left of a life is books and dust.'

It was a few minutes later that the door opened and in walked Inger. 'Hi, everybody.' She tossed her shoulder bag on to a chair. 'What can I do, Victor?'

The moment of reflection had passed and Victor pointed to an ancient bureau in the corner. 'Maybe start there. Henry loved music and art, as you well know. I recall that's where he kept his favourites.'

By seven o'clock they had finished and Perkins had begun to move the boxes on his porter's barrow. 'I fancy a pint and something to eat,' said Owen.

'Good idea,' said Victor. 'Any suggestions?'

'We could go to the Cross Keys,' said Richard. 'They do fish and chips on a Friday.'

The pub was warm and welcoming when they walked in. The television was on and Terry Wogan was hosting the six-and-a-half-hour *BBC Children in Need* marathon. His co-presenters, Sue Cook and Joanna Lumley, were animated companions while telling the audience that the £14 million raised last year had been spent on a wide variety of good causes.

Gradually everyone relaxed with the hot food and a few drinks while the conversation ebbed and flowed. Richard was telling everyone about his new computer. 'It's an Amstrad 6128,' he said. There was excitement in his voice, which was unusual for the precise and moderate scientist.

'I've heard they're expensive,' said Zeb.

'It was £249.99,' said Richard.

Zeb smiled. 'So not *two hundred and fifty pounds*.'

The jocular hint of sarcasm passed Richard by. 'No,' he said. 'A penny less and it's got a colour monitor with seventy-seven free games and a joystick.'

Zeb rolled her eyes. 'A joystick?'

'Yes,' said the phlegmatic Richard. 'You're welcome to call in and try it some time.' The double entendre completely passed him by. There were a few raised eyebrows but the respect for Richard was absolute and no one wanted to make a joke at his expense.

Zeb drank the last of her gin and tonic and got up. 'Well, on that note, it's time to go home. Have a good weekend, everybody.'

'Thanks, Zeb, you too,' said Owen. 'If only we didn't have the Wallop to look forward to next week.'

Zeb stopped in the doorway, a fierce determination in her eyes. 'Guys . . . we're a fire crew in a burning building. It's all hands to the pumps now.'

There was a moment's silence after she left.

'Sadly, Zeb's right,' said Victor. 'Edna is very cunning. She's employing pestilential pressure to make life uncomfortable for us all and I can't see any other outcome.'

It was nine o'clock when the party broke up and one by one they drifted out into the darkness until there was just Tom and Inger left sitting opposite one another and finishing their drinks.

Inger was watching him carefully, clearly picking her moment. 'How are you feeling? You looked pretty upset after your meeting with Edna.'

'A little better, thanks. Sorting out Henry's books took my mind off it for a while.'

'Would you like to talk about it?' She gave him an encouraging smile. 'I'm a good listener.'

He looked into her blue eyes and saw an honest intensity. 'It's just that it's difficult. I felt . . .'

'What?' she asked softly.

'Diminished.'

Inger studied him again. He looked as if he was wearing a cloak of sadness. 'Diminished . . . in what way?'

'She believed I could *renege* on my friends.'

'How?'

'By informing on Victor. Apparently, she's got some new initiatives coming up next semester and presumed he would rebel against them.'

Inger sat back. 'I see . . . and you said no.'

Tom nodded.

'You won't have heard the rest of it. For Edna *no* is a negotiable word.'

'She made an offer of a permanent contract, but only if I agreed. One of the governors, name of Bullock, also collared me this afternoon with a similar veiled threat.'

'I know him, a seedy unpleasant man. It's a pity. Most of the governors seem positive and supportive. He's always been the bad apple.'

'He made it clear my future depended on supporting Edna.'

'That doesn't surprise me,' said Inger forcefully. 'She's just a manipulative woman. But, Tom . . . you must tell Victor. Don't keep this to yourself.'

Tom sighed. 'Thanks. I'm glad to have shared it with you.'

Suddenly there was a softness to her expression. It was as

if for a moment her emotional armour had been removed. 'That's what friends are for,' she said simply.

It was late when they walked back to the university car park. As Inger unlocked her car an owl, like a ghost of the night, flew by. She shivered in the bitter wind and Tom wanted to hold her but instead they said a swift goodbye.

'Thanks, Inger,' he said.

'Glad to help and don't forget: talk to Victor.'

He watched her red tail lights disappear into the distance before he climbed into his car and drove north towards Haxby.

Back in the warmth of his cottage Tom opened his satchel, took out the Tolkien books and sat at the kitchen table with a mug of tea. He opened *The Return of the King* and there at the back of the book, tucked in the flyleaf, was a black-and-white photograph. Curious, he looked at it carefully. A young girl stared back at him. He was puzzled. Her smile was crooked and she appeared to have Henry's Roman nose and pointed chin. It was then he thought back to Zeb's words.

'Books and dust,' he said out loud.

It seemed to be the sum total of Henry's life.

Nothing more and nothing less . . . *or was it*?

Chapter Six

Beautiful Lies

As Tom approached the gates of Claxton Underwood Primary School the first flakes of snow were falling from a gun-metal sky. It was a bitter December morning and his Primary One students were out on another school placement. Beneath the torn rags of cirrus clouds the smell of woodsmoke hung in the air in this North Yorkshire village. In the hedgerow a robin, perched on a branch, sang a mournful song while the red hips of dog roses gave notice of the dark days ahead.

Tom looked around him as children, excited by the falling snow, skipped into school while parents hurried back up the cobbled drive. A group of mothers were exchanging gossip at the school gate as he walked by.

'Ah wouldn't trust 'im as far as ah could throw 'im,' declared a vociferous woman in a tightly knotted headscarf. There were nods of agreement.

'Yer right there, Betty,' said one of them. 'An' t'look at 'im, you'd think butter wouldn't melt in 'is mouth.'

'That's t'problem,' said Headscarf Lady. ''E could tell lies f'England.'

Tom gave a wry smile. He recalled that Benjamin Disraeli was supposed to have once said there were three kinds of lies . . . *lies, damned lies and statistics.* However, at that moment, he was unaware that before the day was out he would discover another sort of lie, an elaborate lie that was the key to a box of secrets. On occasions truth depends on which way you're looking. That was for later, though, as Tom walked into the entrance hall where he was confronted by a grubby, bristle-haired little boy wearing grey shorts, socks round his ankles and a thick sweater. A balaclava hung loosely around his neck.

''Ello,' said eight-year-old Timothy Withers.

'Hello,' said Tom with a friendly smile. 'What's your name?'

'Timothy . . . What's yours?' This was clearly a boy who wasn't backwards in coming forwards.

Tom raised his eyebrows. 'I'm Dr Frith.'

The boy frowned. 'That's a funny name. What 'ave y'come for?'

'I'm here to see the headteacher.'

Timothy nodded towards the door labelled 'Mrs Abrahams, Headteacher'.

'She's busy. M'mam's talkin' to 'er. It's about our Ricky.'

'Ricky?'

'An' it wasn't 'is fault.'

'What wasn't?'

''E frightened m'new teacher.'

'What did he do?'

''E bit 'im.'

'Oh dear.'

''E didn't mean it. 'E were jus' bein' friendly.'

Tom decided to add a touch of common sense to the conversation. 'But biting is wrong, isn't it?'

Timothy was clearly unconvinced. 'Mebbe,' he muttered.

At that moment the door opened and a determined voice said, 'So, thank you, Mrs Withers. Let's say that's an end to it.'

A red-faced lady hurried from the headteacher's office into the entrance hall. She was carrying a wire cage. In it was a white rat with pink eyes. 'Ah told you not t'bring Ricky into school.' She glared down at Timothy and stormed out.

The headteacher, Mrs Abrahams, a tall, slim lady in a tweed suit, was always calm in a crisis. 'Off you go to your classroom, Timothy,' she said, 'and hang up your balaclava on your peg.' Then she smiled benignly at Tom. 'Is it Mr Frith?'

'Yes,' said Tom as realization dawned that he had been discussing an over-zealous rodent.

'Good morning. I'm Mrs Abrahams. Pleased to meet you.'

'Good morning,' said Tom, 'and thank you for offering a school placement. Is it convenient to see Mr Stocks?'

'You've just missed him.' She raised her eyebrows. 'I'm afraid his "Being Kind to Animals" project took a turn for the worse. I've sent him to A & E to check out a rat bite on his finger.'

'Oh,' said Tom. 'That's bad news. I hope it's not serious. In that case, if I may, I'll arrange another visit?'

'That makes sense,' said Mrs Abrahams. 'In the meantime, would you care for a hot drink on this cold morning?'

Tom glanced at his watch. 'Thank you but I had better get off to another school. I have a student at Claxton Bywater.'

'That's only five miles away,' said Mrs Abrahams. 'You can be there in ten minutes.' As Tom walked out of the entrance door she called after him, 'Avoid the ford crossing, of course,' but her words were lost in a gust of wind and sleet.

Tom breathed on his car key to warm up the lock, climbed in and hurriedly checked his Ordnance Survey map of North Yorkshire. He spotted the most direct route and set off. Soon the road narrowed and he had to reverse through a farm gate into a field to let a tractor and trailer drive past. The farmer in a flat cap, undeterred by the bitter weather, gave him a puzzled look as he drove by. Then he passed a sign that read 'Claxton Bywater ½'. 'Thank goodness,' he muttered.

All the way the weather had been worsening, the temperature dropping, and by now a veritable blizzard was sweeping across the frozen land. Tom slowed to a crawl as his windscreen wipers struggled to clear the berms of snow. Suddenly there was a sharp dip and he came to a halt. In front of him a stream crossed the road. It was decision time. Reversing back up the narrow track was not an option. He took a deep breath, chose first gear and eased his Ford Escort forward. The tyres crunched through the ice and all seemed to be well until he reached the centre of the stream, where the water swirled around him and the engine cut out. He tried the ignition again but there was no response. Finally, he opened the driver's door and stared out. There was nothing else for it but to get out and push. The water was freezing and came up to his calves. He staggered around to the back of the car and pushed but to no avail. He was stuck.

The choices were go back to Claxton Underwood or continue on to the next school, which was less than half a mile away. Tom took a deep breath, waded through the stream and walked on.

A church spire came into view, followed by a narrow high street with a pub, a corner shop and a row of terraced cottages with wavy snow patterns on their pantile roofs. Next to the corner shop a school sign pointed up a side road and he staggered up the hill and through the school gate. A blissful and welcome warmth filled the entrance hall. A door opened and a short, plump lady with rosy cheeks appeared. 'Good morning,' she said. 'I'm Mrs Baverstock, the school secretary. Can I help . . .?' She stared down in amazement at the puddles of water that were gathering around Tom's feet.

'Hello,' he said. 'I'm Tom Frith, Ellie MacBride's tutor from the university. My car is stuck in the stream.' He looked down at the woodblock floor. 'I'm sorry about the mess.'

'Don't worry, Mr Frith. Sit down and take off your shoes and socks,' and she hurried away, a woman used to dealing with scrapes and ailments – but this was different. Tom knew she'd be thinking, *Worse than the children . . .*

Tom sat on a chair, removed his sodden shoes and peeled off his socks. When the secretary reappeared she handed Tom a large towel. Then she picked up his socks. 'I'll put these over a radiator.'

'That's kind. Many thanks.'

'I'll tell Miss Frobisher you're here,' she said. 'She's teaching handwriting in the top infant class.'

Tom was left alone. He dried his feet, shivered and sneezed.

It was then that a petite lady in an immaculate two-piece business suit appeared, her blonde hair in a neat French plait. She looked sympathetically at Tom. 'Good morning, Mr Frith. I'm Miss Frobisher, the headteacher. Mrs Baverstock has told me what happened. I'm so sorry. It must have been dreadful for you.'

'Yes, I made the wrong decision on the road. I had to leave my car in the stream.'

Suddenly a tall, rangy figure appeared in the entrance porch. He was wearing a flat cap, an oilskin coat and wellington boots and waving through the window.

The secretary opened the door. 'Hello, Gabriel. Come in.'

'Pardon me but Rose at t'corner shop reckons you 'ave a visitor.' He grinned. 'She said 'e were passin' 'er shop an' looked as though 'e'd been for a paddle. Ah'm guessin' it's 'is car ah've jus' towed out of t'river so ah've left it on the 'igh street t'dry out.'

The secretary turned towards Tom. 'This is Mr Colley from Bramble Farm.'

'And a wonderful supporter of our school,' added a smiling Miss Frobisher.

The rugged farmer blushed slightly. 'Anything to 'elp t'kiddies,' he said with an admiring glance at Miss Frobisher.

Tom stood up. 'Many thanks, Mr Colley. I made a big mistake trying to cross the ford. Your help is appreciated.'

They shook hands and the farmer glanced down at Tom's bare feet. ''Appens from time t'time wi' outsiders. Not t'worry. Jus' remember t'tek turn-off up Sheep Street if y'come again.'

'Thanks, Mr Colley. I'll do that.'

The farmer looked thoughtful for a moment. 'Yer car's

safe where it is f'now but it'll tek a while t'dry out. Either way, good luck. Ah'll get on,' and he walked back down the school drive towards his tractor.

'He's a good man,' said Miss Frobisher. Once again she considered the bare-footed visitor. 'Perhaps it would be better if you wait in the office while you're drying off and Mrs Baverstock will organize a hot drink for you. In the meantime, I need to get back to my handwriting lesson so I'll see you later.'

A bell rang and through the window Tom saw children running out to the playground to enjoy the freshly fallen snow. Mrs Baverstock had left Tom alone in the office while she prepared mugs of coffee in the staffroom. There was a tap on the door and Ellie MacBride walked in.

'Hello, Tom. This is a surprise. I was expecting you next week.' She sat down next to him and then glanced down at the towel wrapped around his bare feet. 'What happened to you?'

'My car broke down crossing the ford.'

Ellie looked concerned. 'I was warned not to go that way.'

'Good advice,' said Tom. 'I made a quick decision to drive on to here from Claxton Underwood.'

'How's Brian getting on?'

'He's gone to hospital. Bitten by a rat apparently.'

'A *rat*?'

'A pet belonging to one of the children.'

'Oh, no! I hope he'll be OK.'

Tom shrugged. 'So . . . it's been an eventful morning.'

The practical Ellie considered the situation. 'What have you got on this afternoon?'

'A couple of tutorials at two o'clock, then a faculty meeting at four.'

She glanced up at the office clock. 'I'm teaching next lesson – maths with the top juniors – but if your car won't start, I can take you back at lunchtime.'

'Thanks. That would be really helpful.'

'Anyway, must go,' she said. 'I want to be well prepared.' She gave a wry smile. 'You never know, my tutor might want to check my lesson notes.'

Tom lifted his socks from the radiator. 'I'll see you soon.'

Ellie hurried away while Tom pulled on his socks and reflected on how this lively woman had such an effect on him. It didn't feel like tutor and student, more like . . . friends.

Ellie's lesson went well. The school had adopted SMP, the School Mathematics Project system of graduated work-cards. The class teacher, deputy head Ralph Conlan, was clearly impressed with the way Ellie supported the wide range of abilities. 'You've got a good one there,' he confided to Tom.

It was 11.40 a.m. when Tom thanked the head and secretary and set off for the high street. His car wouldn't start and he was concerned about running down the battery as he turned the ignition key repeatedly. With hunched shoulders against the flurries of snow, he returned to school. The lunchtime bell had gone and Ellie was waiting for him.

'No luck?' she asked.

Tom shook his head.

'Well, the head has said I can leave early and have the afternoon off, particularly with the weather as it is. So let's go.'

In the school car park was a rusty Austin Metro. It had clearly seen better days. Ellie smiled. 'I know what you're thinking but it gets me to uni each day.'

Tom brushed the snow from the windscreen. 'It's fine and I appreciate the lift.'

Ellie nodded. 'It was my mother's. I use it now.'

Tom recalled the famous television advert back in 1980 when a fleet of them had been assembled on the white cliffs of Dover. They were supposed to repel the invasion of foreign cars from abroad. The strapline was 'A British car to beat the world' but its days were numbered.

Soon they were driving carefully back to York and Tom had an idea. 'We could have some lunch if you like. It would be a way of saying thanks.'

Ellie stared ahead through the windscreen and smiled. She was beginning to see this man in a new light and not as her tutor. He had kind eyes and a warm heart. It was good to relax and perhaps share a little more with him.

Half an hour later they were sitting by a cosy fire with a fish-finger sandwich and a drink in a pub on Goodramgate.

'So,' said Tom as he sipped his beer, 'I guess this is an important time in your life.'

Ellie drank the last of her glass of shandy and smiled. 'It is . . . very special. My mum and dad are thrilled. They still live in a council house in Barnsley and have a fruit-and-veg stall in the market. It gives them a living. Long hours and hard work.'

'They've every right to be proud,' said Tom. Both their glasses were now empty. 'Another?' he asked and Ellie nodded.

Tom returned with two more drinks and the pot-boy put a couple more logs on the fire while Ellie stared into the flames.

'So, go on, Ellie. Tell me. What's the story?'

'Do you really want to know?'

Tom nodded. 'Yes . . . from the beginning.'

'Well . . . I grew up in Barnsley, left school at sixteen and worked in Marks & Spencer's selling women's clothes. I enjoyed it at the time. It was a living but I guess I always wanted more. I just didn't know it then. I was on the same treadmill as my peer group. All my friends were shop assistants or hairdressers and we met up on a Friday night for a drink and a chat and to meet boys.'

'Sounds a regular life,' said Tom.

'It was,' said Ellie, 'until I met Robbie.' She paused and stared once again into the flames. 'I was twenty by then. We hit it off straight away and I was pleased to have a steady boyfriend at last. He was in the navy so we met up when he was on leave. They were good days. Happy times. We were young and free. It seemed a carefree life.'

Then she paused again.

'And what happened then?' asked Tom.

She pushed her hair from her face and sighed. 'I've not shared this since arriving here. It's too personal.'

'I don't want to intrude,' said Tom quietly.

Ellie nodded briefly. 'I know.' She sipped her drink, then she put down her glass and clasped her hands. It looked as if she wanted to unburden her soul. Finally, she took a deep breath and spoke quietly. 'It was on my twenty-first birthday, the fifth of April 1982, when my life changed.'

'In what way?' asked Tom.

'He said he loved me and I thought I loved him. So we decided to get engaged. It was all a bit sudden but we were young and maybe a bit impetuous.'

'It happens the world over, Ellie. He sounds a good guy.'

'Suddenly we were at war with Argentina. He left for the Falklands with the naval task force.' There was a long silence while she struggled to find the right words. 'He was one of those that didn't make it. He died there.'

'I'm so sorry,' said Tom.

Tears formed in her eyes. 'He was a good man.'

'I'm sure he was,' whispered Tom.

She wiped her eyes with a small lace hanky. 'So there was no engagement, no marriage.' A moment of hesitation: 'No children, just an emptiness.' She looked up at Tom. 'I've not been with anyone since.'

Tom grappled with the enormity of the revelation. 'I see,' he murmured.

She shook her head. 'It was tough at home. I remember my mother saying how she felt sorry for the mothers of all those young Argentinian men who died on the *Belgrano* when it was sunk by one of our submarines and my dad told her to shut up. It was the first time I had heard them argue.'

'Difficult times,' said Tom. 'So how did you finish up here?'

'I decided to make a career for myself so I went to night school and got a couple of A Levels. Getting to university was a big achievement. I'm the first in my family to do it.

Coming here means I'll be a teacher by my early thirties. It will be a new life for me. Doing something worthwhile.'

They finished their drinks in silence.

When they walked back to the university car park, Ellie put her hand on Tom's arm. 'Just thinking ahead, Tom. I can take you back tomorrow morning. Your car should be fine by then.'

'That's kind, Ellie, but won't you have things to do?'

There was a pause and she looked thoughtful. 'I can rearrange. Don't worry. You live in Haxby, don't you?'

'Yes, a cottage on the high street. Across the road from the little supermarket.'

'I'll park there, say, at nine?'

'Thanks. See you then.'

When Tom walked through the quad it was carpeted with virgin snow. He followed a group of students who were wearing their warmest coats as they headed for the refectory and the welcome smell of hot soup. In the common room he joined Victor, Owen and Zeb. He sat down beside Victor, who was sipping his tea while the two socialists were complaining about royalty.

'Apparently, Lady Di is trying to persuade her husband to stop shooting pheasants,' said Zeb. 'She wants to make sure her sons don't follow in Charlie-boy's footsteps.'

'No chance,' grumbled Owen. 'That's how the other half live.'

'Actually,' said Victor, 'statistically, it's two point four per cent. In other words, simply the privileged few.'

'There speaks my favourite pedant,' quipped Zeb with a grin.

'Hey, Tom,' said Owen, 'you OK? Didn't see you at lunch.'

'Had a problem getting to one of my schools at Claxton Bywater. My car got stuck in the stream.'

'Bloody hell!' said Zeb. 'How did you get out of that one?'

'With wet feet and a friendly farmer. I'm fine now but I've had to leave my car in the village to dry out. One of my students drove me back.'

'I can give you a lift home after the faculty meeting if you like, Tom,' said Victor. 'Haxby's on my way.'

The afternoon tutorials went well. Over hot drinks Tom helped two of his final-year English students with an extended bibliography for their dissertations on Oscar Wilde and William Golding. As they were leaving he saw Inger in the corridor. She looked stressed and, once again, Tom only wanted to ease her worries. 'Have you time for a coffee, Inger?'

She glanced through the open door at his cosy study filled with books and the coffee cups on the table and made a decision. 'Thanks, Tom. That would be welcome.' She sat down as the kettle boiled.

Minutes later they faced each other and sipped their coffee while snowflakes pattered against the window.

Tom broke the silence: 'How are you?'

'Busy,' she said simply.

Tom changed tack. 'How's your brother?'

Her blue eyes came suddenly alive. 'Back in Norway . . . Exciting times for him.'

'Really? Why's that?'

'He's on television next week.'

'With the orchestra?'

'Yes. It's a new television station, TVNorge. Similar to ITV, supported by advertisements. He said he would record it for me.'

'That's great.'

Inger gave a cautious smile. She'd been avoiding talking too much with her colleagues, but she was glad that she'd said yes to Tom's invitation for a coffee. He was a kind man. For a brief moment as they chatted she had emerged from the dark mist that descended on her each evening when she returned to her empty home. Loneliness was beginning to feed her depression.

'I miss Andreas. He lifts me when I'm down.'

'Is that often?'

She turned to stare out of the window and her blonde hair fell over her face like a golden shroud. 'Sometimes,' she mused. 'When he left he said what he always says.'

'And what's that?

'Listen to the birdsong and rejoice in what we have.'

'He's right. Sounds like you have a great brother.'

Inger brushed her hair from her eyes and looked at Tom. 'He is. He always tells me to stop and think and breathe . . . and remember the good times.'

Tom studied her. 'My mother used to say to me that the best days of my life could begin today.'

'Maybe,' she said.

'You could choose now, Inger. Time only moves in one direction . . . so go with it and choose happiness.'

'Easier said than done.' She gave an imperceptible shake of her head and got up to go.

'Don't leave, Inger. Change is coming. Embrace it.'

She paused by the door. 'I know you mean well, Tom, but at the moment there's no narrative to describe how I feel. Don't worry, I'll get over it.'

It was a lie and she knew it. As she closed the door she recalled nights when it felt as though her heart would burst through her chest followed by days when it was hard to put one foot in front of another. She wanted to tell Tom that her life was broken. *I was humiliated,* she thought as she walked back to her study.

After she'd gone Tom sat in silence and stared at the rows of books that lined the shelves. Perhaps, like the stories before him, love was a worn-out metaphor. Even so, for a brief moment, Inger had shared her pain and Tom felt he had been afforded a glimpse inside her soul.

It was four o'clock and Edna Wallop had adopted a strident voice at the faculty meeting. 'I'm giving you a heads-up on a new initiative.'

Zeb was sitting next to Tom and she sank lower in her chair while Owen shook his head.

'I'm creating an Efficiency Working Party.' Edna was in full flow now. 'Instead of you teaching just two three-hour sessions there is a powerful argument to improve this by timetabling three two-hour lectures each day.' There was a gasp from the audience. 'Each lecture would be followed by a third hour of unsupervised *directed time*.'

Victor raised his hand. 'What does that mean?' he called out.

'It's simple, Victor. You set your students one hour of follow-up work as individuals or groups. They can work in the library. This way each tutor can teach more hours in the day and we can bring in more students from abroad. That's where the money is and I shall have the full support of the governing body.'

'Is she serious?' murmured Zeb. 'Or is she just playing silly buggers?'

Edna had anticipated some resentment. 'OK,' she said with a withering look. 'Cut me some slack here, folks. That's all for now. In the meantime . . . think efficiency, people.'

Tom looked at the back row where Inger was sitting next to Victor and staring down at the floor in a world of her own.

'Thanks, Victor. We're here. I'm opposite the supermarket,' said Tom as they drove down Haxby high street.

Victor eased his Rover 200 to a stop. 'I appreciated you telling me what Edna had to say to you about being her informer. She really is an evil so-and-so and that Cedric Bullock is no better – partners in crime. I know most of the governors and they're fine but Bullock is always out to line his own pockets. He thinks of himself first and last.' He shook his head and then stared at the bright lights of the supermarket. 'Actually, this is handy; I need a few things.'

Tom followed him around. They arrived at the checkout with an eclectic collection. Victor's shopping comprised McVitie's Chocolate Hob Nobs, 61p; a dozen eggs, 99p; a bottle of Tesco vodka, £6.29, and Teacher's Highland Cream Scotch Whisky, £7.99.

As they crossed the road Victor muttered, 'A night to be indoors, Tom.'

'Come in for a few minutes,' said Tom as he opened the front door to his cottage. 'Let's have a coffee and get warm.'

'Good idea,' said Victor, looking appreciatively around Tom's home. It was a world of books, two comfy armchairs, a welcome gas fire, a few Lowry prints and a neat kitchen.

'Love the cottage, Tom.' He pointed to L. S. Lowry's matchstick men in *Going to Work*. 'We have similar tastes. I'm a huge Lowry fan. You've done this up nicely. Bit different to Owen's place. He's an untidy so-and-so. God knows how Sue puts up with him. She's a saint.'

While Tom was preparing two mugs of instant coffee Victor scanned the bookshelves. 'Good taste in literature too. Some great novels here. Particularly like the collection of Penguin paperbacks.' Next to one of the armchairs on a small table were two books, Tolkien's *The Two Towers* and *The Return of the King*.

Victor smiled as Tom came in from the kitchen. 'Absolute classics,' he said.

They sat down facing each other. 'Yes, a great trilogy,' said Tom. 'Henry gave me *The Fellowship of the Ring* just after I started.'

Victor warmed his hands on his coffee cup and looked pensive. 'I miss him. A lovely man. He should have retired a few years ago while his health was holding out.'

'I only knew him briefly,' said Tom. 'What was he like when you first met him?'

'A fine tutor and well respected. Mind you, he was a loner. Difficult to get close to him. Books were his life. He hated the new technology.'

'Which Edna advocates,' said Tom. 'She seems to have made his life difficult.'

'Too true. She bullied him. Ground him down. In contrast to Henry, she's the archetype of an enlightened despot – rather like Frederick William of Prussia. In other words, she's a dictator.'

'I've never come across this kind of leadership before.'

Victor sighed and put down his mug. 'Beware, Tom. It's an insidious process that crushes enthusiasm and blocks progress. She's also an incorrigible liar. That bit about having the support of the governing body just can't be true . . . but you never know. For Edna greed is good.'

He glanced at the clock. 'Well, I had better get home. Pat is making a casserole tonight.'

Tom smiled. 'You're lucky. I could do with some of her cooking.'

There was a pause while Victor slipped on his coat. 'Tom . . . my partner is a man.'

Tom blushed. 'Oh, apologies. I wasn't thinking.'

'No problem. I'm used to it. Most of my close colleagues know, of course. It's only Edna who gives me a hard time.'

'Really?'

Victor looked reflective. 'It's sad; I felt I had to lie when I was first appointed by Henry. They would have called it *obfuscate* in Parliament but opinions have changed in the last twenty years. After all, it's 1988.'

They shook hands and Victor glanced down at the Tolkien novels. 'I'll leave you to Frodo's journey,' he said with a gentle smile.

'Oh, that reminds me,' said Tom. 'There was an old photograph in the flyleaf.'

'Really?'

Tom opened the book and handed it to Victor. 'Maybe Henry was using it as a bookmark.'

Victor stared in surprise at the image of the young girl

and her crooked smile. He studied it for what seemed an age. 'May I hang on to this?'

'Of course.'

Victor placed it carefully in his wallet, buttoned up his coat and walked out into the darkness.

Later that evening, Tom sat reading his book and sipping a glass of beer. In the background Clannad's *Legend* album was playing on his cassette player. It was quiet and soothing and suited his melancholic mood. It had been a strange day, one in which he'd come to feel a new empathy for his friends.

However, realization can be a slow process and sometimes words are not always what they seem. In life some secrets are held close, never to be shared. For Ellie there were simple lies and for Inger more complex lies. Then again, for Victor, on occasions there were *beautiful lies.*

Chapter Seven

Still Waters

Tom awoke to a dawn of silence and light. It was an iron-grey morning and overnight snow had covered the vast Vale of York. As he drove into the city, beyond the frozen hedgerows and skeletal trees a reluctant light spread across the fields towards the stark, desolate high moors of North Yorkshire. It was a harsh winter's morning on Friday, 16 December, and an eventful weekend was in store.

After parking his car he crunched through the frozen snow into the welcome warmth of the reception area.

'Morning, Dr Frith,' called out a cheerful voice. It was Perkins the Porter. 'How are you on this last morning of term?'

'Good morning, Perkins. Fine, thanks.' Tom put his satchel on the polished reception counter and looked at the man who had become a valued confidant over recent months. 'Thanks for all your support. You've been a great help.'

Perkins beamed with pride. 'It's been a pleasure and I was pleased to see you've got on well with Mr Llewellyn. I thought you would.'

Tom smiled. 'He's like you . . . a good friend.'

Peter Perkins looked up with affection at this tall, slightly awkward young man in the familiar crumpled cord suit. 'That's very kind.'

'Have you any plans for Christmas?' asked Tom.

'Usual,' Perkins said with another smile. 'Midnight Mass in our local church. My Pauline's in the choir. Then Christmas dinner with all the trimmings at our daughter's in Bishopthorpe. We watch the grandkids playing with their toys and after a bit of telly we set off home again. Same every year. I love it.'

'Sounds perfect,' said Tom wistfully. 'Anyway, must get on. See you later.'

'Have a good day,' said Perkins. He watched Tom walk away and hoped he might find some peace in his busy life. *The students certainly like him,* he thought.

It was then that Edna Wallop appeared in an expensive fur coat and a matching hat, looking like an upmarket extra in *Doctor Zhivago*. As usual she ignored Perkins completely and strode on.

Perkins shook his head. 'And a merry Christmas to you too,' he muttered.

Tom was walking through the quad when Ellie appeared by his side. She was animated. 'Hi, Tom, guess what!'

'Go on. Tell me. You look pleased with yourself.'

Under her red bobble hat there were flecks of snow on the wavy strands of hair that framed her cheeks. 'There was a Students' Union meeting last night and I'm now an assistant editor for the *Echo*. I'm the first-year rep.'

'That's great news. You're perfect for the job.' The

Eboracum Echo was a popular and vibrant student paper and Tom was familiar with the current storylines.

She grinned mischievously. 'So I'll be relying on you for some juicy stories.'

He stopped under the archway that led to the lecture block. 'You know I'll help as much as I can, Ellie, but there might be confidential stuff involving the staff.'

She frowned for a moment. 'It was just a light-hearted remark, Tom. You know I would never be indiscreet.'

Tom realized he had been too abrupt. 'I'm sorry. That didn't come out as I intended. Just me being cautious.'

She sighed, 'I understand,' and turned to leave.

'Ellie, don't go. I suppose I meant that we may be friends but I need to be loyal to my colleagues.'

She came closer and gave him a knowing look. 'Is that what we are, Tom? Just friends?'

'You know what I mean,' he said softly.

'Do I?'

'Anyway, I'm pleased for you, Ellie. Well done.'

She nodded briefly but as she walked away there was a hint of sadness in her eyes.

Tom climbed the metal stairs to the Cloisters corridor and walked slowly to his study. The conversation with Ellie hadn't gone well. It was the end of the Michaelmas term and he needed to find an opportunity to speak to her once again before the students went down for their Christmas and New Year holiday. He was deep in thought when he opened the door. Owen was standing by the window, his arms folded.

'What was all that about?' he asked.

'Pardon?'

'I saw you talking to Ellie MacBride. After you left her she looked as though she was upset. A couple of her mates arrived and consoled her. Then they set off for the lecture block. So . . . what's going on?'

'Nothing really.'

'Come on. We've shared a lot of stuff in this room. Are you getting involved with her?'

Tom dropped his satchel on the floor and sat down on one of the armchairs. 'It's complicated.'

Owen looked at his watch. 'Are you teaching first session?'

'No. Just tutorials after morning break.'

'Same here,' said Owen. He switched on the kettle and sat down. 'Come on then, let's have it.'

Tom leaned back in his chair and stared at the ceiling. 'Ellie's a great student, really positive.' He paused and shook his head. 'The thing is it's tricky at times because I think she might like me.'

Owen nodded. 'There's nothing unusual about that. Tutor–student relationships go on all the time.'

Tom was surprised. 'Really? I wouldn't want that. Surely it's wrong?'

Owen looked thoughtful. 'I could name a couple now but I won't. Not me, of course. Sue would cut my balls off first . . . and that would be just for starters. But if you fancy her why don't you do something about it? Is she already in a relationship?'

'No.'

'That sounded definite. You've obviously shared a few conversations with her.'

'There was someone a few years ago but he was killed in the Falklands.'

'That's sad. Tough for her.' Owen stood up, spooned coffee into two mugs and poured in the boiling water. 'Is she over it now?'

'I think so.'

'Has there been anyone else since then?'

'Not to my knowledge.'

Owen opened the fridge. 'Damn! We're out of milk.'

Tom picked up his mug. 'This is fine for me.'

'Inger will have some,' said Owen. 'I've borrowed hers in the past.' He nodded. 'You could ask her.'

Tom shook his head. 'No, I'll get some later.' Suddenly there was colour in his cheeks.

Owen sat back. 'Hell's bells! It's her, isn't it? It's Inger. I've seen that soppy way you look at her.'

Tom sighed. 'I asked her out for a drink a while back.'

Owen put down his mug and stared at Tom. 'And . . .?'

'She said no thanks.'

'I'm not surprised. Inger's terrific except she's a closed book – keeps her thoughts and feelings close. She tends not to share. Nobody ever gets close apart from Victor. She trusts him. Even with me she's careful and I've been her colleague since she arrived.'

For a few moments they sipped their black coffee in silence.

'She'll be there tomorrow night,' said Owen. 'There're at least twenty of us going. Victor always arranges a get-together at the end of the Michaelmas term.'

'You mean the faculty night out at the cinema.'

'Yes. Sue's really excited about it. She goes weak at the

knees when Tom Cruise is on the screen. She saw *Top Gun* first time round and they've put it on again for Christmas.'

'I'll be there,' said Tom. 'Victor mentioned it to me last week.'

Silence fell as they sat, each with his own thoughts, until Tom finished his coffee and stood up. Then he grabbed his duffel coat from the back of the door.

'Where're you going?' asked Owen.

'To buy some milk.'

It was lunchtime and for Tom tutorials had ended. He walked into the dining room and scanned the sea of faces. Ellie was sitting with Mo Greenwood and Kath Featherstone. They were deep in conversation when he approached them.

'Sorry to interrupt. Ellie . . . any chance of a word after your lunch?'

She looked curious but nodded. 'Where?'

'Reception,' said Tom.

'OK,' she said simply and returned to her conversation.

In the reception area, Peter Perkins had gone for his lunch and a teenage baggage porter was behind the counter playing with a Rubik's Cube. Tom was sitting on a bench, leaning against the wall and staring aimlessly at the row of heraldic shields when Ellie walked in.

She looked curious. 'Hi, this is interesting.'

'We got off on the wrong foot this morning. I'm really sorry about my reaction. It's just that I've read some of the revelations in the *Echo*.'

Ellie sat down beside him. Her voice softened. 'The paper does a lot of good, Tom. It gives the student body a voice.'

'I agree. It's important and I know you'll be a brilliant editor.'

Ellie smiled. 'Thanks but actually I'm an *assistant* editor. Kimberly's the driving force. She's a real investigative journalist. I'm just writing articles about grants and sports events and the state of our accommodation.'

'Kimberly?' said Tom. 'Do I know her?'

'A scientist in her fourth year. She's great. Total dedication.' Ellie's eyes were suddenly bright with excitement.

'Well, as I said before, you'll be perfect for this.'

'Thanks . . . that means a lot.'

Tom decided to change tack and move on. 'What are your plans for the holidays?'

'I'm staying in York for the weekend to do my Christmas shopping. Then I'm going to Barnsley to see my mum and dad.'

'I'm shopping as well tomorrow morning. Maybe I could buy you a coffee.'

Ellie looked up at Tom, both of them in their private cocoon of space. A breeze sprang up and she brushed a few strands of hair from her face. It seemed to take an age but eventually she said, 'I'd like that.' Then she smiled. 'Because that's what *friends* do.'

'How about outside Bettys Café at ten thirty?'

She raised her eyebrows, a mischievous smile on her face. 'Did you know there's no apostrophe in Bettys?'

'I've never really looked.'

She stood up. 'That's the trouble with certain men. They don't see what's in front of them. See you at half ten.'

*

At afternoon break Tom joined Victor, Owen, Zeb and Inger in the cosy corner of the common room. The television was on and his colleagues were drinking tea, munching on hot scones and catching up on the news. It was dominated by the aftermath of the Clapham Junction rail crash in which thirty-five people had been killed and the mood was sombre.

'Terrible tragedy,' murmured Victor.

'A dreadful Christmas for all those families,' said Zeb.

Tom sat down next to Owen. The Welshman gave him a quizzical look. 'Had a good day?'

Tom nodded and drank his tea while the news moved on to George Bush who was settling into his role as President Elect after defeating Michael Dukakis in last month's election.

'Are you coming tomorrow night, Tom?' asked Victor.

'Yes, looking forward to it.' He glanced at Inger but she was twiddling a strand of her blonde hair and staring at the screen. A picture of Edwina Currie had appeared with the news that she had resigned as a junior Health Minister following the salmonella scandal.

'Good riddance,' said Zeb.

'She might have been right,' said Victor. 'There have been cases of food poisoning after eating eggs.'

Zeb frowned. 'Maybe so, Victor, but she's still a bloody silly woman.'

'I think Zeb means she's a Tory,' said Owen.

'Exactly,' said Zeb. 'Same difference.'

'Come on now,' said Inger. 'Politics always divides us. Let's talk about something more positive.'

'Like Tom Cruise,' said Owen.

'Now you're talking,' said Zeb. 'He could put a notch on my bedpost any night. What about you, Inger?'

Inger merely smiled and glanced up at the clock. 'End-of-term faculty meeting in ten minutes and I need to collect my bag.'

Tom watched her walk away.

A few minutes later Tom and Owen had moved to the rows of chairs in the centre of the common room. Zeb and Inger were in the back row deep in conversation.

'Hey, look at that,' said Owen. Through the window they saw Edna outside in the quad. She had stopped in her tracks, confronted by a tall female student. The young woman was wearing an Afghan coat, knee-length leather boots and a wide-brimmed black hat while clutching a notebook and pen. It was clearly a challenging meeting brought to a conclusion by what appeared to be angry words from Edna.

'Who's that?' asked Tom.

'Kimberly Stratton. Brilliant science student, according to Richard. Been running the *Echo* for the last couple of years. She interviewed me last year for an article on "Physical Education and a Healthy Heart". It was really good.'

'Ellie MacBride mentioned her this morning. Ellie's just joined the editorial team.'

Owen gave his friend a knowing look. 'So you've seen her again since upsetting her this morning.'

'I didn't mean to upset her.'

'So . . . what are you doing about it?'

'I'm buying her a coffee tomorrow morning.'

Owen patted Tom on his back. 'About bloody time!'

*

A hush descended as Edna entered the common room, removed her fur hat and placed it on the table before her. 'Good afternoon, people. We've got the usual end-of-term notices.' Her eyes scanned the room like searchlights. She noticed Victor at the back of the room, sitting alone for a change. He seemed preoccupied.

'So, if I could have your attention, please.' It was more of a command rather than a request. 'Lectures recommence on Monday, the ninth of January, and we'll meet on Friday, the sixth, at one p.m. to confirm any new staffing arrangements.' There were a few puzzled glances. 'Meanwhile there's been inter-faculty agreement for the annual field week. It's to be at the end of April.' She looked down at her calendar. 'Commencing Friday, the twenty-eighth.'

It was then that the mood changed and she turned a glassy-eyed stare towards the back row. 'I note Zeb wishes to take the Drama and Main English students to Stratford and I'll need costings for this as soon as possible and prior to any agreement.'

'There's never been any problem in the past,' muttered Zeb.

While Zeb fumed, a few seats away from the others, Victor was still taking no notice of Edna. Instead, he had slipped out a black-and-white photograph from his wallet and was studying it. He gave an almost imperceptible nod before he replaced it and sat back. Clearly preoccupied with his own thoughts, he stared out of the window.

Edna ploughed on through the list of significant dates for next term but, once again, sensed she was losing her audience. Finally, she raised her voice. 'So, when you leave this meeting keep in mind there will be a paradigm shift next term. The bottom line is we need to benchmark our special practices against other institutions to give us a competitive advantage. This will be a game changer and I'll expect 360-degree feedback. To achieve this it may be time to declutter and trim the fat. Nineteen eighty-nine will see fundamental changes.'

Then a contented smile appeared on her face. 'Finally . . . I've just spoken to the Vice Chancellor and he confirmed the post of Head of Faculty has been advertised and interviews are scheduled for the summer term.' She glanced down at her notes. 'That's it. Thank you, people,' and she walked out.

Zeb leaned over the chairs to talk to Owen. 'Trim the bloody fat,' she said. 'What next?'

Owen shook his head. 'It's getting worse. Does 360-degree feedback mean you don't know your arse from your elbow?'

'Exactly,' said Zeb, 'and it looks like the smug bitch reckons she's already got the Head of Faculty job.'

Tom looked around at his colleagues as they all got up to leave. They appeared dejected. Zeb and Owen were clearly furious while, deep down, he knew the next so-called *paradigm shift* for him was to get ready to move on in six months' time.

He stared forlornly out of the window until there was a tap on his shoulder. It was Inger. She sat down beside him. 'You look sad again,' she said quietly.

'I am,' he said. 'I feel caught betwixt and between. I have great colleagues, and I enjoy my teaching, but this style of leadership is crushing me.'

'I understand,' she said. 'Coping can be difficult.' She was looking at Tom from a fresh perspective. There was a sensitivity about this tall, rugged Yorkshireman that she had not noticed before, a hint of vulnerability. For the first time she recognized another soul in torment.

'Thanks, Inger,' he said softly. 'I'll be fine.' He looked into her blue eyes and smiled.

It was Saturday morning and Tom was driving towards York. Over the distant hills the sun shone like beaten bronze while beyond the frozen hedgerows the trees had lost all their colour and stood like silent sentinels above a shroud of fresh snow. Around him was a stark and desolate world but the harsh winter weather was not uppermost in Tom's mind. He had a mid-morning meeting with an attractive and intriguing woman.

He parked in the university car park and walked down Lendal towards the city centre and into St Helen's Square. He stood outside the famous Bettys Café & Tea Rooms and pulled his scarf a little tighter. It was freezing cold but the locals did not seem to notice it as they hurried towards Parliament Street and the Christmas market.

Ellie arrived wrapped up warmly in a smart winter coat, black cords and a bright blue bobble hat. She was carrying two large shopping bags. 'Hi, Tom. Perfect timing. These are getting heavy.'

'Let's go in. Bettys is always special.'

She smiled and Tom relaxed. It was as if the equilibrium between them had been restored. 'You're right, Tom, this is *special*.'

They were ushered to a table past a display of cakes and handmade chocolates and seated next to the huge curved window. Around them was a haven of wood panelling and art deco mirrors. The waitress looked as though she had just stepped out of an Agatha Christie novel in her cap and starched apron.

They scanned the menu. 'You choose, Ellie. My treat.'

Ellie selected a plate of Yorkshire Fat Rascals, namely fruity scones filled with citrus peel, almonds and cherries. She poured the tea from a silver teapot through the delicate tea strainer and into the china cups. 'Perfect,' she said quietly.

'I'm glad we've done this,' said Tom. He glanced down at the shopping bags. 'So what have you bought?'

She pulled out two heavy books. 'This is for my mother.' It was *Mary Berry's Television Cookbook*. 'A bargain at £4.95.'

'Good gift,' said Tom. 'I might get one for *my* mother as well.'

'They're in WHSmith's,' said Ellie.

'And this one looks useful,' said Tom. It was *The Personal Computer Handbook: The Foremost Guide to the New Home Technology*.

'It's for me,' said Ellie. 'Important to keep up with the new technology, otherwise we'll be overtaken by the children we teach.'

'Very true,' said Tom. 'What's that one?' There was another book at the bottom of the bag.

'It's another for me,' she said cautiously.

'Come on, don't be shy. Let's see.'

Reluctantly she put on the table *Linda Evans Beauty and Exercise Book: Inner and Outer Beauty*. The *Dynasty* star was clearly cashing in on her fame.

Tom shook his head. 'You don't need this, Ellie. You could teach Linda Evans a thing or two about beauty.'

Ellie puffed out her cheeks. 'Oh dear, Tom. Maybe you should have said that yesterday morning,' she teased.

'Mind you, in my experience flattery doesn't come easily to big, tough Yorkshiremen. Ten years ago in Barnsley it was a Babycham, a bag of pork scratchings and a cuddle under the bus shelter, so at least we've moved on.' She waved her hand over the silver service on the table. 'I prefer this . . . so, thank you. This is lovely, a real Christmas treat.' She sat back and studied him carefully. 'So what's your backstory, Tom? You know mine.'

'Nothing special. Born in Yorkshire. Dad got a job near Ipswich. Went to school there, earned extra cash picking French dwarf beans in the fields and worked on the Christmas post delivering small packages on a bicycle. Tried my best at school, then uni, taught in a primary school in Harrogate and finally here.'

'For how long?'

'It's a one-year contract.'

'Then what?'

'Probably back to my deputy headship or maybe look for a village school headship.'

Ellie put down her cup and rested her chin on her clasped hands. 'I was rather hoping you would stay here for the rest of my course. Sounds a bit selfish but you're a good tutor. I've learned a lot.'

'So have I,' said Tom. 'It never stops. I have some great colleagues. I learn something new from them every day.'

Ellie gave Tom the direct look he was beginning to know so well. 'Does that include Dr Wallop?'

'More tea?' said Tom with a smile.

'OK. I know you can't comment but her reputation goes before her. In fact, Kimberly is on her case. She's come across something about her but she's keeping it to herself.'

'I saw the two of them in conversation this morning.'

'In that case Dr Wallop better beware. Kimberly is like a dog with a bone when she gets her teeth into a story.'

The waitress arrived and asked if they would like more tea.

Ellie shook her head. 'I'm fine, thanks.'

They collected their coats and walked out on to the frozen pavements of York. The 1973 Slade hit 'Merry Xmas Everybody' could be heard blasting out on a tannoy system from the Christmas Fayre.

'Well, time to go our separate ways, I guess,' said Tom.

'"Parting is such sweet sorrow",' said Ellie coyly.

Tom grinned. '*Romeo and Juliet*.'

'But why did Shakespeare use the word "sweet"?' asked Ellie.

'I'm guessing this is rhetorical.'

She nodded. 'It meant they would meet again.'

'We shall . . . next term.'

'Some of the girls in our group are going to the New Year dance in the Assembly Rooms. If you're free you ought to come along.'

'Thanks, Ellie, but I'll probably be still at my mother's.'

'Pity . . . I could have taught you a slow waltz.'

'I'm not a dancer,' said Tom.

As they parted she stretched up and kissed him on the cheek. 'See you next year, Dr Frith.'

He watched her walk away and began to understand why Shakespeare talked of 'star-crossed lovers'. Perhaps in another life and another time they could have been more than friends, but not here in Eboracum . . . not now.

*

At six thirty Tom dressed quickly in a clean shirt, a warm jumper and a clean pair of jeans. He grabbed a scarf and his duffel coat and drove steadily into York. The temperature had dropped to minus five degrees and the road was like a ribbon of blue glass. He parked near Micklegate Bar and under the purple hue of a winter evening he walked to the Odeon Cinema. A huge poster for the film *Top Gun*, starring Tom Cruise and Kelly McGillis, was lit up brightly above the entrance. It promised relaxing escapism.

Owen and Sue Llewellyn were at the door as Tom arrived.

'Hi, Tom,' said Sue, 'we got a lift in with Victor,' and then she wandered over to the group gathering in the foyer. Inger was there in a long grey woollen coat and her hair hung loosely over a crimson scarf. Richard Head was resplendent in a bow tie and navy-blue Crombie overcoat that had once belonged to his father, and Zeb had a muscular young man in tow. The colleagues were chattering light-heartedly as they caught up with casual news.

Owen gave Tom a searching look. 'How did you get on with Ellie this morning?'

'Tea and scones in Bettys.'

'Impressive . . . so no expense spared.'

'It was good to chat and there were no hard feelings when we parted.'

'Fair enough. Pleased it went well. Pity you haven't got natural Welsh charm. I could give you a few lessons.'

'I know too many jokes about Welshmen and sheep to go down that road, Owen.'

'Anyway, shut up, boyo, Sue's coming back.'

Sue gave her husband a stern look. 'What are you two grinning about?'

'Nothing, my little daffodil,' said Owen.

'You know where you can stick your daffodils – and your leeks for that matter. Take no notice of him, Tom. Don't let him lead you astray. You're too nice a Yorkshireman for that.' She tugged Owen's sleeve. 'Come on,' she said. 'I want you to meet Zeb's new man.'

As they walked off, Victor approached Tom. 'Pleased you made it. We do this sort of stuff at the end of each term. Good for morale.'

'Great idea,' said Tom. 'Thanks for the invitation.'

Victor looked around and led Tom away from the others. 'Just a thought, Tom, but I was wondering if there were any other photographs in the books you picked up from Henry's study.'

'Don't think so but I'll check.'

'If you would I'd be grateful.'

'Who was the girl in the photo?'

'Not sure but I've got a few ideas. It's certainly intriguing. I'll let you know.'

While Tom had Victor's attention he thought he would ask a question. 'Just thinking . . . will you be applying for the Head of Faculty?'

'It's crossed my mind but it would appear Edna is the favourite. She's certainly got the ear of one or two of the governors.'

'How can that be?' asked Tom.

Victor put his hand on Tom's shoulder and gave an enigmatic smile. 'Still waters, Tom . . . still waters.'

Tom looked puzzled. 'Now you're being cryptic.'

'We'll talk again, Tom. Go and join the others while I sort out the tickets.'

Victor watched Tom walk away. All would be revealed in good time. The photograph of the strange girl was still in his wallet and he thought he knew who she might be ... but that was for another day.

Everyone had arrived and Victor handed in the block-booking tickets at the box office. They all wandered into the darkness of the cinema with Tom following Inger, Owen and Sue up the aisle. Suddenly he received a push from Owen. 'After you,' insisted the Welshman, and Tom followed Inger along the row of seats. When he sat down next to her he was aware of his senses coming alive. As she took off her coat there was the rustle of a silk blouse against her skin and the hint of Dior perfume.

She turned to Tom. 'Do you know what the film is about?'

'Yes,' he said. 'I saw it when it first came out a couple of years ago. Tom Cruise plays Pete "Maverick" Mitchell, a young aviator on a US aircraft carrier. There's a lot of action plus a love story.'

'So you don't mind seeing it again?'

'Not at all. It's a chance to shut out the real world for an hour or two.'

'We all need that, Tom,' she said quietly and then settled back in her seat.

She looked relaxed and her elbow was on the shared armrest between them. Tom tried to imagine it was just the two of them on a date. He guessed that sitting next to this beautiful woman in the shimmering shadows of the auditorium was as close to heaven as he would ever get.

It was over too soon and they gathered once again in the foyer before venturing out into the snow and ice. Then Inger made a sudden and unexpected announcement. 'I'm having a New Year's Eve party in my flat. You're all welcome.' She turned to Tom. 'You too, Tom, if you're free.'

'Thank you,' he said simply.

Victor saw the look on Tom's face as she walked away into the darkness. After the goodbyes and season's greetings the rest of the crowd dispersed and Tom followed Victor and Owen out into the cold night air.

Victor hung back to talk to Tom. He spoke quietly. 'You like her, don't you?'

'Is it obvious?'

'A little,' said Victor.

'Sadly, it's futile. We seem to be walking different pathways.'

'Perhaps you should persevere,' said Victor. 'You need to hope for the best, even in the face of adversity. Alexander Pope put it succinctly in his *Essay on Man*.'

'What was that?'

He patted Tom on his back. '"Hope springs eternal".'

As Tom drove away, heading north out of the city, he reflected on the day. The meeting with Ellie had gone well and they had parted on good terms. Conversely Victor continued to be a conundrum. The conversation with him had felt like a Gordian knot; there was much to unravel. He clearly knew something that he was unwilling to share, particularly about the photograph of the unknown girl and the circumstances surrounding the appointment of a new Head of Faculty. Tom wondered what he'd meant by *still waters*. Meanwhile, Inger's invitation had been unexpected and he smiled in anticipation of spending time with her on New Year's Eve. He turned on the radio and Phil Collins' voice rang out, singing 'Two Hearts' as snow began to fall again.

Chapter Eight

Days of Our Lives

When Tom Frith drove out of Haxby on the last day of 1988, a frigid world of silence stretched out before him. The countryside appeared scoured of life and the hedgerows were rimed with frost. Beneath the wolf-grey clouds was a desolate monochrome land of snow and ice while lazy swirling snowflakes pattered against the windscreen. Finally, as he approached York, his spirits lifted as a sharp morning light filtered through the trees, casting long grey-blue shadows. There are days of our lives that we never forget, and for Tom Frith, Saturday, 31 December 1988, was such a day.

Christmas had been spent with his parents and he had received the usual assorted mix of presents. They included a knitted pullover that would have suited a wartime refugee, a bottle of Zinfandel wine and, incongruously, a key ring from Ipswich Town Football Club, clearly a gift influenced by his father. It had been a joyful time. He was an only child and while there were occasions he wished he had been blessed with siblings, that was not to be. Still, he and his parents were a close and happy family.

He had arrived at his parents' home on 21 December and, along with the rest of the world, had been deeply saddened by the BBC newsflash that evening. Nicholas Witchell announced that a jumbo jet carrying more than 250 passengers had crashed on the Scottish border. It was a seminal moment for them all and he recalled the tears in his mother's eyes and his father's grim expression. When they had turned off the television there was only the ticking of the grandfather clock in the hall to disturb the silence.

The following morning the papers revealed the news that Pan Am Flight 103 had exploded over Lockerbie, killing everyone on board and eleven Scots on the ground. Christmas seemed diminished by the event as talk of a terrorist bombing dominated the news.

Now it was New Year's Eve and Tom had arranged to meet up with Owen and Sue in York. For a Christmas gift they had bought him a copy of *Running for Fitness*. It was a guide by the father-and-son duo of Sebastian and Peter Coe and he wondered if it was an intimation that he ought to get out and do some jogging around the university campus. There was a gravel track around Milestone Lake on the outskirts of the grounds that was popular with the athletics club. He recalled he had been a good athlete at school: maybe he should take the hint. Conversely, Richard Head had bought him one of the festive season's bestsellers; namely, *A Brief History of Time: From the Big Bang to Black Holes* by Stephen Hawking. Richard was keen to share his love of cosmology and over the past few evenings Tom had felt obliged to dip into the mind-bending text in anticipation of his next conversation with his scientist friend.

He parked in the university car park and walked into the city centre. Lendal was busy with shoppers and as he passed the Assembly Rooms he saw a giant poster advertising the New Year dance and he thought of Ellie. She was clearly a talented student and destined to do well. He enjoyed her company and zest for life but there was always the taboo regarding tutor–student relationships. In Tom's view there was a line that should never be crossed. He was deep in thought as he walked down Coney Street until a cheerful voice snapped him out of his reverie.

'Hi, Tom.' It was Sue Llewellyn, waving a greeting. She was standing outside a coffee shop amidst a bustling crowd of shoppers.

'Morning, Sue. Good to see you. Where's the Welsh warrior?'

'Looking for new trainers in JJB Sports. He said he'll catch us up. Let's go in. They do great coffee here.'

Soon they were sitting at a table, munching on hot teacakes and sipping freshly ground coffee.

'So . . . how was Christmas?' asked Tom.

'My mum and dad are excited about the baby.' She patted her tummy. 'It's five months now.'

'And how are you?'

'Generally fine. I get occasional heartburn and times when I feel a bit dizzy but they're few and far between. I've always enjoyed good health so I've no real concerns.'

Tom nodded. It was at times like this he was so pleased he was a man but it was an admission he didn't share. Instead he simply smiled in support.

Suddenly Owen walked in carrying his sports bag. '*Bore da*,' he said as he sat down.

Tom grinned. 'And a *good morning* to you too. What's in the bag?'

'State-of-the-art and seriously cool Adidas trainers.' He held them up, a gleaming white eighties fashion accessory.

'About time too,' said Sue. 'Your old ones stink.'

Suitably humbled, Owen ambled away to buy a coffee.

'He's thrilled about the baby,' said Sue. 'Convinced it's a boy who will play rugby for Wales.'

'And if it's a girl?'

'He will still want her to play rugby. Actually, there's a Welsh ladies team now. They played their first match in Pontypool last year against England. Mind you, Owen doesn't mention it because England won.'

Tom smiled. 'Typical.'

Sue looked up at Owen, who was still waiting in the queue at the counter. She leaned forward and spoke quietly. 'Tom . . . I'm getting concerned about Edna Wallop. She's giving Owen a hard time.'

'In what way?'

'She treats him as a second-class citizen. Physical Education is at the bottom of her list for promoting the university.'

'That's a shame. There's great kudos for universities who produce sports stars.'

'We both know that but there's definitely something else. I think it's because he's a friend of Victor's. I keep picking up the fact she sees Victor as something of a threat. Owen reckons she's really ambitious and is happy to trample on anyone who gets in her way.' She paused and looked at Tom. 'I'm also aware she's making life difficult for you.'

'Sadly . . . yes. It's tough at times. My job is only a year's contract. I wish it could be longer but that's unlikely now.'

Owen had paid for his coffee and was returning to the table.

Sue leaned forward. 'He appreciates your friendship, Tom, so thanks for that.'

Owen sat down. 'What are you two plotting?'

Sue grinned. 'Tom reckons with us sporty types as parents, if it's a girl she could play netball for England . . . or maybe even cricket.'

Owen spluttered over his coffee. 'Bollocks!' he muttered.

Sue raised her cup in mock acknowledgement. 'And that's why you teach PE and Tom teaches English.'

'God Almighty!' said Owen. 'Give me strength! You're beginning to sound like the Wallop!'

Sue winked at Tom as normal service was resumed and they chatted about their hopes for the New Year.

'So, I guess we'll see you tonight at Inger's,' said Owen. 'We've been to a few of her soirées. Bit more upmarket than the ones we host. Ours are more beer and skittles.'

'Yes,' said Tom, 'I'll be there. I was going to take a bottle and maybe an LP.'

'There's a stall on the market,' said Sue. 'Vinyl Pete. Great choice of music.'

Tom raised his eyebrows. 'Vinyl Pete?'

'Sue's right, Tom. Try him before HMV. Great bargains.'

They ventured out into the cold once again and Sue gave Tom a hug. 'Good to talk,' she said with a knowing smile.

Tom walked across Parliament Street and up the cobbled street that led to the Shambles, York's famous medieval shopping street. Before that was the thriving market, full of life, sound and colour. Neatly wedged between Arnie Wainwright's Pork Pies and Bobby Dazzler's Sterling Silver Pendants was Vinyl Pete's Records. The collection of records was huge and stacked so customers could flick through the various selections from Rock & Pop to Classical. A slightly out-of-tune group of handbell ringers stood alongside a roast-chestnut stall playing *The Nutcracker Suite.* However, their rendition tended to be drowned out by the Christmas number one, Cliff Richard's 'Mistletoe And Wine', which was blaring out from a loudspeaker perched on a step-ladder behind Vinyl Pete's stall. He cut a Bohemian figure in a sheepskin coat, a baggy Aran sweater and with long hair held back with a *Dirty Dancing* headband. He was smoking a roll-up cigarette and doing a roaring trade.

Tom finally selected Andrew Lloyd Webber's *The Premier Collection*. It included songs from *The Phantom of the Opera, Evita, Jesus Christ Superstar* and *Cats*. It looked really impressive and Tom felt sure Inger would enjoy the light relief from the classical diet that dominated her work. He slipped the twelve-inch record out of its cover and held it up to the light. There were no scratches.

'It's perfec', squire,' said Pete. 'Elaine Paige, Michael Crawford, Sarah Brightman. Top stars. A bargain at a fiver.' He held out his hand and Tom rummaged in his wallet. He paid and Pete put it in a brown paper carrier bag just as a familiar voice behind Tom said, 'Good choice, Dr Frith.'

Tom turned around. It was Ellie MacBride.

'Well, what a coincidence,' said Ellie with a smile. 'Great minds think alike. This is a terrific market. I always buy my records here.'

'Hello, Ellie. This is an unexpected surprise. How are you?'

'Fine, thanks. I survived my mother's Christmas dinner. Enough to feed the five thousand. What about you?'

'Similar, I guess. My mother always makes Christmas special.'

She looked at the LP. 'Didn't know you were into musical theatre.'

'It's not for me. It's a gift.'

Ellie looked up at Tom expectantly. 'Looking forward to tonight. I'm still hoping you're coming. Should be a great dance.'

'Sorry, there's a faculty gathering. I'm committed to going there.'

Ellie looked sad. 'Oh, I see.' She stared down at the racks of LPs and absent-mindedly picked up Rick Astley's *Hold Me In Your Arms* and stared at the cover. 'Well, maybe you could come on later.'

'I think it will be late when we finish,' said Tom.

'Where's the party?' She was getting insistent.

'Near the racecourse.'

'So . . . not far away.'

Tom was beginning to feel uncomfortable. Ellie was eager . . . almost *too* eager. 'Sorry, Ellie, but I really can't make it.'

'Well . . . you know where I am,' she said. 'I wish you a great 1989, Dr Frith,' and she walked away and was lost in the crowds.

Ten miles away Victor Grammaticus was at home sitting at his desk in his study. He was deep in concentration and staring at a black-and-white photograph.

His partner, Pat, a tall, fair-haired professional artist, was in the lounge sipping mint tea and reading his *Flash Art* magazine. In the background Simon and Garfunkel's 'Scarborough Fair' from *The Concert In Central Park* was playing. Finally, he put down his mug and walked into the study.

'Come on then, Victor. I know that look. What's on your mind?'

Victor smiled up at his handsome partner. 'It's a theory . . . but I think it might be right.'

Pat moved a couple of books from the spare chair and sat down. 'Interesting. You've gone into your cryptic mode.'

'It's this,' said Victor and handed over the photograph.

Pat studied it for a moment. 'A young girl . . . distinctive features . . . quite an old photograph. Who is it?'

'That's the conundrum. I think I may know.'

'Go on . . .'

'It's a conversation with dear Henry that came to mind. He shared something with me . . . a kind of family secret.'

Pat leaned forward. 'I'm intrigued.'

'It was many years ago. He rarely talked about family but he did so once, just after his sister died in a car accident in Cornwall. She had a daughter, but he lost touch with the child when her father remarried. However, later his niece had been in touch. He mentioned her dream was to be a teacher.'

'That's an interesting story, Victor.' Pat pointed to the photograph. 'So do you know who this is?'

'Yes, I think I do and I'll follow it up next term.'

Pat smiled. 'Enigmatic as always.' He stood up. 'Anyway, what are you wearing tonight?'

'Waistcoat and bow tie, of course,' said Victor with a smile of his own.

'Predictable,' said Pat.

Victor looked up at him. 'What about you?'

'My understated blue cord suit. Don't want to appear too outlandish.'

'But of course,' said Victor and gave a knowing smile. They were always careful to dress slightly conservatively when they attended a faculty event.

Pat walked back into the lounge. He called out, 'I'm hoping that dreadful woman won't be there.'

'Definitely not,' said Victor with feeling.

'Thank goodness,' said Pat and he settled once again to Simon and Garfunkel, who were singing 'Bridge Over Troubled Water'.

Meanwhile, Victor returned the photograph to his wallet, sat back and made a decision.

It was nine o'clock when Tom parked on the frosty road outside Inger's home. He rang the bell and Victor opened the door. 'Hi, Tom. Welcome. Inger's in the lounge. Drinks are in the kitchen.'

Tom added his coat to the row of overfilled pegs in the hall and carried his bottle of wine and the LP record into the lounge.

It was a spacious room full of colleagues he knew well and a smattering of people he had never met before. Inger was at her piano in the far corner playing 'Memory' from the musical *Cats*. Her brother, Andreas, was sitting alongside her and playing his violin. His girlfriend, Annika, was leaning on the piano, a glass of *akvavit* in her hand and singing along in a sweet voice.

The walls were filled with colourful posters of popular

shows and over a bookcase full of music manuscripts was a large print of Édouard Manet's *A Bar at the Folies-Bergère*. 'Memory' came to a close and Inger stood up to welcome Tom. 'So pleased you could make it.'

He held up his bottle and passed over the LP record. 'Hope you like it, Inger.'

'That's very kind, Tom. How thoughtful.' She scanned the back cover. 'Some wonderful songs here.'

Her brother stood up. 'Hi, Tom. Good to see you again.'

'So . . . no party in Oslo?'

'Yes, the orchestra always meet up but I wanted to be here with my sister.'

Tom smiled. 'Good decision.'

Andreas nodded towards the door. 'Help yourself to a drink.'

Tom walked through the hall to the kitchen and passed Zeb sitting on the stairs and smoking a cigarette. She was deep in conversation with Richard Head, who had clearly made an effort towards sartorial elegance in a black shirt, black trousers and a purple tie. The lanyard around his neck was swinging free. They both looked up and gave a friendly wave.

In the kitchen a group of men were chatting and enjoying glasses of red wine. Victor and Pat were sharing news about their recent weekend trip to London with some friends who worked at the Theatre Royal in York. They had been to see the revival of Cole Porter's *Can-Can* at the Strand Theatre.

'You must go,' said Victor.

'It's on for another three weeks,' said Pat. He was a

supporter of the theatre scene in York and on the committee of the Joseph Rowntree Theatre.

Tom selected a Younger's Special Ale from the worktop, opened the can and poured it into a pint glass while the lively banter continued around him.

Victor broke away from the others and came to stand next to Tom. 'You really must come to the theatre with us some time, Tom. Pat's enthusiasm is a joy to behold.' He gestured with his glass towards the animated group. 'They all love him, you know.' The pride in his voice was obvious.

'I'm so pleased for you, Victor. You have a wonderful partner.'

'That's kind of you to say, Tom. I do appreciate it. It's not always been easy, but attitudes are changing. Fortunately, we only come across a few bigots these days.' A burst of laughter exploded from the group around Pat. 'I love to see him as happy as this.'

'Good to be here,' said Tom and raised his glass. They clinked glasses.

'Cheers, Tom,' said Victor with a warm smile. He sipped his drink and then his voice took on a serious tone. 'Tom, it's clear to me you like Inger and it would be great if she could find a friend who cared for her. She's a wonderful woman.'

Tom sighed and shook his head. 'Maybe.'

Victor looked stern. 'You must try.'

For a moment Tom looked distraught. 'But I tried.'

Victor put his hand on Tom's shoulder. 'Yes, Tom, but you must never *fail* to try.'

There was a call from Pat. 'Victor, come here. George has a great idea for a *Songs from the Shows* evening.'

'Excuse me, Tom.' He looked calmly at his young colleague. 'We'll talk again.'

The next two hours were filled with music and laughter. Tom met some of Inger's neighbours, including the couple from the upstairs apartment along with a few of her friends. There were musicians, artists and teachers, all full of life and conversation, and Tom gradually relaxed as the evening progressed. Eventually he wandered into the small conservatory that linked the lounge to the garden and Inger appeared by his side.

'Tom, there's something I'd like to share with you.' They were in a private space and out of earshot of the rest of the party.

Tom was curious. 'Of course. What is it?'

'It's a sensitive matter but I felt I ought to have a word . . . as a friend and a colleague.'

He put down his glass of beer on the coffee table. 'I'm intrigued.'

'I overheard a couple of my students in the choir talking about you.'

'Really? I can't think why.'

'They mentioned Ellie MacBride.'

'Oh, I see.'

'Do you, Tom? They thought something was going on between you. This is something that could damage your career.'

'I can assure you that's not the case. Ellie is a great student, vibrant and full of determination. I want to help her succeed but there's no other relationship between us.'

Inger's blue eyes softened. 'That's good to hear but we

have to be careful of encouraging our students in a manner that could be misinterpreted.'

Tom leaned back against the wall and became pensive. 'I understand . . . or at least I think I do. Perhaps I ought to mention I had a coffee with her in York a couple of weeks ago. Also . . . she invited me to the New Year dance in the Assembly Rooms.'

Inger considered this for a moment. 'I see. She's clearly keen on you, Tom. You won't be aware but there was a case just after I arrived when a student in the art department told her friends she was having an affair with her tutor. It was idle gossip but it swept through the faculty. The guy was completely innocent as it turned out – the girl was lying – but it damaged his career. He moved down south in the summer and took up a new post.' She leaned closer. 'I wouldn't want this to happen to you.'

The reality of what she was saying hit him hard. Tom realized that his *friendship* with Ellie could easily be misconstrued and he began to question the wisdom of some of his earlier actions. Going to Bettys now seemed to have been an ill-advised idea. He would have to be very careful of what he said and did in the future.

Suddenly their conversation was interrupted by Owen tugging Tom's sleeve. 'Come on, Englishman. Nearly midnight and we're gathering to sing that bloody awful Scottish song.'

'I'll be right there,' said Tom as Owen lurched away into the lounge, can of beer in his hand.

Inger tucked a strand of her long blonde hair behind her ear. She sipped her wine and looked intently at Tom. 'I hope you didn't mind me mentioning this.'

Tom returned her gaze. He was increasingly captivated by this woman. 'Not at all. I'm grateful. This is a new world for me.'

She smiled. 'You're going to get a few of the girls falling for you, Tom. Just be wary.'

The television was on in the corner of the room. On BBC One *Clive James on 88* had come to a close: his quirky review of the past year was over. The image of Big Ben appeared on the screen and as it began chiming out the midnight hour everyone gathered in a circle in the lounge. They sang 'Auld Lang Syne' and then broke away and began to hug whoever was nearest.

Sue Llewellyn reached up and kissed Tom on the cheek. Owen shook his hand and patted him on the shoulder. 'Here's to next year, Tom,' he said. 'Let's hope it's a good one.'

Tom shook hands with Victor and Pat while Zeb left lipstick on his cheek after an over-enthusiastic embrace. Richard Head gave him a smile. 'Happy New Year, Tom. I should be interested to hear what you thought of the Hawking book.'

Tom moved around the room in the chaos of the moment.

Then Inger was before him. He held her hand and said, 'Happy New Year.'

There was a brief moment of hesitation and then she moved closer. She squeezed his hand and kissed him lightly on the lips, softly and with feeling. It was a moment Tom would never forget and he stood there, stunned, as the crush of friends swirled around him.

When the evening ended, he drove home under an ethereal night sky, knowing his life had turned on its axis.

Chapter Nine

Beneath a Wolf Moon

It was a bitter winter morning when Tom arrived at the university on the first day of the new term. He had passed a copse of hazel trees where the lambs' tails of catkins quivered and hung like teardrops while small animals had stripped bare the fallen branches. Even so, hope stirred. Beyond the hedgerows there was the promise of snow-drops. It was a view that froze the body but healed the soul. He parked and hurried towards the entrance. In a trough outside reception Perkins had planted some pansies. The bright splash of yellow was a cheerful welcome on this Monday, 9 January, and an eventful 1989 stretched out before Tom Frith.

'Morning, Dr Frith, and a Happy New Year,' said a cheer-ful Perkins.

'Thanks, Perkins, and the same to you. How was your Christmas?'

'Perfect. My Pauline sang like an angel in the choir for Midnight Mass and I got some thermal socks that would suit a polar explorer.' He stamped his feet as if to emphasize the point.

'Good to hear,' said Tom. 'Anyway, have a good day,' and he heaved his satchel over his shoulder and set off for the frozen quad.

Perkins called after him, 'Mr Llewellyn is already in, said something about skiing.'

Owen was scribbling on an A4 notepad when Tom walked into their study.

'Hi, you look busy,' said Tom.

Owen looked up and smiled. '*Blwyddyn Newydd Dda*.'

'And a *Happy New Year* to you too, Welshman,' replied Tom.

'Well done,' said Owen, impressed with the translation. 'Just making sure I'm ready for the meeting at lunchtime today. I'm taking the final-year PE students to Chamonix for field week. We alternate each year with camping in the Brecon Beacons and skiing in the French Alps. It's a great trip but I'm having to bring it forward from the end of April to March with the baby due in early May.'

'Sensible,' said Tom. 'How's Sue?'

'Fine. Intending to carry on teaching up to Easter if all goes to plan.'

'Have you cleared it with the Wallop? I heard Zeb struggled to get the Stratford field week sorted.'

'No, I bypassed her. She won't be pleased but she's not Head of Faculty yet. I went to the Vice Chancellor. He was understanding. Gave me the go-ahead straight away. Loves rugby and played a bit in his younger days at Cambridge so we get on.' He stared out of the window as if seeking divine inspiration. 'You know . . . I really ought to go to one of his Sunday morning services by way of a thank-you.'

Tom grinned. 'The shock would probably kill the old boy.'

Canon Edward Chartridge was a friendly soul and his sherry evenings along with compulsory poetry readings in the Lodge were legendary. Tom had taken some of his English groups there on occasions.

He glanced at the clock. 'I've got English One at nine so I'll catch you later. Good luck with the meeting.'

Tom enjoyed his first session. It was good to be back with the students and teaching again. This morning's subject was *The Mill on the Floss* by George Eliot and a comparison with her later novel *Middlemarch*. A few of the women, including Ellie MacBride, were sceptical about the female author, Mary Ann Evans, using the pseudonym George. Tom explained that, after discussing this with her editor, she had decided to use this name to conceal her gender and to avoid the attention that would come from an unmarried woman living with a married man.

This brought on a barrage of complaints from the liberated women in the group. One of the nineteen-year-old females declared in strident tones that it was an affront to her sex. She was wearing a badge that read 'Sex is not just for Christmas', which, although factually correct, had created a modicum of curiosity on arrival.

When the ten o'clock bell rang, Ellie MacBride hung back to catch Tom's attention. 'Tom, I'm about to write my first article for the *Echo*. Please don't misinterpret this but I wondered if I could check out the Cloisters corridor.'

Tom looked puzzled. 'Yes, of course . . . but why?'

'Kimberly wants me to write an article about student accommodation in the old Victorian part of the building. All our rooms are in a pretty poor state, a big contrast to the new build.' She took a sheet of paper from her shoulder bag. It was a plan of the top floor that ran around the quad far below. 'There're seven corridors including Cloisters and Alcuin where the tutors have their rooms. Students are in the other five: Sterne, Benedict, Tuke, Rowntree and Terry. My room on Benedict has seen better days but I've done my best with it. Tuke corridor, where Kimberly hangs out, is by far the worst.'

'Sounds like it's important to highlight the problem,' said Tom. 'I've never been up the stairs on the other side of the quad so I've no idea what it's like.'

'It's rare for tutors to go up there, although Dr Wallop occasionally appears on patrol.'

'I wonder why?'

'To keep an eye on us, I guess.'

'So when do you want to come up to Cloisters?'

'Would after last lecture this afternoon be OK? It shouldn't take long.'

'Yes, that's fine. Come to Room Seven at, say, four thirty.'

She smiled. 'See you then . . . and a Happy New Year.'

On the other side of the campus in the science block, Richard Head was working with a group of his final-year students when Victor Grammaticus tapped on the door and walked in.

'Hello, Victor. This is a pleasant surprise.'

'Sorry to disturb you but could I have a quick word?'

They walked to the side of the room behind his desk. 'How can I help?' asked Richard.

'I need to speak with Kimberly Stratton. Nothing serious . . . just some information for her newspaper.'

Richard nodded. 'Well, we're just finishing up so you can catch her now.'

The tall, confident editor of the *Echo* gave Victor a level stare when he approached her. 'Good morning, Professor Grammaticus, how can I help?'

'Hello, Kimberly. Actually, it's the other way round. I have some information that may support your editorial work.'

Kimberly was immediately on her guard. 'And what might that be?' she replied crisply.

'It would be better to discuss what I have to say elsewhere. There's a coffee shop on Goodramgate round the corner from St William's College.'

'I know the one,' said Kimberly, her interest rising.

'Would you be willing to meet me there?'

Kimberly was eager to agree. Her scrutiny of corruption in the university was progressing well but this was too good an opportunity to miss. She guessed it might be simply a ruse on the part of a senior tutor to discover how much she knew and get her to stop. 'Yes,' she said. 'When would you like to meet?'

'Is lunchtime convenient?'

'Shortly after twelve would be fine.'

Victor remained perfectly calm. 'Thank you . . . until then,' and Kimberly watched him walk away.

At morning break Tom collected a coffee and joined Inger, Zeb and Victor in the far corner of the common room.

'Hi, handsome,' said Zeb. 'Come and join the malcontents.'

Tom sat down. 'Morning, everybody.' He looked at Inger, who smiled back. 'So what's the news?'

'It's Edna,' said Zeb, puffing vigorously on a cigarette. 'Makes my blood boil.' She nodded towards a ring of chairs on the other side of the room near the arch window. Edna was sitting with a group of Japanese students. 'When I walked past she was fawning all over them in sympathy for Emperor Hirohito.'

Tom recalled his recent death in Tokyo, after a sixty-two-year reign, had been reported on the BBC *News* last night.

'Looks like she's done her homework and is keen to impress,' said Inger.

Tom glanced at her again. Her hair was centre-parted with long braided pigtails. In a thick white polo-neck jumper and green cord trousers she looked great and he recalled their New Year kiss.

'There was a note in my pigeonhole this morning from the Vice Chancellor,' said Victor. 'It said six students were visiting today from Japan. Apparently, they're keen to attend a university in England. He's having one of his sherry evenings for them this evening and I'm invited.'

'And presumably the Wallop will be there,' said Zeb, stubbing out her cigarette in anger.

Victor nodded. 'Inevitably, I guess.'

'Trust her to get her sticky fingers into that initiative,' said Zeb, getting up to leave. 'Just listen to her trying to impress.' Edna's voice had risen and the students were staring at her, apparently impressed.

'Ignore it,' said Victor. 'It's another one of her Faustian moments.'

'Just white noise,' murmured Inger. 'Nothing more,' and she sat back and sipped her coffee, her mind elsewhere.

They all watched Edna as she led the students into the quad, and then they got up to leave. Tom walked out with Inger. 'Thanks again for the New Year party,' he said. 'I really enjoyed it.'

'So did I,' she said, and smiled.

He wondered if she had enjoyed it as much as he had. He had a few minutes to spare before his tutorial sessions with English Three so he walked back into the reception area. Perkins was dusting the heraldic shields on the wall.

'Hello again, Dr Frith.' He waved his feather duster. 'Important to keep them looking bright. Shows we respect history.'

'I agree,' said Tom. 'I'm guessing you know a lot about the original building.'

Perkins was a modest man. 'Well . . . I've got some knowledge. Depends what's on your mind.'

'I'm seeing a student later who's writing an article about the state of the corridors on the top floor.'

Perkins nodded sagely. 'It's a proper rabbit warren up there. I go up with the maintenance team to give it a check now and then.'

'I've never seen the student corridors. Cloisters seems fine and I'm really happy with my study.'

'Alcuin is the same,' said Perkins. 'Lovely rooms, especially the one at the end. That's Dr Wallop's. There's a door from there that leads to Tuke corridor but it's always locked.'

'I didn't know that.'

'Yes. Just outside the door is a steep metal staircase but no one uses it. All the students go up the main wooden staircase. It's wide and gets plenty of use. One day they'll replace the carpets and give the walls a lick of paint but it's never been a priority. I think it ought to be but I've no say in the matter.'

'So who does?'

'That'll be the governors.'

'Oh well, thanks, Perkins. It was just a thought.'

'Any time, Dr Frith,' and he returned to his dusting.

At lunchtime Tom was sitting alone in the refectory when Richard Head stopped at his table and sat down beside him. 'Hi, Tom. How are you getting on with Stephen Hawking?'

'OK,' said Tom hesitantly. 'It's a bit complicated in places.'

Richard looked surprised. 'Really? I've always found it quite straightforward. All he's saying is that after the Big Bang black holes appeared, some as tiny as protons, and all this action is governed by general relativity and quantum mechanics.'

'I see,' said Tom . . . but he didn't.

'By the way,' said Richard as he got up to leave, 'it's a wolf moon tonight so don't miss it.'

'Is it?'

'Yes, the first full moon of the year.' He looked excited. 'The American Indians named it after hearing wolves howling at the moon owing to winter hunger.'

'Sounds a bit sinister.'

'I've also heard it called the ice moon.'

'That's appropriate, considering the weather.'

'Yes, I suppose so.' Richard paused, clearly animated. 'I've always been fascinated by the moon. There it is,

240,000 miles away, but you feel you could stretch out and grab it in your hand.'

'I know what you mean,' said Tom, who always had empathy for the faculty's boffin.

'And it always shows us the same face,' added Richard for good measure. 'So make sure you look out for it.'

'OK,' said Tom. 'Will do.'

'Anyway, must rush. I've been summoned by Edna. She's showing some students around the science block.' He gave an impish smile and stroked his stubby goatee beard. 'Did you know January is Edna's favourite month . . .? Named after Janus the two-faced god.' Chuckling to himself, he headed across the quad to the door marked 'Alcuin'.

On Goodramgate shoppers stooped like Lowry figures under grey skies that promised more snow as Victor walked towards the coffee shop. Kimberly was already seated with a hot drink alongside a notebook and pen. He collected a coffee and sat down in front of her. 'Sorry if I've kept you waiting.'

Kimberly looked thoughtful. 'Not at all. I simply came early to jot down a few questions.'

Victor looked around. It was the perfect venue to speak, away from any prying eyes.

Kimberly wasted no time. 'So, Professor Grammaticus, what is it that you want to talk to me about? Could it be to do with the sudden surge of foreign students that are beginning to swell our student numbers?'

Victor gave a wry smile. He could see why she made such a good editor. 'Please call me Victor. I know that you are not in any of my tutor groups but those who are call me by my first name.'

'Of course, Victor, but the question remains the same.'

Victor remained silent and then with deliberate care he took the photograph from his wallet and placed it on the table in front of her.

Kimberly stared at it for a moment and then looked up. 'Where did you get this? And more to the point, why are you showing it to me?'

'A colleague of mine found it in one of Henry's books when we cleared out his study and it reminded me of something that he once told me.'

'What was that, may I ask, and what could it possibly have to do with me?'

As he looked at the distinctive features of the woman before him he became more convinced he was right.

'In answer to your first question, Kimberly, he told me in confidence that he had a much-loved niece. Sadly, he saw little of her after the death of his sister. Her husband later remarried. He told me that the girl had dreams of becoming a teacher.' He paused and studied her reaction. 'And in answer to your second question . . . I think we both know what it has to do with you.'

Suddenly Kimberly's eyes filled with tears and Victor gave her a handkerchief.

It took a little while for her to recover and she looked at the photograph once again. 'Henry must have valued your friendship a great deal for him to share this information with you.'

'I would like to think so. He was a dear friend and colleague and I miss him greatly. Our friendship was professional but important to us both. I admired him for his integrity and honesty. It saddened me greatly to see how he was diminished by Edna Wallop in his later years.'

Kimberly sighed and shook her head. 'I agree. She made his life hell.' A silence followed as they both considered the implications. 'So, Victor, you're right. I am that niece and he was a wonderful uncle. I didn't see him a great deal after my mother's death but I remembered all the fun times we had together when I was young. He knew that I wanted to be a teacher and so I applied to this university, hoping that I could be near him once again. We met quite a few times. But he was very anxious that Edna should not find out about him being my uncle. She had a hold over him. He told me that she was involved in something irregular but then Edna threatened him. She told him she would provide false evidence to put the blame for it on him. He didn't say exactly what this was but he was worried that if she knew I was related to him she would somehow ruin my chances of doing well. I kept quiet for him. But now he is no longer with us I'm determined to find out what the issue was. I am sure that the stress of everything contributed to his death.'

'I agree with you but I also agree with Henry. Don't let her know who you are. She'd do something to harm you, I'm sure. She is also convinced that she will get his position. That would be disastrous for the university.'

'I appreciate you being so frank and I understand why.' She looked down at her notebook and flicked back a few pages. 'I know that I'm on to something but it's not possible to share it with you at this stage. I don't want to put you in any difficulty by knowing what I know.'

'I understand,' said Victor quietly, 'but you must be careful. I'm convinced she is a dangerous woman.'

'On that,' she said with determination, 'we are agreed.' She sat back and looked at Victor, who returned her gaze with quiet assurance. 'It's been good to talk, Victor. You have a certain sangfroid . . . It's a great quality. I hope to emulate you in this one day.'

'There's no need to copy me, Kimberly. You've handled this well. You have your own style. Be yourself and follow your dream. That's what Henry would have wanted.'

Kimberly sipped the last of her coffee and closed her notebook. 'Thank you, Victor. In the meantime, the *Echo* will be out a fortnight today. I'm putting the cat among the pigeons.'

'I guessed you might. So what's the underlying intention?'

'To see Dr Wallop's reaction. The front-page article will not be just *words*, Victor . . . It's a challenge.' She stood up and gave a determined smile. 'No doubt we'll talk again.'

'Yes, we shall, and meanwhile take this.' He held out the photograph.

'Thank you,' she said and put it in her pocket and walked away.

At afternoon break Tom walked across the quad and collected a hot chocolate in the common room. In the television area Inger and Zeb were sitting on one of the sofas drinking tea and chatting while the television set was burbling in the corner.

The news had been dominated recently by the blight of AIDS, now in its eighth year, along with the Berlin Wall and the memorial service for those who'd died in the Lockerbie air disaster.

'Pretty dismal news,' said Zeb as Tom sat down.

'Never-ending,' said Inger quietly.

'So has anyone got any news to cheer us up?' asked Zeb.

'Well, I got a call from a school colleague last night,' said Tom, 'and a group of us are going to the theatre in Harrogate at the weekend. It's *The Importance of Being Earnest*.'

'Perfect,' said Zeb. 'One of my favourite plays.'

As they walked out into the quad, Inger fell into step beside Tom. 'I absolutely love Oscar Wilde. If your friend organizes future theatre visits, perhaps I could come along.'

Tom's heart leapt. 'But of course – and you would like my friends.'

Inger smiled. 'I'm sure I shall.'

By 4.30 p.m. darkness had fallen. Tom was in his study and in the quad below all was still. Owen had called in briefly, happy that his meeting about his skiing trip had gone well and keen to get home to Sue. Victor was giving him a lift these days.

There was a knock on the door. 'Come in,' said Tom. It was Ellie MacBride, clipboard in hand.

'Much more salubrious up here, Tom. Fitted carpets, subtle decor, all very different to where I live.'

'So, what can I do to help?'

'I'm not sure I need any after all. I've walked up the corridor and jotted down my impressions.'

'In that case do you want a coffee before you go?'

Ellie sat down in one of the armchairs. 'Yes, please.'

Tom boiled the kettle, found two reasonably clean mugs and a half-bottle of milk plus a few fig biscuits. Soon they were relaxed and enjoying the hot drinks. Ellie stared out of the window at the bleak rooftops beyond. 'You could do with some curtains. It would make it cosy in here. It's a nice room but a bit, well . . . sparse.'

'Functional, I guess,' said Tom. 'Owen and I don't really discuss interior decoration.'

'It shows,' said Ellie with a mischievous smile.

Tom decided to share what was on his mind. 'Ellie . . . just thinking . . . I didn't want to give you the wrong impression about . . . about you and me. If I've done that I apologize and hope you understand.'

Ellie put down her mug and gave a sad, knowing smile. Tom could see that she was considering her reply.

'Yes, I do understand. Having said that, you're new in the role of tutor and maybe a bit naive on occasions.' She saw the surprise on his face. 'But at least you're honest, unlike some men I've known.' She leaned forward and touched his hand lightly. 'And you never know . . . maybe when I have finished my course, and you are no longer my tutor, things could be different.' With that she stood up. 'Thanks for the coffee, Tom,' and she turned away and left.

It was an hour later when Tom pulled up outside his cottage. Sharp moonlight lit up the frozen pavement. He picked up his satchel, locked the car and walked to the front door. On impulse, he stopped and looked up to the heavens. The full moon appeared behind the scudding clouds. All was silent and a few flakes of snow began to fall, each one a perfect hexagon and different from another until they joined together to form a white shroud over the silent village.

He reflected on the day. The conversation with Ellie had gone well while the elusive Inger seemed less distant. With hope in his heart, he turned the key in the door. Then, with a last look at the moon, he smiled. There were no wolves howling on this bitter winter night.

Chapter Ten

The Honey Trap

'Morning, Dr Frith,' said Perkins. 'They're going like hot cakes.'

On the counter was a pile of the new edition of the *Eboracum Echo* and Tom picked up a copy. The headline read:

CASH COW CORRUPTION!

Is There an Endowments Scam in Universities?
Evidence is emerging of unconditional offers being made to overseas students regardless of academic results . . . Kimberly Stratton investigates . . .

'They'll need to print some more at this rate,' said Perkins as another student hurried past and collected two copies.

'I'm not surprised,' said Tom. 'It's a powerful headline.'

'Dr Wallop didn't look too pleased. I had six copies on display when she arrived and she picked up the lot. Had a face like thunder. Fortunately, I had another hundred under the counter.'

Tom scanned the first paragraph. 'It doesn't mention this university directly.'

Perkins nodded. 'True . . . but there's an implication. Clever young woman is that Miss Stratton. She certainly knows how to put the cat among the pigeons. I spoke to her this morning. It was early when she came in. I asked her if she was ready for a reaction.'

'And what did she say?' asked Tom.

'She said, "Let's wait and see." '

As he walked away Tom murmured to himself, 'I wonder who will blink first.'

It was Monday, 23 January, and on this freezing winter morning a bitter confrontation was in store.

Tom climbed the stairs to the Cloisters corridor and walked into the study where Owen was sitting in an armchair. 'Have you read it?' he asked, holding up a copy of the paper.

Tom dropped his satchel on his desk and sat down. 'Just skimmed through it so far.'

'It's dynamite!' Owen opened his copy to page two. 'Quite subtle, the way she's done it. Doesn't mention Eboracum directly, or any member of staff for that matter, but with the Wallop playing mother hen to all these foreign students lately it doesn't leave much to the imagination. You don't have to be Sherlock bloody Holmes to see who she's getting at.'

'If that's the case, Edna will be on the warpath. She won't want anything to spoil her chances of getting Henry's job. The governors would take a dim view of all this.'

Owen stood up and grabbed a clipboard. 'Definitely . . . but this is the Wallop we're talking about. There will be a reaction – just wait and see. She can be an evil bitch when she wants.'

'Sadly, yes she can,' said Tom.

Owen looked at his watch. 'I've got a practical session first thing so I'll catch you at break.'

'See you then,' said Tom and he packed his satchel with the Primary Three essays he had marked last week.

At morning break Tom collected a coffee in the common room and sat down to read Ellie MacBride's article at the foot of page three. Titled 'The Corridors of Power' it was a succinct, factually correct summary of the state of the top floor of the old building around the quad.

She had described the narrow Victorian passageways that created a warren of foot traffic from one part of the university to another, interspersed with flights of stairs, some of them narrow staircases with a thick rope attached to the outer wall for balance. Even so, there was a distinct *edge* to the writing, particularly when comparing the quality of the student corridors with those of the lecturers. Tom was pleased for her. It was a good start. However, compared with the power of the front page exposé, it faded into insignificance.

Kimberly had given specific details revealing a possible examination scam along with hints of entrance 'endowments'. She had remarked that one of her sources had mentioned that a certain senior tutor had simply fuelled the conspiracy of silence. It was easy to guess whom she meant. He was browsing through the more general articles about the spread of AIDS, the state of the economy and the fact that George Bush had been sworn in as the 41st President of the United States, succeeding Ronald Reagan. Then he moved on to a more disturbing article about attacks on gay men in the city centre when Victor sat down beside him and took out of his pocket a colourful A5 poster. It was advertising *Songs from the Shows* at the Joseph Rowntree Theatre.

'Thought you might be interested in this, Tom. Pat is drumming up support for the opening night. It's an am-dram music evening next month on Valentine's Day. I'm passing a few of these out among colleagues who might be free.'

'Joseph Rowntree Theatre?' said Tom. 'I've never been there.'

'It's a lovely place, just over the bridge and before the chocolate factory. They do lots of great shows. Pat absolutely loves it. Anyway, just turn up if you're interested. Should be a crowd of us going.'

Suddenly the seats around him filled up. Zeb, Inger and Richard had arrived.

'My drama group are furious,' announced Zeb.

'The choir want action,' said Inger. 'I've never seen them so disgruntled.'

'Likewise,' said Richard. 'I worked with Science Four this morning and they said they were going to protest. They've worked hard to achieve their qualifications to get here and they don't want students turning up who have simply bought a ticket. So Kimberly is mustering the troops.'

Tom put down his coffee cup. 'The rumour mill about Edna was gathering pace in the conversations at the end of my session.'

'*Fama nihil est celerius*,' said Richard, who, like Tom, had studied Latin at A Level.

'Quite right,' said Tom with an understanding nod. 'Nothing is swifter than rumour.'

Not to be outdone, Victor, another Latin scholar, added, '*Ovem lupo committere*. You don't trust a fox to guard the sheep.'

Zeb lit up another cigarette and shook her head. 'So how did Edna get into this?'

'It was the Vice Chancellor,' said Victor. 'The governors were seeking ways to increase funds so he tasked Edna with encouraging more overseas students to be enrolled in order to swell the kitty. What he shouldn't have done is give the job to someone who would then be in a position to exploit it for her own ends.'

'And Kimberly has gone after her,' said Richard. 'It's a clever piece of writing. She told me it was a honey trap. I think we can deduce what she means.'

'It's what happens next that should be interesting,' said Inger.

'I wonder where she's getting her information?' asked Owen. 'It's what's left out of the article that catches the eye.'

'She won't reveal her sources,' said Richard.

'I agree,' said Victor. 'She's too astute for that.'

'How about having a quiet word with Perkins?' asked Tom. 'He might have some inside knowledge.' He looked at Victor. 'I'm guessing you know him well.'

'Really well,' said Victor. 'He's been a friend for twenty years. Knows everything, does Peter . . . A wonderful source of information. He doesn't miss much.'

'Tom's right,' said Owen. 'It's worth following up and there's no love lost between him and the Wallop.'

'It looks like Kimberly has clearly stumbled on something,' said Inger.

'She's one of my best students,' said Richard, 'and she will have used her own style of scientific methodology to discover the facts. I definitely saw her talking to some of those Japanese students that were here at the beginning of term.'

'It's looking more and more as if Edna's been taking a few backhanders,' said Zeb.

'I agree,' said Richard. 'The article talks about corruption linked to endowments.'

'Some of my students were in early making posters in the art block,' said Inger, 'so it's almost certain there will be some sort of response.'

'Definitely,' said Zeb, 'and my drama students are a volatile lot.'

'Bit like last November in London,' said Inger. 'A dozen of my students went down there to protest against tuition fees.'

'That was one hell of a demonstration,' said Zeb. 'I remember it well.'

Tom recalled the news coverage. Ten thousand students had brought London to a standstill. They were carrying placards that read: 'We Don't Need No Education – Obviously', 'Thatcher, Education Snatcher' and 'Stuff Your Loans – Education is a Right'. Eventually they had been dispersed by mounted police wielding batons and preventing them from reaching Parliament.

'Let's hope it doesn't get to that,' said Tom.

Zeb stood up to leave. 'Don't be too sure.'

'Time to move on,' said Owen and he hurried to his next session.

Victor and Richard walked away deep in conversation while Tom and Inger drank the last of their coffee. It was then Tom had an idea. 'Inger . . . just a thought. You know you said if there was a group going to the theatre you might come along?'

'Yes?'

He took out the *Songs from the Shows* poster. 'Victor mentioned this. Apparently, Pat is involved and he's drumming up support.'

'Oh, I recall now. I think he mentioned it last week.' She studied the poster. 'I love the Joseph Rowntree Theatre. I've seen a few shows there.' She looked up from the poster at Tom. His eagerness was obvious, almost infectious. 'Thanks, Tom. I'll have a think about it.' She glanced at the clock. 'Anyway . . . must go.'

He watched her walk away with mixed feelings in his heart.

After lunch Tom and Owen were working at their desks when Owen suddenly caught sight of what was happening below them. 'Hell's bells!' he said. 'It's started.'

They both jumped up and opened the window to stare out. Other top-floor windows were being opened on the scene below them. About a hundred students had marched into the quad and crunched across the frozen grass. They were chanting, 'We want the truth,' and holding placards that read 'Degrees Not For Sale', 'Thirty Pieces of Silver' and 'Merit Not Money'. Many were waving copies of the

Echo. Tom recognized some of his students, including Ellie MacBride, who looked up and waved.

Kimberly had borrowed one of Richard's loudspeakers from the science department. She was standing on the steps in front of the archway that led to the front of the university and speaking in short powerful sentences. The tall, slender young woman cut an impressive figure in her dyed jeans, denim jacket, biker boots and long red scarf and bobble hat. 'We have to show unity with our fellow universities,' she said. 'This must not be allowed to continue.'

'Hear! Hear!' shouted the crowd.

'It smacks of corruption,' said Kimberly. She held up a copy of the *Echo*. 'We have evidence.'

A reporter and photographer had arrived from their office at the *York Post* and were busy writing notes and snapping pictures. They were excited. This would be front-page news for the city newspaper that evening.

'There's a conspiracy of silence about entrance endowments,' said Kimberly. 'We need answers.' There were more cheers. 'So sign the petition, tell your friends, and we'll present it to the governing body.'

Tom saw a few students holding up clipboards and moving around the crowd.

Owen leaned further out of the window. 'Hey! Look who's here. It's the Wallop.' From a window to their left Edna Wallop was surveying the mayhem below her with a face like thunder. Suddenly she withdrew her head and slammed the window shut. 'Wait for it,' said Owen. 'She's not happy.'

Moments later she appeared on the step of the Alcuin doorway. 'I want you to disperse immediately,' she yelled, 'or there will be consequences.' All heads turned towards her.

'Do you deny the charges?' shouted Jenny Middleton, a second-year Geography student.

'And do they apply to this university?' bellowed her boyfriend, Nick Thompson.

'Yes . . . and no, of course,' retorted Edna with malice. 'This is nonsense. Now get back to your rooms. Leave before you regret it.' No one moved. It was then she spotted the local press taking photographs and speaking to students. The situation was escalating.

The chanting continued, louder and louder. It was rising in a crescendo. 'We want the truth . . . We want the truth.'

'Go away!' shouted Edna. 'Go away!'

Then it happened! A brown paper bag was thrown from the back of the crowd. It was half filled with flour and it sailed over their heads and hit Edna on the shoulder of her fur coat. She screamed an obscenity and yelled, 'Whoever started this will be dealt with. That's a promise.' Her face was a mask of fury. Then, with a hate-filled glare at Kimberly, she stalked inside.

Owen leaned back in and sat on the windowsill. 'Edna looked bloody frantic. I wouldn't like to be in Kimberly's shoes.'

Further along the corridor Victor was watching the same scene from his window. He recalled Kimberly had remarked how he remained calm under pressure but at that moment he would have cheerfully throttled his Acting Head of Faculty.

*

At afternoon break all was quiet again in the quad. The majority of students had gone to lectures or met up in the refectory to discuss their next strategy. The atmosphere was less charged but the determination to seek answers was still evident. At one of the tables Kimberly was talking to a few of her *Echo* team. The excitement among them was palpable. Then, on the far side of the refectory, she caught sight of Victor. He was sitting alone and looking preoccupied, drinking tea and writing in a notebook. She made a decision, stood up and walked towards him.

'Excuse me, Victor, may I have a quick word?'

Victor nodded. 'Of course.' He smiled. 'It's been an eventful day. That was a brave performance this morning.'

Kimberly glanced around her. 'I won't stay here. It's too public and I've no wish to inadvertently implicate you.'

'I fully understand,' said Victor quietly. 'How can I help?'

Kimberly leaned forward and spoke rapidly: 'Could we meet again . . . where we met before?'

'We could if you wish . . . but when?'

'Are you free now?'

'I am.'

'Perhaps in ten minutes.'

'See you then,' said Victor and returned to his notebook as Kimberly strode out of the refectory. He was intrigued. It had to be important. Then he glanced at his watch and decided to wait a moment before leaving.

Kimberly paused in reception to speak with Perkins.

'Good afternoon, Miss Stratton. I thought you were very brave earlier today.'

'Thank you, Perkins. I have a query.'

'Here to help,' said the cheerful porter.

'Outside my study, at the end of the corridor, there's a door that's always locked. It leads to Alcuin and Cloisters where the tutors have their studies.'

'That's right. It's always shut tight. You wouldn't choose to go through it with that metal staircase in the way.'

'I was wondering who has a key for it.'

'Well, definitely Charlie Cox, the caretaker, and probably the maintenance team. I've not got one but I've been up there with Charlie just to check it occasionally.'

'I'm asking because Dr Wallop suddenly appeared through it today. It's not happened before.'

'That's unusual. Maybe she's got one in case of a fire risk.'

'Thanks, Perkins. It was just a thought.'

'Are you OK? You look a bit concerned.'

'I'm fine, thanks. I appreciate your help.'

'Any time, Miss Stratton.' He held up a copy of the *Echo*. 'And good luck with this.'

'Thanks, Perkins.'

He watched her as she strode confidently away. *That's the future,* he thought with a wry smile.

Kimberly walked out of reception and shivered. Snow had gathered in gentle curves around the doorway. Across the icy road sharp moonlight lit up the city walls with a luminous glow. Her breath steamed before her as she set off, unaware her departure had been noted.

It was a relief to enter the warmth of the coffee shop. She bought a hot drink and found a quiet table in the far corner. Then from her shoulder bag she took out her Sony portable microcassette player and recorder. It was a recent model, the M-455, one she used frequently to record her interviews. After inserting two new AA batteries she pushed the eject button and inserted a cassette labelled 'EW1'. Then she plugged in her earphones, pressed play and listened for a few moments. All was ready. She sat back, sipped her coffee and waited.

A few minutes earlier, when Kimberly had walked down the drive, Edna Wallop had been standing by her window and smoking a cheroot. Cedric Bullock was in the visitor's chair, smoking a cigarette and looking thoughtful. 'It will blow over, Edna,' he said reassuringly. 'These students are irresponsible at the best of times.'

'You don't know this Stratton girl,' she said. 'She's trouble and she's devious. I don't want her preventing me from getting Henry's job.'

'I may be able to sway a couple of the governors.'

'But what about the rest?'

He stubbed out his cigarette, stood up and joined her by the window. 'You're doing the job now. That counts for a lot.'

'It's not just Stratton; it's Victor – that pony-tailed professor is a thorn in my side.'

Cedric stared out of the window. 'Speak of the devil, it's him.'

'I wonder where he's going,' said Edna. 'It can't be a coincidence that I saw Stratton leaving just before him.'

Cedric grabbed his coat and scarf from behind the door. 'Let's find out, shall we?'

Once outside he turned up his collar and pulled down the brim of his black trilby hat as a malevolent wind whipped across his face. Beneath the trees on either side of the driveway was a smooth blanket of frozen snow patterned by the tracks of midnight foxes and creatures of the night. It was with caution that he followed the tall figure of the professor.

A pewter-grey sky was gradually turning dark when Victor walked into York. He pulled his scarf tighter as the bitter rhythms of winter continued with a cold wind blowing in from the north-west. Goodramgate was busy with shoppers negotiating the slippery pavements. As he approached the coffee shop and the unexpected meeting he wondered what could be so important. The bell above the door jingled as he stepped inside and queued for a coffee. The shop was brightly lit and the warmth was welcoming. He greeted Kimberly with an imperceptible nod, collected his hot drink and sat down.

'Thank you for coming, Victor.'

He said nothing, simply stared down at the recorder.

'Victor, I have a recording of a conversation that took place in my room immediately after this morning's demonstration. I would like you to listen to it. It lasts less than a minute.'

Again, Victor remained silent and pressed one of the proffered headphones to his ear. There was a flicker of recognition almost immediately. When the recording ended he handed back the headphones and sat back, shaking his head. 'This is remarkable. Can you give me some context?'

'You probably know there's a door that links Alcuin to Tuke. It's always locked but I heard heavy footsteps coming from that direction and stepping across the metal walkway above the staircase. For a moment it was unnerving. Then

Edna walked into my room and closed the door behind her. My recorder was on my desk behind a pile of books. It was an automatic reaction. I pressed record and stood up to face her.'

Victor pursed his lips and pressed his hands together. 'Kimberly, thank you for sharing this with me.' He tapped the recorder with a long, elegant finger. 'I don't need to tell you that this is dangerous. For now put it somewhere safe.'

Kimberly gave a cautious smile. 'Thank you, Victor. I'll take your advice.'

There was a copy of the *Echo* on the table in front of Kimberly. He pointed to the headline. 'Excellent report, by the way. You were right about a so-called honey trap but keep in mind there may well be a sting in the tail.' He stood up. 'We'll speak again.'

When he walked out into the silent, hostile world he failed to see the figure in the darkness across the street. Cedric Bullock had observed their conversation with keen interest, particularly when Victor had picked up the headphones. Kimberly too, as she packed away her cassette recorder, was unaware of the watcher in the shadows.

Chapter Eleven

From Riches to Rags

It was early on Tuesday, 14 February, and the world outside Inger's window was still as stone. Across the road the silence of snow lay heavy on the frozen fields of the Knavesmire and dormant trees shivered in the bitter wind. Beyond the horizon a spectral sky was filled with grey clouds that promised more snow. As she dressed in her warmest clothes she recalled it was Valentine's Day and memories flooded back.

It had been on that day she had said farewell to her parents and left for England. Her parents had been kind and caring and she recalled their last conversations after she had decided to move on with her life. Her father had given her a gentle hug and whispered, 'Have the courage to pursue your dreams.' Her mother had followed her out to the taxi with tears in her eyes and whispered, 'Remember, Inger, we can only learn to love by loving.' It was then Inger had wondered if her mother knew more about that which had always remained unspoken.

When she opened her door and walked out to her car, above her head in the high branches rooks squawked their cries of danger. Her little red Mini appeared frozen solid and nothing happened when she turned the ignition. 'Blast!' she muttered, then slammed the door, returned her car keys to the hall table and set off to walk to the university.

It was a hazardous journey on the frozen pavements, but as she approached reception she stopped and smiled. Members of her choir were outside dressed as medieval jongleurs and singing 'Greensleeves' while rattling collection tins. It cheered her to see the students and she opened her purse and donated a few coins. It was the university's Rag Week and this was one of many events. When she walked into reception, Perkins was behind his counter beneath a huge poster advertising 'Jail Break', 'Blind Date' and 'Pub Crawl'.

It was well known that the concept was to raise money for the less advantaged people in society and the students had entered into the spirit of it wholeheartedly. Inger was aware that Rag was an acronym for Red Amber Green, where red was a warning and green meant good to go. All the events on the poster were printed in bright green. They had passed the acid test as far as the students were concerned.

'Good morning, Dr Larson,' said Perkins cheerfully.

'Hello, Perkins,' said Inger. She always felt uplifted by this charming man. He stood there almost to attention in his immaculate white shirt, regimental tie and blue blazer. 'You always look so smart,' she said with a smile.

'As my dear mother used to say, slovenly dress leads to a slovenly mind.'

'I'm sure it does,' said Inger.

'And may I say, your choir have brightened up this rather bleak morning.'

'They certainly have.' She glanced up at the poster. 'There's a lot going on this week.'

'Yes,' said Perkins and paused. 'Although I'm not too sure about the Pub Crawl. Apparently, the challenge is a half-pint in twenty different pubs. They call it the Micklegate Mile. Still, I suppose they're only young once.'

'Very true,' said Inger while thinking she couldn't imagine Perkins doing anything like that in his younger days. He would have been too busy polishing his boots.

'Have a good day,' said Perkins as Inger set off towards the quad.

A few minutes later Edna Wallop frowned at the choir as she walked into reception and approached Perkins. 'Is Grammaticus in?'

'Good morning, Dr Wallop,' said Perkins evenly.

'I asked if Grammaticus was in.'

Perkins hated her abrupt manner and lack of formality. '*Professor* Grammaticus was in early,' he replied. 'He passed me half an hour ago.'

Edna strode off towards the quad.

'Have a good day,' he murmured with little conviction.

On the Cloisters corridor, Victor was in his study at his desk when there was a tap on the door. He turned as it opened uninvited. It was Edna with a stern expression on her face. 'A word,' she said abruptly and beckoned with a nicotine-stained forefinger. Victor was not in the habit of following Edna's demands, but he didn't have the energy this morning to be confrontational. Sometimes it was better just to go with the flow. It was also common knowledge that Kimberly's petition had been signed by hundreds of students and delivered to the Vice Chancellor and he knew this had not put Edna in the best of moods.

He followed her along Alcuin corridor and entered her spacious but desperately untidy study. It was a shambles and he could not imagine how anyone could work efficiently in such chaos. There was a bureau with a drop-down lid in the corner of the room. It was open, revealing a bottle of whisky and two crystal tumblers among a pile of books. As ever, she didn't mince her words.

'I'm not happy with this excuse for mayhem in the guise of Rag Week, Victor,' she growled. 'So I want you to speak to your colleagues in the faculty. Traditionally it's been typified by noisy, disorderly conduct in defiance of authority. I'm giving you fair warning . . . This will not happen.'

'I see,' said Victor impassively.

Edna was determined. 'You appear to have some sway with the students. I want you to limit its remit. I do not want a repeat of previous atrocious behaviour. Eboracum has a reputation to maintain.'

Victor folded his arms and sighed. 'I agree they do get up to the usual shenanigans but they're young and like to let their hair down. We have to remember they raise a lot of money for those less fortunate in the city.'

'I've seen some of the posters. What's this about a blind date?'

'It's a programme on television hosted by Cilla Black that began a few years ago. Very popular, I understand. The students will be be doing something similar, I expect. It appears harmless enough.'

'It has to stop,' demanded Edna.

Victor shook his head. 'The point is, Edna, this is *tradition*. It's a national event and I'm sure you would not want the press to hear that you are suppressing the students' activities when in other universities they are encouraged.'

'Really?' she retorted. 'I regret to say I'm fully aware that the mob uses charitable works as an excuse for unruly behaviour. I want all events to be orderly and I shall hold you responsible if they are not.'

Victor gave her a stare. 'Fortunately, I am not the one who is Acting Head of Faculty. So if any heads roll it won't be mine, Edna.' He turned to leave but, as always, she was keen to have a last word, which was heavy with sarcasm.

'Yes, of course . . . A fitting comment from someone who was unsuccessful for the post when you were interviewed with Henry. I gather you have not applied this time. Probably a sensible decision.'

Victor stopped dead in his tracks. Edna was delighted with the reaction and knew that she had hit home. He turned slowly and spoke with quiet authority. 'The better man got the job when I was interviewed. I was honoured to serve under Henry and learned a great deal. However, I am not sure who is supplying you with information, Edna, but the closing date for the post of Head of Faculty is tomorrow, I believe.' He closed the door behind him while Edna clenched her fists, shaken by the implication.

At morning break, Zeb and Inger were having a planning meeting in the common room. Along with Royce Channing, the Head of the Art Faculty, they were the directors of the annual summer arts festival.

'Early June would be ideal,' said Zeb. 'We could reserve the quad for two nights and hope for the best with the weather.'

Inger scanned her notebook. 'So you've decided on *The Merchant of Venice* . . . a great play.'

Zeb took a last drag of her cigarette and nodded. 'We performed it a couple of years before you arrived and it worked really well.'

'We would need to get it in the faculty diary,' said Inger with a frown. 'That means consulting Edna.'

Zeb stubbed out her cigarette with some force. 'Not this time. I'll talk to Canon Edward over a friendly sherry. He loves our drama performances.'

'Good idea,' said Inger. 'Let me know how it goes and we can start planning rehearsals.'

Zeb got up to leave. 'By the way, I heard you had car trouble and walked in this morning.'

'Yes, my Mini struggles in this weather. The guy in the upstairs apartment is good with cars. He's having a look at it this afternoon. I'm keeping my fingers crossed.'

'OK, good luck, catch you later.'

In the teaching block, Tom's session with English One had gone well. However, when the bell sounded for morning break, the conversation turned away from the poetry of Adrian Henri, Roger McGough and Brian Patten to the fact that Ellie MacBride was one of three women taking part in Blind Date that evening. He left the excited chatter behind him and headed for the warmth of the common room where Zeb was collecting her mail. Tom checked his pigeon-hole but it was empty, unlike Zeb's. She held up three brightly coloured envelopes that were obviously Valentine cards. 'Randy students,' said Zeb with a grin as she lit another cigarette and headed out to the quad.

Tom collected a coffee and spotted Inger writing in her notebook. 'Hi, Inger, may I join you?'

'Hello, Tom, of course. I've just been planning the summer festival with Zeb. You might want to get involved.'

'I'd like that. What are you doing?'

'*The Merchant of Venice*.'

'Brilliant. One of my favourites. "The quality of mercy is not strained" and all that.'

'That's the one. Early days, obviously, but I'll let you know.'

Once again Tom looked into her blue eyes. 'It's *Songs from the Shows* tonight at the Joseph Rowntree Theatre. Did you decide to go?'

There was a pause. 'Not sure,' she said. 'I'll have a word with Victor. In any case, my car is playing up. I walked in this morning. I'm hoping to get it fixed this afternoon.'

'I could collect you at seven if it would help.' The words came out suddenly. 'My car is coping well in this weather.'

'That's kind, Tom. I'll let you know.'

He sipped his coffee and watched her leave with hope in his heart.

It was lunchtime and Owen was working at his desk when Tom walked in.

'Just booked the flights for Chamonix,' he said with a grin. 'Can't wait. It'll be brilliant.'

'That's good,' said Tom and sat down. 'So . . . how's Sue?'

'Fine. Six months gone but still fit and active. Quite a girl is my Sue. Just worried about her in this bloody weather. The pavements outside our house are like the Cresta Run. Fortunately, Victor's helping out with lifts.'

'Are you going to the theatre tonight?'

'Sadly, no. Sue was keen but her mum and dad are coming round and staying over for a few days because of the weather. They're really good at helping out, shopping, great meals, tidying up. You get the picture.'

'Sounds good.'

'I saw you chatting up Inger at break. Is she going?'

'Maybe. I've offered a lift.'

'Oh well. Good luck with the ice queen.'

Tom gave a shy smile. 'How about some lunch?'

'Great idea. We can discuss how Wales are going to beat England in Cardiff next month.'

'Or we could have a chat about how they've just lost to Ireland.'

Owen grinned. 'The thing is, Englishman, we always show some *hwyl* against the old enemy.' Tom didn't know the word but guessed it must have something to do with blood and guts.

When they walked into the quad students dressed as silent-movie prisoners in striped uniforms were about to be chased around the university campus. The so-called Jail Break had begun.

A few minutes later Tom and Owen had sat down to a warming lunch of steak pie and chips. 'Have you heard about Sky telly?' asked Owen. 'It'll never catch on. I already pay a TV licence. Word has it this guy Murdoch is going to charge us for films and sport. Bloody cheek if you ask me.'

Last week Sky television, courtesy of Rupert Murdoch, had begun broadcasting as the first satellite TV service in Britain.

'My neighbour said he was going to buy a Sky dish,' said Tom. 'He's having it fixed outside his house to pick up the channels.'

'Not for me,' said Owen. 'I'm not paying a subscription to an Aussie millionaire.'

Meanwhile, at a far table, members of the university's rugby 1st XV were plotting the route of their evening Pub Crawl. Word had it there was a pub for every day of the year within the city walls so there were plenty to choose from.

Afternoon lectures had gone well and it was five o'clock when Tom finally arrived home and switched on the television for company as much as anything else. It burbled away in the background as he prepared cheese on toast and a mug of tea. On BBC One the pupils of Grange Hill were going on a study trip to the Isle of Wight and he smiled, recalling many of the school trips he had been in charge of in past years.

When the news came on, it sounded like problems were in store for the author Salman Rushdie following the publication of his controversial book *The Satanic Verses*. It had caused outrage among the Islamic community, and Ayatollah Ruhollah Khomeini of Iran had placed a *fatwa*, an order to kill, on him. Tom guessed Rushdie's days were numbered.

He was trying to find a clean shirt when the phone rang. 'Hi, Tom,' said a familiar voice.

'Inger, good to hear from you.'

'If it's not too late, I wondered if there was still a chance of a lift to the theatre. My neighbour couldn't fix my car and it would be good to support Victor.'

'No problem. I can be outside your place at seven if that's OK.'

'If you're sure. It's pretty dreadful out there.'

'That's fine. Wrap up warm and I'll see you soon.' Tom put down the phone and smiled. The temperature might have been minus five outside but, inside, he felt a warm glow.

Three miles away Victor and Pat were at home in Easingwold getting ready for the concert. Pat had laid out his magnificent cerise three-piece corduroy suit with a white collarless shirt while Victor was selecting a red bow tie, an azure waistcoat and his best grey suit. He was deep in thought.

'Come on then,' said Pat. 'Out with it. What did she say?'

'She wants to curtail the students' activities during Rag Week.'

'Why? What's the problem?'

'She disapproves of their noisy behaviour.'

'Nonsense.'

Victor was struggling with his bow tie. 'In fact, she went into a splenetic rant about it.'

Pat smiled. He loved Victor's use of language. It was one of his professorial partner's most endearing habits. 'Come here. Let me do that for you.'

Victor relented. He knew he was letting Edna's taunting get to him.

'Surely you have to at least try to stop that despicable

woman getting the post.' Pat stood back to appreciate the perfect knot in Victor's bow tie. 'And if she got it, would you leave?'

'Of course not. I have a duty to the students.'

'In that case you must apply. I'll dig out your old application and tidy it up. You could get it in by tomorrow.'

Victor looked at Pat. His enthusiasm was infectious. 'Why not?' he said. 'Let's do it.'

Pat smiled. 'I'm so pleased.' He gestured around their beautifully furnished room with its original watercolours, velvet drapes and elegant chairs. 'You know, Victor, whatever happens at the university, we're very lucky . . . We have a life of riches.'

Tom set off for York with an air of anticipation. He drove past the Joseph Rowntree Theatre where members of the orchestra were beginning to arrive with their instruments. As he crossed the River Ouse over Lendal Bridge a flurry of snow pattered on his windscreen. Taxis were in demand outside the railway station as commuters to Leeds returned from work. Finally, the familiar sight of Micklegate Bar came into sight as he turned right towards the racecourse. There was a bright light in the porch above the front door of Inger's apartment and he pulled up outside.

Inger smiled when she opened the door. Tom's long hair was matted with snow after the short walk from the car. 'Thanks, Tom, I'm glad you're driving and not me. The forecast isn't good.' She wore a scarf over her head, a long woollen coat and thick, fur-lined boots.

Tom drove into the car park near to the theatre and they hurried towards the bright lights that lit up the steps outside the entrance. As they went through the doors, Inger said, 'You'll love this place, Tom.'

He was immediately impressed. Opened in 1935, it was a beautiful art deco building. Founded on chocolate, the theatre had been commissioned by the Joseph Rowntree Village Trust for the workers of the Rowntree & Company chocolate factory. It had become one of the cultural centres of the city. 'Perfect,' he said, but it wasn't just the theatre he was admiring.

Victor and Pat were in the foyer welcoming friends. Pat was in his element, an effusive, ebullient man, a figure of sartorial elegance and charm. He was obviously an important and respected member of the theatre's team of voluntary helpers. Pat shook Tom's hand and kissed Inger on the cheek. 'So pleased you made it. Thanks for your support.'

Tom sat next to Inger, who seemed more relaxed than on previous occasions. He had bought two programmes and they discussed the wide variety of music featuring songs from *Kiss Me Kate, My Fair Lady, Les Misérables* and *Cats*. A couple of years ago Inger had gone to see *Les Misérables* with her brother. 'It was a wonderful show,' said Inger and Tom could sense she was sharing a happy time.

It was an entertaining evening and the amateur performers were outstanding. They were an eclectic group of teachers, shopkeepers and civil servants with a shared love of music, and their enthusiasm shone through.

At the end there was a standing ovation. Finally, after the goodbyes in the warmth of the foyer, everyone hurried out to the car park. The drive back to Inger's was slow and uneventful. All the traffic was moving at a snail's pace.

'Thank you for coming out of your way, Tom.'

'A pleasure,' said Tom as they finally arrived outside her apartment. He hurried round to the passenger door and opened it.

Inger stepped out and paused for a moment. 'I would invite you in for coffee but perhaps not tonight,' and she gestured towards the flurries of snow banking up against the front bumper of her Mini.

'Perhaps another time,' said Tom. 'What about tomorrow morning? Do you need a lift?'

'My neighbour is bringing me in and then he's taking my car to get a new battery. So thanks anyway.'

'Well, just let me know if you need some help.'

'That's kind, Tom.' She leaned forward and kissed him on the cheek. 'I've enjoyed tonight,' and she stepped carefully through the snow to her front door. Tom drove away, smiling.

It was quiet now in the theatre and there was just Victor and Pat in the foyer. Only the caretaker and theatre manager remained in the auditorium.

'A triumph,' said Victor. 'I'm so pleased for you. I know how hard you've worked.' He gave him a hug.

'A team effort,' said Pat, 'and wonderful to have a full house.'

Victor opened the entrance door and peered out. 'Wait here,' he said. 'I shouldn't be too long. I'll get the car started and bring it to the front,' and he turned up his collar and hurried out into the snow. He stepped carefully down the steps and crunched up the frozen driveway to the tall metal gate lit up in the streetlights. Then he turned right and crossed the road by the roundabout. The car park was in the shadow of the high walls of the local swimming baths. As he stepped into the darkness of the vast empty spaces of the car park, he became aware of hurried footsteps behind him.

The two brothers, Jason and Donny Blackburn, were local thugs. Theirs was a life of petty theft, drugs and violence. The sight of two men embracing beneath the bright lights of the theatre foyer had attracted their attention. Then one of them began to make his way to the car park. The fact he wore an expensive coat suggested he might have money in his wallet. It was an opportunity too good to miss and the prospect of a savage attack on a vulnerable man filled them with drunken pleasure.

Victor realized the danger too late. He was standing next to his locked car searching for his keys when the brutality began. He barely had time to cry out before Jason punched him in the stomach and Donny kicked his legs from under him. What followed was a ruthless and relentless beating. It ended with a final kick to the head but by then Victor was in oblivion. As they dragged him out of sight beside the car his coat and trousers ripped on the frozen tarmac. After emptying his wallet they wandered off into the night to seek another victim.

Pat said goodnight to the theatre manager, collected his coat, scarf and trilby hat from the cloakroom and waited for the car to appear. Minutes passed by. 'Oh dear,' he muttered. 'I hope he can get it started.'

He stepped outside and walked across the road to where the car was parked. Then he stopped and stared. Victor's car was there and a drift of snow had gathered against the front tyres. The lights of distant streetlamps gave an eerie orange glow to the surroundings and in the distance he saw the shadows of two figures running away towards the chocolate factory and the road beyond. They were large men wearing bobble hats and bomber jackets and what appeared to be heavy boots.

Pat looked around him and wondered if he had missed Victor when he was saying goodnight to the manager in the auditorium. He stood there like a silent sentinel, feeling perplexed. The wind blew snowflakes in his face. Around him the car park was a vast, deserted space. He shivered, deep in thought. Something was wrong.

On impulse he walked towards the car. It was then he saw something that froze his blood. A still figure was lying on the ground on the far side of the car. Pat skittered through the snow and looked down at Victor. He was lying on his back, arms outstretched. His coat was open and his shirt was torn. The knees of his suit were in rags as if he had been dragged. He knelt down. 'Victor, Victor!' he cried. He stared in horror and felt for a pulse. Then he saw the pool of blood staining the snow around Victor's head and he looked to the heavens and screamed.

Chapter Twelve

A Walking Shadow

A few snowdrops shivered in the bitter wind and winter jasmine clung to the wall as Tom left his cottage on the morning of Monday, 6 March. The season was turning and winter no longer held the land in its iron grip. There had been many dark days after the brutal attack on Victor but now spring felt just around the corner. He had made a good recovery and the two culprits had been caught.

They had been targeting gay men in York for the past few months. Their decision to run from the theatre car park and continue their night of violence on High Petergate met with a painful end. They hadn't counted on the Rag Week's Pub Crawl. A few burly members of the university rugby team had left the Guy Fawkes Inn nearby and rushed across the road to help the unfortunate man who had just left the Hole in the Wall public house and was being punched and kicked. The young men meted out similar retribution and detained the two drunken thugs until the arrival of the police. Since then Victor had confirmed their identities and life was slowly returning to normal.

Pat was driving Victor to York down the A19. He glanced across at his partner and gave an encouraging smile. 'You look so much better now.'

'I do feel almost like my old self,' he said as he stared out of the passenger window. 'But it's a little strange going back to work.'

'That's understandable,' said Pat. 'I'm just relieved they caught those bully-boy muggers. I hope they lock them up and throw away the key.'

'I agree. In the meantime, I'm looking forward to catching up with my students once again.'

'And what about the Head of Faculty interviews? I'm pleased I delivered your application to Miss Frensham in the Vice Chancellor's office. It just met the deadline.'

Victor nodded. 'Thanks for that. I can't imagine how you remembered with everything that was going on.'

'Victor, you know it was important.' There was determination in his voice. 'We need to at least try to stop that woman ruining all the good work done by Henry and yourself.'

Victor sighed. 'No doubt she will have spent the last fortnight trying to establish her credentials with the governing body.'

'Probably . . . but truth will prevail. It always does.'

Victor wasn't so sure but thanked Pat when they arrived in the university car park and he stepped out to greet the new day. Elegant as always in a new blue shirt, red bow tie, mustard waistcoat and a burnt sienna cord suit, he picked up his leather shoulder bag and strode into reception.

'Good morning, Perkins,' he said.

Perkins looked up in surprise. 'Well, that takes the Garibaldi,' he said. 'Only a minute ago Dr Wallop was asking if you were in.'

'Really?'

'And she wasn't exactly polite. Suddenly she turned up like the proverbial bad penny, if you don't mind me saying, and questioned me as if I was the enemy.'

You probably are, thought Victor. 'I'm sure there was a reason,' he said with cautious restraint.

Perkins paused for a moment and stared up at the man he respected so much. 'Anyway . . . welcome back, Professor.'

'It's good to be back.'

'We've missed you and you're looking well.'

'Thanks,' said Victor. 'I was wondering about my mail?'

'I collected it for you. It's quite a pile. I have it here.' From beneath the counter Perkins produced a bundle of envelopes tied with a red ribbon.

'That's very kind,' said Victor. He added them to the papers in his shoulder bag.

'I'm glad they caught those villains,' said Perkins.

More like psychopathic homophobic skinheads, thought Victor. 'Yes, a big relief,' and he set off for the quad.

'Have a good day, Professor,' Perkins called after him.

Owen was completing his itinerary for the Chamonix field week when Tom walked in.

'Have you heard?' said Owen. 'Victor's back today.'

'That's great news.'

'I walked in with the Vice Chancellor this morning. He was asking about the skiing and mentioned it. He looked pleased.'

'I hope Victor is well enough to cope with his lectures.'

'One thing's for sure: the students love him and they will be sympathetic.'

'That's good to hear. How about you? Is Chamonix sorted?'

'Yes, fine. To be honest it was a relief to come in to work after yesterday's fiasco.'

'How come?'

Owen shook his head in despair. 'I'm in the dog house. Slipped up badly for Mother's Day. Spent £4.99 on an azalea basket from Woolworth's for Sue's mother, then got talking with a rugby mate and left it in the shop. Who thought up Mother's Day, I'd like to know? They've got a lot to answer for.'

'I played safe,' said Tom. 'I just sent a card.'

'Yes, but your mum doesn't live with you. Our house is looking like a bloody show home. Everything in its place. She's just bought some serviettes.'

Tom nodded. He guessed the napkins really were the final straw.

At morning break Victor stopped in the quad to talk to one of his students. It was Giovanni Filippo Carmichael, the President of the Students' Union. A popular figure around the university, everyone knew him as Gio.

'How are you, Victor?' he asked. He was a tall, dashing

young man with an English father and an Italian mother. With over 70 per cent grades throughout his Mathematics course and an outstanding dissertation in progress concerning financial modelling and functional analysis, he had been identified by Victor as a very likely candidate for a first.

'Much better, thank you, Gio,' said Victor. 'It was a painful first week but I've recovered from the bumps and bruises.' There was a small scar on his forehead above his right eye. That apart, he was back to his old self. 'So I'll be seeing you this afternoon for your tutorial.' Victor looked at his watch. 'Shall we say two o'clock?'

'Thanks. I'll be there.'

'And how are you?' asked Victor. It had been over two weeks since they had spoken.

'I'm fine but Kimberly is in a bit of a state.' It was well known he and Kimberly were an 'item'. 'I'm going up to Tuke now to see how she is. She was very concerned last night. Reckoned someone had been in her room. She never locks it, of course, with the editorial team always going in and out but this was different . . . stuff being moved around.'

Victor looked thoughtful. 'I see,' he said quietly. 'Yes, you must check all is well.'

Gio swept his long black hair from his eyes and nodded. 'Thanks, Victor. I'll see you at two.'

Victor watched him walk away and decided he would speak with Kimberly at the earliest opportunity.

In the common room, Inger had arranged to meet Zeb to discuss rehearsals for *The Merchant of Venice*. The performance dates had been booked: the dress rehearsal on 9 June and two presentations on 10 June; the main parts had been cast; and Royce Channing had already begun to prepare the scenery in his art department.

'So . . . any thoughts?' asked Zeb.

Inger opened her notebook. 'I'm thinking of woodwind, percussion and strings. My orchestra have some good ideas.'

Zeb nodded. 'Both Portia and Lorenzo say music is made more beautiful by the night-time. Maybe you could come up with something.'

'Bit of good news. My brother is coming over for a holiday and said he would help. A violin solo would be perfect. He's already composing some original pieces based on the three plot lines: the bond, the casket and the ring.'

'Brilliant!' said Zeb. 'Sounds perfect.' She sat back, drank the rest of her coffee and searched in her shoulder bag for a new pack of cigarettes. 'I read it's opening as a musical in New York in December. We ought to go. It would be fun. Think about it.'

'I will,' said Inger. 'What's this, by the way?'

There was a copy of the BBC holiday guide *Holiday '89* on the table.

Zeb lit a cigarette and flicked through the pages. 'I thought this looks interesting. Thailand for £399 all in.'

Inger smiled. 'What does "all in" mean?'

Zeb grinned. 'I guess you use your imagination. It's my new boyfriend, Rocky, who's given me the brochure.'

'Rocky?'

'Lead singer for Rocky and the Caretakers.'

'Caretakers?'

'Yes, Tony and Peter . . . They're caretakers at a secondary school. Great guys. They're trying to get a gig in Edinburgh.'

'Sounds good,' said Inger. It seemed the right thing to say.

'What about you?' said Zeb. She gave her an enquiring look. 'Tom's a nice guy.'

'He is,' said Inger. There certainly was something engaging about the man, with his long unkempt wavy hair and hazel eyes, but she wasn't going to say so. She picked up her notebook. 'OK. Things to do. Maybe we could meet with Royce next time to check out the scenery?'

'Will do,' said Zeb and she continued to peruse her holi day guide. Ibiza looked good but she had done that and didn't want to bump into any previous lovers.

It was lunchtime when Victor caught up with Kimberly. He was standing by the door of the dining room and she walked over to greet him. 'Welcome back. Gio said you were much recovered.'

'Yes, I am and it's good to be back.' He looked around. The clatter of crockery and the hum of student conversation surrounded them. They were invisible in plain sight. 'There is something I wanted to discuss with you.'

'Yes?'

'When I spoke with Gio he said you thought someone had gone into your room.'

'Yes. To be honest, I'm feeling a little nervous.'

'Why is that?'

'Someone has definitely been in. It's happened a couple of times. I didn't want to make a fuss with Gio. He tends to be overprotective and I don't want him to be distracted from his studies. It's so important to him that he does well.'

'I can understand that but what exactly has happened?'

'A few small things. My desk wasn't as I left it. My notes for the next edition of the *Echo* had been disturbed.'

'Perhaps it's one of the editorial team. Don't they go in and out?'

'Yes, I suppose they do and my door is never locked.'

'Then maybe it's as simple as that.'

She frowned and pursed her lips. 'Actually, Victor, that's not all. There was just a hint of a smell of cigarettes and none of my friends are smokers.'

Victor frowned. 'I think you should start locking your door.'

At afternoon break Tom was drinking tea in the far corner of the common room near the television set. A copy of the *Radio Times* lay on the table with the headline 'Comic Relief Special Issue'. On the front cover was a photograph of Billy Connolly in Africa prior to the second Red Nose Day on Friday.

Suddenly Inger appeared and sat down beside him. She pointed to the magazine. 'This could catch on,' she said. 'It raised millions last time.'

Tom smiled. There was something very special about this beautiful woman that raised his spirits. The fact that she was always out of reach made her even more appealing. 'They may do it every year in future,' said Tom. 'It certainly caught the imagination of the nation.'

'This might be a little out of your comfort zone, Tom, but I've heard from Owen that you play the guitar.'

Tom blushed slightly. 'I used to play in school assembly. It was the usual three chord stuff: "Kumbaya" and "Puff, The Magic Dragon" and not much more. I play at home, mainly for relaxation . . . a sort of a poor man's Bob Dylan.'

'Perfect,' said Inger with a grin. 'That's all we need.'

'For what?'

'Red Nose Day.'

'Go on.'

'Are you up for a bit of busking with a few of my choir?'

'You're joking!'

'No, quite serious, Tom. It could be fun.'

'Where?'

'St Helen's Square outside Bettys. We've decided to meet there during the lunch break on Friday. No big commitment, probably only half an hour.'

'What will you be singing?'

'They mentioned Joan Baez; Peter, Paul and Mary; Pete Seeger; Joni Mitchell . . . So, mainly folk songs.'

'I would need to practise,' said Tom a little hesitantly.

'I expect there might be a couple of other guitarists so you needn't worry and I can scribble some chords for you if you wish.'

'That would help.' Tom was warming to the idea.

'Good,' said Inger. 'That's settled. See you later.'

As she walked away Tom realized he was about to play in public for the first time. 'Bloody hell,' he muttered to himself.

It was 4 p.m. and Canon Edward Chartridge was in the Lodge pouring sherry into two crystal glasses. His home was a distinctive Victorian red-brick dwelling in the university grounds. It had ornate gables, churchlike rooftop finials, a canted bay window and a pair of octagonal towers. Inside it was filled with mahogany bookshelves, watercolour paintings and comfortable furniture.

'Do take a seat, Victor,' he said with a seraphic smile.

'Good of you to call by. I was very concerned about the dreadful incident that caused your absence. Are you sure you are well enough to return?'

'Yes, thank you, Edward. I'm fine now.'

'It must have been a terrible shock.'

'It was. Life can be cruel sometimes.'

Edward sipped his sherry and gestured towards a shelf of classic poetry books. 'Ah, yes, Victor. Such is the vagary of life. Percy Shelley said it stained the white radiance of eternity.'

Victor smiled. 'I have to agree and that poem, "Adonais", is one of his very best.'

Edward nodded. It was always good to converse with this well-read if slightly unconventional professor. 'So, I see you put in an application for the Head of Faculty.'

Victor smiled. *So this is the reason for the invitation,* he thought. 'Yes, I wanted to put my hat in the ring.'

'And so you should.'

Victor sighed. 'I just wish Henry was still with us.'

'As do I. He was a true Christian spirit.'

Victor noticed the reference to Christianity but Edward had always been accepting of his agnosticism. 'I miss him terribly.' He leaned forward in his chair and sipped the last of his sherry.

Edward stood up. 'Let's have another,' he said. 'This really is excellent sherry.' He gestured towards a wonderful print above his drinks cabinet. It depicted Sir Francis Drake standing proudly on Plymouth Hoe and surveying his fleet before departing for Spain. 'He knew what he was doing,' said Edward while holding up the decanter. 'Left with three thousand kegs of sherry after raiding Cadiz.'

Victor settled back once again. Edward clearly had more to discuss.

The conversation drifted from university examinations, preparations for field week to the need to increase the number of foreign students. Finally, it came back to the interview, now only a few weeks away.

'I'm aware you don't always see eye to eye with Edna.'

'We have different views,' was Victor's neutral reply.

'The thing is I believe she has the support of a good number of the governors.'

'I can understand that.'

'There are also governors who disapprove of your personal circumstances.'

So this was it, thought Victor. 'It will soon be the last decade of the twentieth century, Edward. The attitudes of society move on.'

'Perhaps,' said Edward. His voice sounded almost sad. He respected this man and knew his value to the university. 'In the meantime, Edna is a determined lady. Reminds me of Proverbs three, sixteen. She has the length of days in her right hand and in her left hand riches and honour.'

Victor pondered this for a moment, wondering if there was a message there.

They finished their drinks and stood up.

'Oh well, the interviews will soon come around,' said Edward. They shook hands. 'So good luck and, of course, the governors will have the final say.'

'Naturally,' said Victor.

Darkness had fallen and Edna Wallop was sitting on the window ledge in her study and smoking a cigarette. She was staring out at the students and tutors making their way home. On the other side of the room Cedric Bullock was sitting in an armchair and sipping a glass of malt whisky.

'I've spoken to a few of the governors,' he said. 'Some have a listening ear; others are keeping their cards close to their chest. I have to be cautious.'

'It's disappointing that Victor recovered so quickly,' said Edna.

'Yes. I heard from one of the secretaries that he had a meeting with Edward this morning. Apparently, it went on for about half an hour.'

'That doesn't worry me. The Vice Chancellor is always in a neutral corner. He continues to see the good in people. Occasionally his naivety is remarkable.'

Cedric pondered this. 'But doesn't he have influence?'

Edna shook her head. 'Not any more. We've got a new breed of powerful business types on the governing body now. They would eat him alive.'

Cedric nodded. 'Yes, I've met a few of them.'

Edna blew smoke towards the closed window. 'It's that Stratton girl who might cause me trouble.'

Cedric finished the last of his whisky and stood up. 'By all accounts she's still poking her nose in where it's not wanted.'

Edna stubbed out her cigarette. 'Not for much longer.'

It was late and Richard Head was sitting in his study in the far corner of Alcuin corridor. His room was organized to perfection. On his bookshelf the books were arranged according to strict Dewey Decimal Classification and each evening his spiral-bound notebook was always left so it was parallel with the edge of his desk. The pictures on his wall of famous scientists were all in identical frames and regularly checked with a spirit level to ensure the top of each frame was horizontal and in perfect alignment with its neighbour. They were also arranged from left to right according to their date of birth, so Galileo came before Newton, Darwin and Einstein. Richard loved order and hated chaos.

After his scientific work his passion was astronomy. In the far corner of his room he had a quirky skylight window that overlooked the quad. From it he could look down towards the common room and the offices above it on the first floor. On the top floor was a narrow arched leaded window that gave some light on to the metal staircase that opened up on to the landing outside Tuke corridor. Occasionally he would spot a fleeting figure crossing the metal walkway at the top but this was not his focus of interest. Richard had erected a powerful telescope which enabled him to study the heavens and the movement of the stars and planets. The winter months were the happiest times for this amateur astronomer and most evenings he would settle down for a quiet hour peering up at the sky.

He was aware that a partial solar eclipse was forecast for 7 March but he would have had to travel to America to enjoy the full spectacle. So it was a lonely and rather unproductive vigil for Richard tonight, and he had to admit there had been little of interest since the supernova back in 1987. The fact that it had occurred in a satellite galaxy of the Milky Way some 160,000 light years distant had given him the biggest thrill since he had made copper sulphate crystals as a nine-year-old in his mother's kitchen.

He was closing the skylight for the night when, on the

other side of the quad, he saw a shadowy figure appear at the top of the metal staircase outside Tuke corridor. It struck him as strange, as surely no one would dream of being there in the darkness, and he wondered who it was. Richard hadn't read Shakespeare's *Macbeth* since he was at school so didn't recall that towards the end of his tragedy the Bard had described life as 'a walking shadow'. If he had, it would have sent a shiver down his spine.

Chapter Thirteen

The Valley of Decision

When Tom drove into York on Friday, 17 March, the morning was sombre and grey and the taste of rain was in the air. There had been a brief halcyon period of fair weather but now he was in his study and the rain was coming down like stair rods and the sash window rattled in its frame. It was the last day before the Easter break and he was alone. Owen had left last weekend for the field week in Chamonix. His PE group were due to return tomorrow morning and Owen had insisted they spend the afternoon together at his home watching Wales play England in the Five Nations Championship.

Meanwhile, today was different. On arrival he had checked his mail in the common room. There was a note from Edna asking him to come to her office during the lunch break. It wasn't an inviting prospect. He stared at it in dismay, then put it in his pocket. He had students to teach.

*

As he was walking to the English block, Tom was met by the cherubic figure of Canon Edward Chartridge. 'Just the person I wanted to see,' he called out.

'Oh . . . good morning, Vice Chancellor.'

'Good morning, Thomas. I'm pleased I've caught up with you. I was looking through the timetable and spotted you're meeting your English One students this morning. It occurred to me that I've not invited them to one of my literary soirées yet, which is remiss of me. So perhaps we can determine a convenient date when you call in after lectures today. You will be there, of course.'

Members of the Education Faculty had received an invitation to call into the Lodge at five o'clock for an end-of-term get-together.

'Yes, looking forward to it,' said Tom.

Edward gave a rosy-cheeked smile. 'And mention to your students that if a few of them wish to volunteer a poetry recital, so much the better.'

Tom took the hint. 'Yes, Vice Chancellor, I'll mention it.'

'Splendid, Thomas. I'll let you get on. What's the subject this morning?'

'Metaphysical poetry.'

Edward beamed. 'John Donne, of course, but perhaps also Henry Vaughan and Andrew Marvell?'

'Plus George Herbert,' added Tom with a smile.

'But of course,' said Edward. He looked to the heavens. '"Easter Wings" is one of my favourites. Enjoy your metaphysical morning, Thomas,' and he walked away as if his head was still in the clouds.

*

The students in Tom's English One group were receptive and he appreciated the relaxed atmosphere. It was a gathering of eager young minds and he was enjoying his teaching in this new world of higher education. However, he could tell, towards the end of the session, that it was the thought of the Easter holiday rather than the poetry which really caught their imagination. Even so, the life of Henry Vaughan, the Royalist and Civil War poet, was discussed at length until the bell rang, then a hubbub of conversation rose, and cheerful goodbyes. Tommy Birkenshaw and Billy Whitelock, two Liverpudlians, were looking forward to supporting Liverpool in the FA Cup and Amy Fieldhouse and Liz Colby had got an Easter holiday job in Bridlington selling ice cream from a kiosk on the seafront. It took Tom back to his own university days when friends were plentiful and they all thought they would live for ever.

Ellie MacBride was the last to leave. 'Any plans for the holiday, Tom?' she asked as he packed his satchel.

'Visiting my parents plus preparation for next term. There's a lengthy teaching practice coming up and the placements have to be confirmed. It's turned out to be a really complex job, particularly when we try to place those students with a young family closer to home. What about you?'

'Home tomorrow to help my mum and dad with their stall over Easter. Then a short holiday in Whitby.'

Tom smiled. 'I love Whitby. It's one of my favourite places . . . the harbour, great beaches, the 199 steps, the abbey, Captain Cook . . . There's so much to see and enjoy. How long are you going for?'

'Not sure yet. Probably a long weekend.'

'Well, enjoy it.'

She paused as if seeking the right words. 'I'm going with Dave.'

'Dave?'

'David Hardisty, another *mature* like me. Main History. I met him during Rag Week. He picked me, unseen of course, at the Blind Date event. We both hit it off. It's not serious but he's a nice guy.'

'I'm pleased for you, Ellie.'

She gave Tom a searching look. 'Thanks,' she said quietly and then left without another word.

At morning break, Inger was in the common room when Tom collected his coffee. He joined her at a table under one of the huge arched windows.

'Morning, Tom. How's things?'

'Fine except I've just been told I'm coming apart.'

'What do you mean?'

'One of my students mentioned it this morning.' He pointed to the brown leather patches on the sleeves of his cord jacket. The stitching was unravelling. 'She said she could fix it for me some time.'

Inger pursed her lips. 'Oh dear, Tom, so you obviously didn't do needlework at school?'

'Boys didn't do that stuff in my school. It was woodwork and metalwork with a bit of bricklaying.'

'Pity. It would have come in useful. Still, it's not too late to learn.'

'Not sure about that.'

'Well . . . I've got a needle and thread in my study. Call in before Edward's soirée. You know what he's like. Very fastidious. Probably not a good idea to turn up with your jacket falling apart.'

'Thanks. You're right, of course.' Then a thought struck him. 'After the busking in York I don't think I ever thanked you for all the guitar chords. I've had fun at home widening my repertoire. It's been quite soothing playing a few folk songs.'

Inger smiled. 'That's great. Maybe we should buy a capo for you. It makes such a difference.'

'I know what it is but have never thought to use one.'

'It's a really useful device. Takes its name from the Italian word for *head*. It simply clamps on to the neck of the guitar and shortens the length of the strings so you can raise the pitch. If you're singing along it can make such a difference in depth and variety.'

'In that case I'll get one.'

'Go to Banks in York. It's on Lendal. The oldest music shop in Britain. I go there regularly.'

Tom smiled. 'Thanks. I'll go tomorrow.' A thought struck him. 'Might you be going as well?'

Again there was that familiar pause. 'I might,' she replied cautiously. 'Not sure of my plans yet.' She glanced up at the clock. 'I've got violins in ten minutes. What about you?'

'Yes, tutorials until lunchtime.' He sighed. 'Then I've been summoned by Edna.'

Inger frowned. 'Whatever for?'

'No idea . . . but it won't be good news.'

She finished her coffee and stood up. 'Best of luck and remember: talk to Victor if there's a problem.' She tapped the flapping leather patch. 'And I'll sort this out for you.' He watched her walk away, lithe and purposeful.

At 12.30 p.m. Tom ascended the stairs to Alcuin corridor and approached Edna's study. He tapped on the door, waited for the muttered 'Come' and walked in. As usual there was a smell of stale tobacco. Edna was seated behind her desk. It was littered with a detritus of papers, files and memos.

She gestured towards a visitor chair. 'Sit, please.' It was a request reminiscent of Crufts dog show.

'I prefer to stand,' said Tom quietly. 'I'm teaching at one o'clock.'

'Then we have plenty of time for the business in hand,' she said and leaned back in her chair. 'Tom . . . let's put the past to one side for a moment. Please do sit down. This won't take long.' She glanced down at the timetable before her. 'And I'm aware you don't want to be late for your seminar with English Two.'

Her words were conciliatory but her tone was a parody of pity.

Tom relented and sat down.

Edna focused on him with her steel-grey eyes and leaned forward. 'Tom, the purpose of this meeting is because I care about the reputation of Eboracum. The university is dear to my heart and its future is in the balance.'

Tom remained silent. He knew the denouement was coming.

'I regret to say there are dissident factions in the faculty. They could cause great harm to those of us who are working hard to make this university one of the leaders in higher education. I'm aware you are a newcomer to this world but you are still ideally placed to support some of these initiatives.'

'I'm unclear,' said Tom tersely. 'What exactly is it that you are asking of me?'

Edna paused, weighing the moment. 'I know you have a loyalty to Victor. He has taken on the role of unofficial mentor and it's clear you take notice of his guidance.'

Tom nodded briefly. 'Professor Grammaticus has been very helpful to me.'

'I'm sure he has but you need to be mindful of the wider perspective.'

'Which is?'

Edna twitched at the abrupt response. She picked up her cigarette packet, thought otherwise and placed it firmly to one side. 'Kimberly Stratton and the *Echo* have begun to damage the reputation of our university. She is causing trouble and I have it on good authority she has been meeting with Victor.'

Tom glanced at his watch, then looked up. 'Why are you telling me this?'

'I want to know what's going on.'

'Then surely you should speak to them and not me.'

Edna gave a condescending smile. 'If only life was that simple. I doubt they would communicate with me.'

Tom stared at her and realized this woman was still living in her own cul-de-sac of devious dreams. 'I'm not sure I can help you and, if you'll excuse me, I need to get to my next session. So, was there anything else?' He looked at his watch again. 'It's time.'

Edna snapped, '*Time?*' She looked up at Tom with hostility in her eyes. 'Let me save you some time. You are aware that, if you don't do as I ask, you will not have your contract extended.'

'You've made that very clear.'

'It would appear that doesn't seem to worry you a great deal.' Edna stood up and pushed back her chair. 'However, this will. If you don't cooperate I will not give you a positive reference. So, think hard. When I have finished, you will be unemployable.'

Tom walked towards the door and turned to face her. 'Intimidation and blackmail do not suit you, Edna,' he said quietly. He closed the door behind him, walked down the corridor and descended the stairs. The rain blew into his face as he walked through the quad. By the time he reached the English block he had quelled his anger and begun to focus on the poets of the sixteenth century.

Soon his students were immersed in the wit and wisdom of William Shakespeare, Edmund Spenser, Christopher Marlowe and Ben Jonson. John Donne cropped up once again and as Yvonne Platt, an effervescent young woman from Bristol, reminded everyone that no one is 'an island', Tom cast his mind back to the conversation with Edna. Siobhan agreed with John Donne that just by being human, everyone is part of humanity. However, it occurred to Tom that there were exceptions and Edna Wallop was one of them.

After lunch Edna returned to her study with Cedric Bullock.

'So what was his response?' he asked.

Edna poured two tumblers of Teacher's Scotch Whisky. 'He's a weak character, young and idealistic. Sad really. He could have been useful.'

'He doesn't sound as if he's in tune with the realities of

higher education. It's obviously a quantum leap from his previous experience.'

'Quite right. His naivety is something to behold.'

'So what next?'

'Well, his days are numbered but he will, no doubt, report back to Victor. His little band are thick as thieves but by this time next year I will have rid the faculty of all these troublesome characters.'

'You sound confident you will get the job.'

'I am.'

'And what about the Stratton girl?'

'She must be stopped, of course.'

'How?'

Edna drank deeply and slammed down the tumbler on her desk. There was brimstone in her words. 'Never fear. I have my ways.'

After his seminar Tom walked into Victor's study and leaned against the door. His meeting with Edna had come flooding back. He was incandescent. 'Just how low can she go?'

Victor looked up from his desk and pushed aside a student dissertation on number theory. 'Sit down, Tom,' he said calmly. 'Let's talk. I presume you've had a meeting with Edna.'

'Yes and it was dreadful. Once again she wanted me to inform on others for her. When I refused she threatened to make me unemployable by not providing a positive reference. She's trying to destroy my future career. Surely she hasn't got that power? I just walked out.'

Victor stood up, filled the kettle and switched it on. 'Coffee or tea?'

'Ah . . . coffee, please.' The normality of the question brought him back to the here and now. 'Sorry to burst in.'

'That's not a problem,' Victor said with calm assurance. He collected two china cups and saucers from the Welsh dresser on the other side of the room and placed them on his coffee table along with a jug of milk, a bowl of brown sugar and a plate of Bettys Yorkshire shortbread biscuits. Then he gestured towards the neat grouping of Scandinavian armchairs. 'Please, Tom . . . take a seat.'

Tom sat down and put his head in his hands. 'It's as if she's clearing out anyone who stands in her way.'

Victor was measured in his response. 'Maybe it's not as bad as it seems. There are a number of scenarios. For example, it's not definite she will get the job. There will be other candidates and no one has been invited for interview yet.'

'But she talks as if she's already got it.'

Victor spooned Maxwell House into the cups and added boiling water. 'Think about it, Tom. If she does get it no one will want to work for her. We have talented colleagues who would be snapped up by other universities, perhaps Leeds or Nottingham or Sheffield. There are many opportunities elsewhere.'

'It would be drastic if many left,' said Tom, adding milk from the jug and a spoonful of sugar.

'Yes. Very true. It's the students I feel sorry for. The impact on their coursework would be huge.'

Tom sat back and sipped his coffee. 'I feel as though I've been through the wringer with her.' He looked up at Victor. 'Thanks for listening. It seemed like my future was in tatters when I left her study.'

Victor held out the plate of biscuits and Tom took one

gratefully. 'Don't worry about references. That's in your hands. It's up to you who you put down. You could use me or the head of your primary school in Harrogate.'

Tom sat back and munched his biscuit, feeling more normal.

Victor waited until he was sure his young colleague's equilibrium had been restored. 'Try to move on, Tom, and I'll see you later at the soirée.'

It was just after four o'clock when Tom returned to his study. It had been a busy day and there was still a lot of work to do. He sat at his desk and opened his huge school placement folder. After a few minutes he switched on the Grundig transistor radio perched on his bookcase. The voice of a news reporter drifted in and out of his consciousness as he matched schools to students. Earlier in the week Bob Geldof's wife, Paula Yates, had delivered a baby, a sister for Fifi Trixibelle, and the newsreader was wondering what name would be given to their new daughter. Then Jason Donovan began singing his hit record 'Too Many Broken Hearts' and he stood up, switched off the radio and picked up his jacket from the back of the chair. The leather patches on the elbows were literally hanging by a thread. He smiled. Inger's study was just down the corridor and school placements could wait a little longer.

At five o'clock Tom and Inger walked into the warm, inviting entrance of the Lodge and he felt a sense of inner contentment. Inger had agreed to meet him in Banks music shop on Saturday morning at ten o'clock. The troubles of the day seemed behind him and, with the patches on his sleeves now neatly sewn, life didn't seem quite so bad after all.

The spacious lounge was full and Edward was the perfect host as he drifted from one conversation to the next. Tom stood with Victor admiring the neat bookshelves when he felt the presence of the Vice Chancellor.

'Hello again, Thomas. Do you like my book collection? Quite a lot of first editions here. It's a hobby of mine.'

'It's wonderful, Vice Chancellor. I love books.'

Edward looked around the room. Everyone appeared deep in conversation and they were away from the main throng. 'I've heard good things about your work from Victor.'

Tom glanced at Victor, who simply smiled. 'Yes, Victor has been very helpful.'

'You appear to have settled in well.'

'Yes, and I've enjoyed working with the students.'

'And what of the future?' asked Edward.

Tom wondered how to progress this conversation. 'I love my teaching so I would like to stay on a little longer but, of course, that decision is out of my hands.'

Edward smiled and raised his glass. 'Ah, Thomas. Decisions . . . decisions. I'm reminded of Joel, chapter three, verse fourteen.'

Tom looked puzzled. 'I'm afraid you will have to enlighten me.'

'The day of the Lord is near in the valley of decision.'

'What does it mean?'

'Simply that God challenges us to make a decision and he will hand down his judgement.'

'I see,' said Tom hesitantly.

'Anyway . . . must circulate,' said Edward benignly. 'So

do remember, Thomas . . . life is a myriad of special moments so hold them tightly in your hand because they are fleeting.' And with that he was gone.

'Interesting,' said Victor. 'Come on, let's join the others before they all leave.'

Soon the gathering ended and everyone drifted off with messages of good wishes for the two-week holiday.

That evening in Easingwold, Pat had prepared an excellent beef stroganoff and Victor was relaxing after the meal with a glass of Merlot. 'Thanks,' he said. 'Simply superb.'

'A pleasure as always.' He gave Victor a knowing look. 'Cooking takes away the stresses of the day, don't you think?'

'You know me so well,' said Victor.

'But of course.' He topped up Victor's glass and they both retired to the pair of armchairs by the log-effect fire. 'Now, shall we talk?'

Victor nodded.

'In that case,' said Pat, 'one thing is for certain. The present situation at the university can't continue. Something has to be done.'

'If I get an interview,' said Victor with assurance, 'I'll be very well prepared.'

'That's good to hear but what's happening with Kimberly Stratton? Her article in the *Echo* won't go away. Surely Edna will respond in some way.'

'I'm sure she will and the situation may well get worse. It's become clear to me that Kimberly has something very significant on Edna.'

Pat leaned forward. 'Would it stop that dreadful woman getting the job, particularly if the governors become aware?'

'It may come to that, which is why I need to speak with Kimberly again.'

Pat nodded thoughtfully. 'How did the soirée go?'

'Excellent sherry,' said Victor.

'Naturally . . . but come on, tell all.'

'To be honest, I felt sorry for Tom. Edna has pretty well destroyed him. He came to see me today stuck between a rock and a hard place. Then to top it all the Vice Chancellor was giving him a lecture on decision-making. He was quoting all the biblical stuff about the valley of decision.'

'The valley of decision?'

'I don't think Tom knew what he was talking about but I'm pretty sure Edward was passing on discreet messages. He's a wily old cove. There's more there than meets the eye. We covered it in philosophy a long time ago. Apparently, the Valley of Decision is a biblical name given to the Valley of Jehoshaphat by the prophet Joel. It was the location of Zion's enemies.'

'How do you remember all this?'

Victor looked thoughtful. 'I'm not entirely sure! But sometimes I think Edward knows more than he lets on.'

'I always presumed he was just a figurehead for the university . . . a bit distant, perhaps.'

'Maybe so, but when he talks about the valley of decision I think he's making a subtle point. He's saying that when God was handing down his judgement, wickedness will be dealt with swiftly.'

They both sat back, enjoying their wine and deep in thought.

*

Meanwhile, three miles away Tom was drinking a glass of beer and enjoying his takeaway fish and chips while watching *Dallas* with Larry Hagman as the infamous J. R. Ewing; he was making sure the innocents were caught in the crossfire of the Southfork Ranch war. However, Tom had no such problems. He had forgotten about biblical quotes, school placements and that Ellie MacBride had moved on with her life. Even Edna Wallop had been pushed to the back of his thoughts.

He was going to Banks music shop in the morning to buy a capo under the direction of a beautiful Norwegian woman.

Chapter Fourteen

No Strings Attached

By the time Tom drove to York on the first day of the summer term the season had moved on its axis and the first breath of new life was in the air. It was an expectant dawn with the promise of light and colour and warmth. The hedgerows were bursting into life and the yellow petals of forsythia reflected the pale sunshine that gilded the distant land. It was Monday, 3 April, and spring had arrived in all its glory. So it was with a fresh optimism that Tom walked into reception where Perkins gave him a cheerful smile.

'Good morning, Dr Frith, and welcome back. I trust you had a good vacation?'

'I did, thanks, Perkins. How about you?'

He grinned and shook his head. 'No rest for the wicked. I've been busy with Charlie doing safety checks. The students need to be safe when they move around the campus.'

'Good to hear. So, any news?'

Perkins glanced left and right to ensure no one was within earshot. 'Yes, there is.' He lowered his voice. 'Dr

Wallop came in early. Told me to look out for two interviewees. They're arriving at morning break.'

'Interviewees?'

'Yes, a man and a woman, apparently. They've been shortlisted for the Head of Faculty post. I have to take them straight to the common room.'

'I see. That's interesting. Perhaps I'll meet them later.'

'You probably will.' A crowd of students wandered in accompanied by excited chatter. 'Anyway, have a good day, Dr Frith.'

'You too, Perkins,' said Tom and hurried across the quad to mount the stairs to Cloisters.

Owen was already at his desk when Tom walked in. 'Morning, Owen.'

Owen looked up from his summer-term timetable. 'Hi, Tom. Welcome back.'

'How's Sue?'

'Bit tired. Only a month away now. We were discussing names for the baby last night. She's picked William or Elizabeth.'

'Sounds OK.'

'I'd prefer Gareth.'

Tom smiled. 'I thought you might. What if it's a girl?'

Owen shook his head. 'It won't be.'

Tom dropped his satchel on the coffee table and sat down. 'I've just spoken to Perkins and he said a couple of interviewees for the Head of Faculty are visiting this morning.'

Owen put down his pencil. 'Yes. I met Victor on the way in – he told me he'd heard from the Vice Chancellor that he's one of four shortlisted. The interviews are next month.

So it will be Victor, the Wallop or one of the two arriving today.'

'Fingers crossed for Victor.'

'Don't hold your breath.' The Welshman scowled. 'Edna will have it all sewn up.'

Tom picked up his satchel. 'Anyway, Primary One beckons, so see you later.'

In the common room, Inger and Zeb were checking their mail when Victor appeared. He was the image of sartorial elegance with a cream shirt, yellow bow tie, a mustard-coloured waistcoat and neatly pressed chestnut-brown jeans.

'Morning, Victor,' said Inger. 'How are you?'

'Fine, thanks.'

'You're looking good,' said Zeb. 'Love the outfit.'

He smiled. 'Pat chose it. He reckons he's better than me at colour coordination.'

'How was the holiday?' asked Inger.

'Interesting. Lots happening. I've got an interview for the Head of Faculty.'

'Brilliant!' said Zeb, lighting up a cigarette.

Inger smiled. 'I'm so pleased. Well done. I presume Edna has been shortlisted as well?'

Victor gave a wry smile. 'Yes, she has. There's four of us. The Vice Chancellor rang me to let me know I had been shortlisted along with Edna and a man and a woman who are calling in this morning to have a look around.'

'That should be interesting.'

'Definitely, particularly as Edward left it to Edna to arrange their preliminary visits.'

'No surprises there,' said Zeb. 'The Vice Chancellor has his head in the clouds most of the time.'

'So maybe we'll see the other candidates,' said Inger.

Victor looked thoughtful. 'I've heard Edna has lined up Richard and Selina from the science department to act as hosts. They're meeting them at morning break, showing them round and then taking them to lunch.'

Inger sighed. 'That's very clever on the part of Edna.'

'I'm guessing she wants to make sure they don't meet us,' said Victor. 'They might get the wrong impression. We might say something that didn't reflect well on the faculty.'

'Well, she's right there,' said Zeb.

Inger looked puzzled. 'In that case I'm surprised she picked Richard.'

Victor considered for a moment before responding. 'Actually, I heard she was secretly impressed with his speech last autumn about us tutors being the unique selling point of the faculty.'

Zeb smiled through a haze of cigarette smoke. 'That would have appealed to her vanity.'

'Too true,' said Victor.

Zeb gave Victor a knowing look. 'But Selina is another story. With her reputation, there's no second-guessing which candidate *she* will be showing around. Her nickname is "Sadistic Selina".'

'Really?'

'Yes. Perfect for Edna. Selina will be taking the guy around and he's certain to be put off.'

'Why's that?'

'She hates all men, wants them all neutered. That's why we call her "Sadistic".'

Everyone got the message and the conversation ended.

Edna Wallop was in her study, staring out of the window. Sunlight lit up the city walls and the skyline of York stretched out before her. Meanwhile Cedric Bullock was reclining in one of the armchairs and smoking a cigar.

Edna looked down at the list in her hand. 'The two of them are coming in at morning break: Colin Goodenough from Oxford and Felicity Capstick from Ely. I've told Perkins to take them straight to the common room and I'll meet them there.'

'You seem to have it all in hand,' said Cedric with a contented smile.

'It's tricky,' said Edna. 'I have to be seen to be welcoming and providing an opportunity for them to look around the various departments. It has to appear that everything is above board. Thankfully they will be gone after lunch.'

'They appear well qualified,' said Cedric. 'The rest of the governors seemed quite impressed when the shortlist was compiled.'

Edna shook her head. 'They're adequate but no more. My proposal to increase the number of foreign students will sway it. The governors won't turn their backs on a pot of gold.'

Cedric stubbed out his cigar in the ashtray. 'And Victor? What about him?'

'Victor's invitation is simply a token gesture. By the end of this term I may well move him on.'

'And what about the Stratton girl? I read her piece in the

January issue of the *Echo*. Maybe she knows more than we think.'

'Don't worry,' said Edna. 'I have plans for her.'

Cedric nodded and smiled. 'Are you sure Richard Head is a good choice as a tour guide?'

'He's perfect. A nerdy oddball. He'll do the job well but will leave Felicity Capstick confused. Meanwhile Selina will work her unique form of magic on the poor unsuspecting Colin Goodenough.'

Cedric gave a grimace. 'The poor bastard. He'll be shredded piece by piece.'

'I hope so,' said Edna and lit up a cigarette.

Tom was in the education block with his Primary One students. They were full of anticipation as school placements were announced.

'This will be your longest teaching practice to date,' he said. 'It's a four-week placement and you will need to be well prepared. Preliminary visits are next week. Keep an eye on the noticeboard and I'll be seeing you individually to check your teaching files.'

When the bell rang at the end of the session, catch-up conversations broke out as friends shared their news. There was excitement as Alison Littlewood announced she had got engaged to a Durham policeman over Easter and was showing her engagement ring to a group of her friends. Meanwhile Tommy Birkenshaw and Billy Whitelock, the two Liverpudlians, were excited about the progress of Liverpool in the FA Cup. They were looking forward to their forthcoming visit to Hillsborough in Sheffield for the FA Cup semi-final against Nottingham Forest.

Ellie MacBride caught up with Tom as they walked through the quad. She looked different; her hair had been cut short into a neat bob.

'Hi, Ellie. Like the new look.'

'Trying to make life a little less complicated,' she said. She stroked her fingers through her hair. 'This is easier to look after.'

'So . . . how was your holiday?'

She stopped for a moment and stared up at Tom. 'Mixed, to be honest. My mum and dad appreciated my help on the market but the few days in Whitby with Dave didn't go well.'

'Sorry to hear that.'

'Don't be, Tom. It's fine. Nice guy . . . but not for me. Anyway, must rush. I've offered to help out with *The Merchant of Venice*. There's a meeting in the drama studio.'

'That's great. Have you got a part?'

Ellie grinned and pulled out a sheaf of papers from her shoulder bag. 'I'm the prompt, Tom. I sit out of sight following the script, line by line,' and she hurried away.

At morning break, Tom met up with Owen in the common room. They sat there, sipping coffee while watching Edna Wallop fussing like a mother hen over the two interviewees. One was a short blonde woman in her forties, wearing a fashionable blue linen trouser suit. She carried a Filofax with a purposeful air. The other candidate was a very tall beanpole of a man who carried himself awkwardly. He was all angles, with sharp elbows and a prominent Roman nose. His business suit with flapping trouser legs looked a little too small for him and his white socks and black leather shoes were definitely a vestiary faux pas.

'Richard looks committed to the task,' said Tom.

'He'll take this very seriously,' said Owen. 'I almost feel sorry for the woman.'

Richard was introducing himself to the blonde interviewee while she kept casting curious looks at the plastic identity card swinging from his lanyard. Next to them the beanpole man was staring at the tall, athletic and intense woman by his side. She had curly permed brown hair and wore a bright blue smock over tight black jeans. Her Doc Marten boots completed the ensemble. The image was definitely one of *don't mess with me.*

'The poor sod,' said Owen, shaking his head. 'He's got Selina for company.'

'Who's Selina?' asked Tom.

Owen grinned. 'Dr Selina Morton. You've obviously not met her . . . a legend in her lifetime. She works part-time with Richard and is just a crazy scientist.'

'I'm glad we've never met,' said a wide-eyed Tom.

'Keep it that way, boyo. She would happily castrate the whole male population. I heard she had a fiancé once and insisted he had a vasectomy before the nuptials. She didn't want to add to the overpopulation of the human race and encourage a subsequent famine. She also runs a course on "Euthanasia in a Future World" at U3A and suffers from hypertension. I heard she takes a bucketload of pills and is a slave to her beta-blockers.'

'Sounds extreme.'

'Too right, but Selina will no doubt work her charms on the unsuspecting guy. In fact, neither of them know what they're in for.'

'What about Richard?' asked Tom. 'Surely he's OK?'

'You mean apart from always walking in straight lines and not being able to touch door handles? By the time the interviews come round they may well have dropped out wondering what kind of alternative universe we live in here.'

Tom leaned back in his chair, perplexed. 'All sounds a bit strange.'

Owen was on a roll. 'Selina is convinced that it is only a matter of time before we are obliterated by a Russian nuclear strike. Also a rumour went round a while ago that she was working on a drug to shrink a man's testicles and I wouldn't put it past her to succeed. By the way,' he added, 'her doctorate was in gene technology. You don't mess with Selina.'

'So a clever choice by Edna,' said Tom.

'Definitely,' said Owen. 'Edna will use every trick in the book to eliminate the opposition. Then when she's got the job she can enjoy an abuse of power followed by an inflation-linked pension. It's a load of bollocks!'

Tom smiled warily. 'Don't let Selina hear you say that.'

Owen glanced nervously at the misandrist doctor but fortunately she was out of earshot.

In fact, Selina was assessing the lanky specimen before her. Colin Goodenough, despite his DPhil in History from Oxford, stood awkwardly waiting for instructions. 'Colin, come with me.' It was a command rather than a request. 'Let's have a few minutes in my study. Then you can ask questions without being disturbed before we tour the campus.'

The beanpole academic with his neat side parting and trousers flapping like sails in the wind stumbled after Selina in an apparent state of bemused enchantment. He was told to sit down.

'Coffee?' asked Selina sharply.

'Yes, please,' said Colin.

'I take it black.'

'So do I,' said Colin with a whimpering smile.

'That's good,' said Selina.

She served up two mugs of coffee and sat back to survey the nervous interviewee sitting with his knees level with his shoulders.

'I have to make it clear to you that I'm hoping a woman will secure this post. In our world of academia the male has suppressed the female for too long.'

'I couldn't agree more,' said Colin, sipping nervously on his coffee. 'I believe females have been downtrodden for too long, to the extent that I'm often embarrassed to be of the male persuasion.'

Selina's eyes widened. There was more to this man than met the eye. 'Really?'

'Oh, yes,' said Colin. 'The world is changing.'

Selina decided to press home her views. 'You will be aware women have more brain cells. I've made a study of this.'

'Yes, it's a known fact. I bow to your superior wisdom,' said the gallant but subservient Colin. 'Even so, as a mere man I have to keep trying.'

Selina smiled. It was a rare occurrence but here at last she had met a man who was a maelstrom of contradictions. He was different. 'I have some Brontë biscuits in my cupboard. Would you care for one?'

'My favourite,' said Colin with a doe-eyed smile.

*

Richard Head had taken Felicity Capstick out to the quad. A gregarious woman from Ely, the cathedral city in Cambridgeshire, she was puzzled by this possible future colleague. Richard removed an A4 sheet from his clipboard. 'Here's the plan,' he said. It listed, minute by minute, the proposed tour of the various departments starting with the science block.

'You appear to be very organized,' said Felicity with approval.

'Thank you. Being organized means I'm in control. The variables are within my sphere of influence.'

Felicity raised her eyebrows. 'I suppose they are.'

'Before our tour I've arranged for you to see something special.'

'Yes?'

'I was hoping you might like to see my telescope?'

Felicity took a step backwards. 'Pardon?'

'My telescope. It's magnificent.'

'I'm sure it is but perhaps we ought to check out the campus first?'

Richard acquiesced. It wasn't a problem. He had allowed sixteen minutes of time for random variables.

It was Kimberly Stratton in the science block who provided Felicity with enlightenment.

'Let me introduce you to Kimberly, one of our outstanding students,' said Richard. 'This is a visitor, Dr Capstick from Cambridgeshire.'

'Pleased to meet you,' said Kimberly.

'Likewise,' said Felicity.

'Perhaps you would like Kimberly to show you our science facilities?' said Richard. 'They're really impressive.'

'Thank you,' said Felicity.

'This way,' said Kimberly with a smile and they walked towards the storeroom filled with a magnificent array of equipment.

'Thank you, Kimberly. You obviously appreciate Professor Head as your tutor.'

'Definitely. A great man. Utterly dedicated to science and, of course, one of the country's leading astronomers. He would spend every night peering through his telescope if he had the chance.'

'Ah, that's good to know,' said a much-relieved Miss Capstick.

At lunchtime Zeb and Tom had enjoyed a speedy lunch together and then found a quiet corner of the common room. Zeb opened her notebook, stubbed out her cigarette and studied her copious notes. 'So, we're almost there. Stratford is just about sorted. I've ordered the coach for nine o'clock on Friday, the twenty-eighth of April. There're sixteen students from Dance/Drama plus fifteen from your English Four group.'

Tom was impressed. 'What about theatre tickets?'

'All in hand, booked and ready for collection at the box office. The students will be in the youth hostel. We've got accommodation in a hotel, cheap and cheerful. So it should be fine.'

'Can I do anything? You seem to have done it all.'

Zeb smiled. 'It's like shelling peas. Done it so many times, it runs like clockwork now. We can leave the students to their own devices. All they need to do is turn up at the theatre.'

'Bit different to the school trips I used to organize.'

'Just bring some beer money, Tom. It's usually a good break from this place.' She got up and hurried away to the drama studio.

In a private alcove of the dining room Edna was sitting with Colin and Felicity. He was enjoying sausage, mash and onion gravy while Felicity was picking carefully at a green salad. Much to Edna's chagrin both seemed remarkably content.

'Thank you for the visit, Dr Wallop,' said Felicity. 'It's been an illuminating morning. Richard was the perfect host and it was a pleasant surprise to discover we share a love of astronomy.'

'Really? That's good to hear,' muttered Edna through gritted teeth.

Colin looked up. 'And Selina and I got on really well.'

'Did you?' Edna could barely mask her surprise.

'Yes, a remarkable lady. I am sympathetic to her views.'

Edna stared at this strange man and couldn't believe what she was hearing. It was a relief to her when their taxi arrived to take them to York railway station.

At afternoon break Owen was in the common room supping a mug of tea and reading his *Daily Mirror* when Zeb sat down beside him. She peered over his shoulder at the incongruous photograph of Soviet leader Mikhail Gorbachev drinking Guinness with Irish Premier Charles Haughey. The Russian had declared that he was not only a European but also an advocate of reducing military confrontation.

'It must be the Guinness talking,' said Owen.

'Mind you . . . it always tastes better in Ireland,' said Zeb, who was recalling an amorous weekend in Dublin. 'So . . . anything else of interest?'

Owen grinned. 'You'll love this. Fifty-two-year-old Bill Wyman of the Rolling Stones wants to marry eighteen-year-old Mandy Smith but five churches have turned him down.'

'Why?'

'She's a Catholic and he's C of E and divorced. Apparently, he's known her since she was thirteen.'

'Oh dear,' muttered Zeb.

'Meanwhile,' said Owen, 'check this out. Neil Kinnock and his shadow cabinet colleagues are going to make a record of their new campaign song. They're hoping it will be a hit.'

'And pigs might fly,' said Zeb.

'Maybe, but don't forget we Welsh are great singers,' insisted Owen.

Zeb shook her head. 'I've heard you singing in the pub. Like Kinnock . . . you're the exceptions.'

Owen closed the paper. 'So . . . any news about the interviewees?'

'No doubt Victor will let us know.'

'They looked an interesting pair,' said Tom. 'Certainly Edna was making a fuss of them.'

'She's simply a calculating bitch,' said Zeb. 'They won't stand a chance.'

It was the end of the day and Tom and Owen were in the common room preparing to go home when Victor walked in with Zeb and Inger. They were smiling.

'So, one in the eye for the Wallop,' said Zeb.

Victor nodded. 'You could say that.'

'Why? What's happened?' asked Owen.

'Things didn't work out as Edna planned,' said Inger.

Tom noticed she looked relaxed and was enjoying the moment. 'So come on . . . Tell all.'

Victor glanced around the room and lowered his voice. 'You know what Robert Burns said about "best-laid plans"? Well, it backfired on Edna. Perkins heard them in reception when they were leaving. Apparently, Felicity Capstick considered Richard to be an inspirational genius and Colin Goodenough thought Selina was simply wonderful.'

'Selina . . . wonderful?' exclaimed a bemused Owen.

'So a good result,' said Victor. He turned to leave and then paused. 'By the way, I heard from Perkins the dinner-dance tickets have been printed. So I'll collect our allocation next week.'

'Dinner dance?' said Tom.

Owen was suddenly animated. 'Yes, at the end of term for the Education Faculty. It's a posh affair, Tom.' He looked at Tom's crumpled cord suit and the frayed collar of his shirt. 'You'll need to smarten yourself up. It's black tie in the Assembly Rooms in York.'

'That's right, Tom,' said Victor, 'and take no notice of this unshaven Welshman. Ticket allocation is limited to one hundred and they sell like hot cakes but there's usually plenty for all the tutors plus partners.'

Owen looked enthusiastic. 'Sue will be up and about by then, Victor, so put me down for two.' He turned to Tom. 'It's always a great night. I'll teach you a few of my dance moves.' He stood up and gave a twirl.

'On the other hand,' said Zeb, 'maybe not.'

Victor smiled. 'Owen's right. It's a special night. The Vice Chancellor always attends plus a few VIPs. So put it in your diary. It's on Friday, the seventh of July.'

Zeb turned to Tom. 'All you need is a partner and sadly I'm already taken.'

There was a moment when Tom looked expectantly at Inger and their eyes met. 'Will you be going, Inger?' he asked.

Everyone turned to hear her reply.

'Yes, I'll be there. The last couple of years Andreas has been my partner. I guess he will be coming again.'

Tom sighed and felt a little sad.

As everyone departed for home Victor was speaking to Inger with a new intensity and they both looked back at Tom as he headed for the car park.

That evening Tom was back home watching television. *The Education Programme* was on BBC Two and they were discussing green issues with a forceful reminder that we should treat the planet with respect. It said an environmental crisis was imminent if humans did not change their behaviour and the next generation would suffer. It was a sobering thought.

Earlier he had opened his diary to the end of the first week in July and stared at the page. It was empty apart from a question mark. He guessed it would be his last day as a tutor at Eboracum. Suddenly his thoughts were interrupted by a ringing telephone.

'Inger, this is a surprise.'

'Hi, Tom. I've just spoken to my brother and he says he is coming to the faculty dance.'

'Oh well, that's good,' said Tom without conviction.

'The thing is he's bringing Annika with him so I'm free after all.'

'That's brilliant. So does that mean you might be able to come with me?'

There was a pause. 'Yes, it does.'

'Are you sure you haven't another partner in mind? I'll understand.'

'No, that's fine, Tom. I've been to previous dances but always with my brother. This will make a change and we seem to get on well – with no strings attached.'

'Only if you're sure. There must be dozens who would like to be your partner.'

'That goes both ways, Tom.'

'Well . . . thanks for the call. It's in the diary.'

'And in mine, Tom . . . goodnight.'

'Goodnight, Inger.'

Chapter Fifteen

Sweet Sorrow

It was lunchtime on Friday, 28 April, and bright sunshine gilded the rooftops of Stratford-upon-Avon. Zeb looked at her notebook and nodded in satisfaction.

'Let's check in, Tom, and then have a drink and a sandwich.'

Tom stared up at the impressive Moat House Hotel. 'This is much better than I expected.'

The hotel was situated between the Bridgeway and the River Avon and was clearly a popular destination for business meetings. With over two hundred bedrooms and spacious meeting rooms, it was definitely a far cry from the youth hostel where the students had been dropped off half an hour earlier. Zeb had made a good choice. The reception area was busy but Zeb was an experienced traveller and soon they were in the lift to the second floor. They had rooms opposite one another at the end of a long corridor.

'See you back in reception in a few minutes,' she said. 'I'm hungry.'

Tom was impressed by his tidy room with its double bed, writing desk and spotless shower. It was very different from his cottage. He tried out the television set and there was a report on Gorbachev's visit to Downing Street. The USSR had completed the withdrawal of troops from Afghanistan and it looked as though the Iron Curtain that had blighted Europe since the 1940s was lifting at last. Tom switched off and unpacked his old sports bag. It was a simple task that took seconds. He merely tipped the contents on to the shelf in the wardrobe. Then he put the complimentary notepad and pen in his jacket pocket, picked up his door key and walked out.

He took the stairs back to the ground floor where he found Zeb. She had ordered sandwiches and drinks at the bar and they sat down in a comfortable lounge outside the dining room. There was a copy of the *Stratford-upon-Avon Herald* that had been discarded on a coffee table and Zeb picked it up and scanned some of the front-page articles. There were still snippets relating back to the Hillsborough disaster from earlier in the month. Over ninety Liverpool supporters had died during the terrible event that had stunned the nation.

Zeb shook her head and sipped her gin and tonic. 'So what happened to your two first-year students who went up to Sheffield for the football? Dreadful to think of such a huge loss of life.'

Tom supped on his glass of beer and then placed it on the table. He clasped his hands and leaned forward.

'Thankfully, they're fine. It was Tommy Birkenshaw and Billy Whitelock in Primary One. They're good lads, both keen students. It's hard to understand how they must be feeling. They didn't see those poor supporters crushed in the pen behind the high wire fences. They only heard the screams and the sirens. It was a day they will never forget.'

Zeb put down her drink. 'Oh, Tom. This is almost too hard to comprehend.'

Tom sighed. 'I've spoken to them over the phone and told them to stay with their families in Liverpool. They were in too much distress to come back. I informed their teaching-practice schools they wouldn't be attending their preliminary visit. So that's in hand.'

Zeb stared down at the newspaper. 'I saw the images on television. The grief of those poor families must be beyond belief.'

Tom nodded. 'They were definitely two of the lucky ones. Apparently, they arrived at the ground but couldn't get in. The crowds were too great. Just as well. The scenes inside were heartbreaking.'

Zeb picked up her drink again and looked thoughtful. 'I'm not really into football, Tom, but I saw the Home Secretary's response on the telly.'

It had been widely reported that Douglas Hurd had recommended all-seater stadiums.

'Watching a game of football will be changed for ever,' said Tom quietly. He stared out of the window at the scudding cirrus clouds above the rooftops of this busy market town. A party of loud and lively American tourists were disembarking from their coach outside the hotel. As Tom and Zeb sat back to eat their sandwiches the light and shade of life revolved around them.

Zeb had arranged to meet up with the students at the Shakespeare Centre that afternoon. As everyone gathered, Tom stared up at the huge poster of the world's greatest playwright. There was a brief history of his life from his birth here in Stratford-upon-Avon in 1564 and his marriage to Anne Hathaway at the age of eighteen. Finally, thirty-seven plays later, at the age of fifty-two, he had found his final resting place in a special grave in Holy Trinity Church. It was a life like no other and Tom wondered about the great man and the power of his words.

Zeb called out to the students, 'Gather round and listen in, everybody. Let's spend an hour together here in the Centre and then you're free until we meet up at just before seven outside the Royal Shakespeare Theatre for tonight's performance of *A Midsummer Night's Dream*. I'm not expecting any problems but if something does crop up you've got the contact details for Tom and myself at the Moat House Hotel. Any questions?'

Tamara Robinson and Pixie le Fevre waved their arms. They were close friends, both from Manchester. 'Zeb, there's a local dance tomorrow night,' said Tamara.

'Do you fancy coming after the performance?' shouted Pixie. There were a few knowing grins from some of the other dance students.

'No, thanks,' said Zeb. 'I'll be in the hotel bar.' She smiled. 'Just remember . . . if you can't behave, be sensible.' There was laughter as everyone dispersed.

Tom took in the scene. 'Zeb . . . this is quite an experience.

Bit different to my school journeys when everyone lined up and walked in pairs wearing bright red caps. There was a teacher at the front of the crocodile and one at the back. This amount of freedom is almost scary.'

'They're adults, Tom. We have to trust them. Problem is students like Tamara and Pixie can be a bit wild. In fact, rather like I was at their age.' She smiled and tugged Tom's sleeve. 'Anyway, come on, handsome, let's enjoy the Centre.'

Tom was impressed with the dedication of the students and watched as they made notes while wandering through the costume displays and the library. He was also finding it unusual to be clearly the second-in-command rather than always being the leader on an educational visit. He spent the next hour talking to his English Four students and, aside from William Shakespeare, they discussed the merits of Marlowe's *Dr Faustus* and Jonson's *The Silent Woman*. He was gradually realizing the true value of this long weekend when students could relax together and enjoy informal conversations with their tutors, who, later in the term, would be assessing their final dissertations.

At six o'clock, Tom met up with Zeb in the hotel reception. She was wearing a diaphanous dress of sapphire blue that contrasted beautifully with her flaming red hair. A warm black shawl completed the ensemble along with the predictable chunky leather boots.

'Wow! You look great!' said Tom.

'Thanks, Tom.' She looked him up and down. 'Well, at least you've brought a clean pair of jeans. One day someone needs to take you in hand and organize your limited wardrobe.' She strode towards the entrance. 'Come on then, Romeo, the Mucky Duck awaits.'

It was one of Zeb's traditions to enjoy a drink in the White Swan Hotel before going on to the theatre. It was already full of theatre-goers when they walked in: women in colourful frocks and men in cream linen suits. There was a lively *joie de vivre* about the place while a few students were propping up the bar. Tamara and Pixie were drinking wine and studying a colourful flyer. It had a smiley-face logo on the top. They waved as Tom and Zeb walked in.

'What's that?' asked Zeb, pointing to the flyer.

'It's the dance we mentioned,' said Tamara.

Zeb recognized the advertisement with its familiar logo and frowned for a moment. 'You mean a rave party.'

'Maybe,' said Pixie cautiously.

Zeb gave them a hard stare. 'Just be careful.'

Tom was excited when he walked into the foyer of the Royal Shakespeare Theatre. It was many years since he had been here and it rekindled memories. Zeb led the way and the students followed her to their seats in the dress circle. Tom had bought a programme and, once again, checked out the plot for one of Shakespeare's most popular and widely performed plays. The comedy was set in Athens and it was clear to see why Zeb had made this choice in preference to *Hamlet* and *Cymbeline*, the other plays currently being performed. Along with the students, Tom sat there transfixed by the various subplots revolving around the marriage of Theseus and Hippolyta. There was no doubt the evening was a huge success and everyone joined in the standing ovation.

Zeb was full of enthusiasm when they all walked out and gathered in a group in the cool of the evening. She waxed lyrical about the quality of the performances and the forest scenes in which the fairies had manipulated the humans with effortless ease.

'By the way, tomorrow afternoon I'm walking to Anne Hathaway's Cottage. If anyone wants to come along, meet me outside the Mucky Duck at one o'clock. It's about a mile and a half up the Shottery Road. The weather is fine so it should be a nice walk. It's a spectacular place with a thatched cottage and a lovely garden. It was Anne Hathaway's childhood home, so well worth a visit. No pressure, come if you wish. Otherwise, we meet outside the Swan Theatre for tomorrow night's *Romeo and Juliet.*' She gestured to them all with a theatrical wave. 'As Juliet would say, parting is such sweet sorrow, but maybe not for you at this moment . . . so go off and enjoy yourselves.' There was laughter as they drifted away, some holding hands as new relationships emerged.

Under a firmament of stars, Zeb and Tom walked slowly back to the hotel. 'Let's have a nightcap, Tom,' said Zeb. 'It's been a long day.'

They relaxed in the bar before returning to their rooms where Tom welcomed the comfortable bed, free coffee and biscuits and the late-night film, *Paradise Alley* with Sylvester Stallone.

On Saturday morning Tom went out for a walk after breakfast. The sun was shining and children with padded knees and safety helmets rode past on their BMX bicycles to their local track on the Warwick Road. It was good to enjoy the sights and sounds of this special place but his mind drifted back to Eboracum and he wondered what Inger Larson might be doing on this perfect morning.

After Tom had enjoyed a relaxed lunch with Zeb in one of the cafés on Henley Street, they set off to walk to Anne Hathaway's Cottage with around a dozen of the students. It was just as Zeb described and the gardens and orchards around the cottage were a surprise. Nine acres of Warwickshire countryside spread out before them and it was a peaceful time with the hand of history on their shoulders.

On Saturday evening Zeb appeared in yet another dramatic outfit with an off-the-shoulder sweatshirt and sky-blue Jane Fonda leggings. This was the performance she had earmarked as very special for her drama students. On this occasion they were in the Swan Theatre and, as the play began, it was noticeable there was a minimum of props. That mattered little as Mark Rylance captivated the audience with his portrayal of Romeo. As the intermission approached, his frenzied stabbing of Tybalt clearly shocked everyone and the drinks at the bar provided a welcome release. At the end of the second half, once again there was a standing ovation followed by a buzz of excitement as everyone left the theatre.

Zeb found a quiet space away from the foot traffic and gathered all the students around her. 'Well . . . a brilliant night, everybody. You can see why I was keen for you to experience this performance. When we get back to York on Monday I want you all to think back on this play and make your own notes on what has impressed you the most. Try to describe the stagecraft you have just witnessed and ask yourselves why the colours of the costumes were so muted.' Zeb was clearly animated and gestured back towards the theatre. 'We can learn so much from this experience. For example, think back to the pool of downstage light that lit up the two lovers. Why was it so effective? The enormous height of the balcony, over twenty feet above the stage, was striking and the fight scenes were full of tension. There was so much to take in.'

She looked around at their eager faces. It was time to let them off the leash. 'So remember this: when we perform *The Merchant of Venice* in six weeks' time we can all be better for this experience.' Then she paused and scanned the crowd. 'Now go and enjoy yourselves, but for God's sake be sensible. And if anyone wants to join Tom and me tomorrow morning, we're going to have a look around Holy Trinity Church where Shakespeare is buried. Otherwise, Sunday is free for you to enjoy Stratford and the coach will leave your hostel on Monday morning at ten sharp.'

Tom had stood and watched Zeb at work and was reminded how Owen had said she was a brilliant tutor. The students evidently respected her, regardless of her sparky behaviour. She really was a special woman and utterly dedicated. It was obvious to Tom that, for someone as talented as Zeb, working with Edna Wallop must be completely disheartening. They were opposites and, unlike magnetism, there was no attraction.

Once again Tom and Zeb relaxed with a few drinks before going up in the lift to their rooms. 'Thanks, Zeb,' said Tom. 'I've loved this visit. Well planned; great plays. Everything has gone so smoothly.'

He spoke too soon. He was fast asleep at four in the

morning when he unexpectedly heard a muffled knocking on his door.

He rolled out of bed and stepped across the room in his boxer shorts. Pixie and Tamara were outside in the corridor, both looking the worse for wear but particularly Pixie who was being held up by Tamara.

'Sorry, Tom,' said Tamara. 'We couldn't get into the hostel and we're freezing. Zeb gave us two room numbers, 201 and 202. It's her we need.'

Tom looked at Pixie. She was in a poor state, sweating and staring vacantly with dilated pupils. He propped open his door with a chair and stepped across the corridor to Zeb's door. He tapped on it until there was a response.

'What the hell!' shouted Zeb.

'Sorry, Zeb,' said Tom. 'It's important.'

She stuck her head around the door. Her red hair was dishevelled and limp. She yawned. 'What is it, Tom?' Then she saw Pixie and Tamara and understood the situation.

'OK, Tom. Leave it to me. You two get in here.'

'Can I help?' asked Tom.

'No, thanks. I'll make sure they're safe. They can kip on my floor. I'll see you in the morning,' and she closed the door.

Zeb told Tom about the events of the previous night over Sunday breakfast. 'Don't worry, Pixie and Tamara are fine and sleeping it off in my room. I'll take them back to the hostel later today.'

'So, what happened?' asked Tom.

'A few of my drama group attended an unlicensed rave party in a local warehouse. It was advertised mainly by word of mouth although organizers have started using the new mobile pagers as well as distributing lots of cautiously worded flyers featuring the smiley-face logo. That's the big clue.' She gave Tom a knowing look. 'Like I told you before. It's the so-called Second Summer of Love with all the hedonism and freedom of San Francisco in 1967.'

'So what went on last night to get them in that state?'

'They were enjoying the usual acid house music and the marathon dancing. Apparently, staff were giving out lots of water and Lucozade to combat dehydration. They were even serving up ice pops.'

'Sounds a good idea,' said Tom. 'It must be hot as hell in there.'

'The problem is, Tom, that's not all that was given out and Pixie fell into the trap. Thank goodness Tamara was more sensible.'

'Why? What was it?'

'The drug MDMA. It's pretty well part of the new youth culture.'

'Drugs?'

'Yes, Tom. MDMA tablets were handed out . . . or to give it its more common name, Ecstasy. It affects the nervous system, increases energy and stimulates pleasure.'

Tom looked puzzled. 'You seem to know a lot about it. So . . . have you tried it?'

'Of course. Why not? It's an experience. I did something similar when I was younger, but I wouldn't these days. Definitely not. The main thing is not to get hooked on it. Sadly, some of these kids will be and then go on to harder drugs.'

'What can we do?'

'Educate, listen, talk, share – all the usual stuff, Tom.'

She finished her coffee, lit up another cigarette and leaned back against her chair. 'It's just modern life. Maybe not what you've experienced in your primary school.'

Tom nodded. 'I guess so. I had a couple of girlfriends a few years back who experimented with drugs but nothing on this scale.'

She gave Tom a hard stare. 'So, come on. Open up for once. Have you had many relationships?'

Tom gave Zeb a quizzical look. 'You're pretty direct, aren't you, Zeb?'

'Is there another way?'

He pondered before replying. 'Well . . . the answer is yes. I've known a few women but nothing serious.'

Zeb nodded knowingly. 'Talking of girlfriends, I was pleased Victor had a word with Inger.'

'What do you mean?'

'The dinner dance at the end of term. Victor told Inger you were a great guy and she would be safe with you.'

'So that's why she rang me to to say she was happy to be my partner.'

'That's right. Her brother, Andreas, was always her security blanket. I'm guessing there's stuff in her past that has made her cautious. What is certain is that you're not a guy to take advantage. I'm pleased for her and pleased for you.'

Tom smiled. 'Thanks, Zeb. I appreciate that.'

Later, in the Old Town, Zeb, Tom and around twenty of the students made their way towards Holy Trinity Church with its elegant spire. Beyond the avenue of lime trees they discovered many ancient graves, including Shakespeare's burial place. Beneath the dappled light they stood in a shroud of silence where for the past eight hundred years the folk of Stratford had worshipped. It struck Tom there was a sense of awe and wonder in this special place where the prayers of people long gone echoed down the centuries.

'Thanks for bringing us here, Tom,' said a quiet voice. It was Chris Appleyard, an introverted and sensitive young man from Leeds. 'It's amazing to think what he did with his life and then finished up here.'

Tom smiled. 'I know what you mean. I've been to Stratford before but never here.' They stared at the gravestone. 'Fifty-two doesn't seem so old these days. Amazing what you can do in one short life.'

Chris gave a shy smile. 'I was just thinking that. It's made me want to make something of my own life.'

A breeze rustled the branches of the trees and shadows flickered across the gravestones. 'So what do you want to do? You've clearly made a decision about teaching and by all accounts you've had success in the classroom, according to all your reports.'

'Yes . . . it's strange, isn't it? My mother always used to say I wouldn't say boo to a goose but I'm fine in front of a class of ten-year-olds who are keen to learn. It's just that I love to write. It's my hobby. I was thinking about having a go at a screenplay. What do you think?'

'It's a great idea. What would it be about? Presumably you'll go for a subject you know.'

He nodded. 'Yes, class and money. I was brought up in Chapeltown in Leeds and we were a desperately poor family: Dad out of work with his war injuries and Mam working in Sharp's toffee factory to make ends meet. I'm here sitting alongside people like Tamara and Pixie whose families are rolling in money with big houses in Cheshire. They're great girls but their outlook on life is different.'

'I understand,' said Tom. 'Come and see me when we get back. I've got a copy of Willy Russell's *Blood Brothers* on my shelf that I can let you have. Once you've read that, we'll talk again.'

Chris looked relieved and content as if a weight had been lifted from his shoulders. 'Thanks, Tom. I appreciate you listening.' He looked at the crowd around him. 'I haven't got many friends.'

'Come on,' said Tom. 'This calls for tea and cake,' and they headed back to the town centre. He gestured towards one of the students. 'We must talk to Beth Kirby. She spoke to me a while ago about writing screenplays.'

Half an hour later it was a happy group of students who sat down with Tom and Zeb to enjoy a pot of tea and a slice of fruit cake in one of the riverside cafés. Chris Appleyard gave Tom a hesitant thumbs up as he discussed his new-found enthusiasm for writing with the studious and petite Beth Kirby from Durham, who had discovered an equally new-found interest in this gawky young man.

Finally, on Monday morning they all boarded the coach and left behind the superb Warwickshire countryside as they headed north. As the miles flew by, Tom found he was looking forward to returning to York, yet it also occurred to him that parting really was sweet sorrow.

Chapter Sixteen

Divided We Fall

Victor Grammaticus was apprehensive. It was an unfamiliar feeling for this confident, erudite academic. He was wearing his best dark-grey three-piece suit as he climbed into his Rover 200. After an evening of gentle rain the morning had dawned bright and clear and Pat was there to wave him off. He drove out of Easingwold and south towards the city of York. It was a journey he had done a thousand times but today was different. The season had shifted and gave notice of warmer days to come. Beyond the hedgerows lambs were bleating in the fields and the distant woods were carpeted with bluebells, but Victor was oblivious to the sights and sounds of nature.

He pulled up in the university car park and walked slowly along the winding path to reception. Beside him the trigger of life had opened the closed buds of the cherry trees but his head was bowed. He was apprehensive because the unknown awaited. Many years had passed since he had been interviewed and now it was happening again. It was Monday, 15 May, and an eventful day was in store.

'Good morning, Professor,' said Perkins with an encouraging smile. 'Good luck today.'

Victor nodded. 'Thank you, Perkins.'

'The other interviewees have arrived and are in the common room.'

Victor nodded again with a strained smile and strode quickly towards the quad.

In the common room, Edna Wallop was holding forth to Felicity Capstick and Colin Goodenough. A secluded corner had been reserved for them and Edna in her latest power suit was gesturing expansively out of the window. She ignored Victor when he joined them whereas Felicity moved towards him with a warm smile and shook his hand. Colin nodded nervously in his direction and turned back to Edna, who was waxing lyrical about the perfect lawn that was the centrepiece of the quad.

Moments later the Vice Chancellor's private secretary, Miss Hermione Frensham, appeared. She was looking particularly smart today in a new M&S navy business suit and holding a clipboard with a list of the interviewees. It read:

9.30 a.m. Dr Felicity Capstick
10.15 a.m. Dr Colin Goodenough
11.00 a.m. Professor Victor Grammaticus
11.45 a.m. Dr Edna Wallop

Conversation ceased as attention turned towards her.

'Good morning and welcome to Eboracum. Interviews will commence shortly in the Lodge, which is the Vice Chancellor's residence. There is a comfortable anteroom, the Temple Studio, and I'm taking you there now. Coffee and refreshments have been prepared. You will be interviewed in alphabetical order, after which you are free to leave. Later today you will receive a telephone call regarding the outcome of your interview. Please follow me.'

They walked through the quad and out towards the imposing gabled porch of the Lodge. Edna walked beside Miss Frensham as if it was she who was leading the way. The Vice Chancellor's secretary had her own views concerning the over-confident Acting Head of Faculty but kept them to herself. A few paces behind, Felicity Capstick and Colin Goodenough were chatting amiably while Victor brought up the rear. He was preoccupied and unaware of a thrush with a speckled breast trilling out its morning song. Above his head swallows had returned to their nesting places in the eaves of this imposing dwelling and, as they approached, the heavy scent of wallflowers filled the air beneath the leaded windows.

When they entered Temple Studio motes of dust hovered in the bright shaft of sunlight that split the room. An arrangement of dried flowers on the dark mahogany table provided an almost funereal atmosphere and conversation was both brief and stilted. Miss Frensham excused herself and the four candidates settled in the comfortable armchairs. A few minutes later the efficient secretary reappeared and announced, 'Dr Capstick, please.' The two of them left the room and once again silence descended.

*

The Vice Chancellor was behind his desk and flanked by four men and one woman. A single carver chair had been placed facing the semicircle of expectant faces. He rose to greet Felicity. 'Good morning, Dr Capstick. Do take a seat. Welcome and thank you for your attendance. Representatives of the governing body are on the panel and they will introduce themselves. Our secretary Miss Frensham is here to record notes. At the end of the interview there will be an opportunity for you to ask questions. Perhaps you could begin by providing a few details of your current work and why you have applied for this post.'

At morning break, Tom went into the common room and found Inger.

'Have you heard anything?' asked Tom.

'Only that Perkins said the four candidates were all in the Lodge. So I guess it will be some time this afternoon when we hear.'

'Fingers crossed,' said Tom.

Inger frowned. 'I'm not hopeful.'

'I don't know the governors well enough,' said Tom, 'and it's in their hands. Let's hope they make the right decision.'

'I'm sure Victor will have a good interview,' said Inger. 'He's sure to be by far the brightest candidate there.'

They both sipped their coffee thoughtfully.

'So, any news?' asked Tom. 'How are rehearsals going?'

'Fine. I'm meeting Zeb at lunchtime to check the music again. She came up with a new idea for the scene when Portia declares her unfaithfulness so I'll have to work on that. Also my brother rang to say he will be coming over for the play so I may get him involved.'

'How is he?'

'Busy with a performance for the visit to Norway of Pope John Paul the Second on the first of June. After that he and Annika are staying with me for a few weeks. He also said that last week the ban on skateboarding in Norway was lifted and it's one of Annika's favourite pastimes. So she's happy.'

'And what about you?' asked Tom. 'Are you happy?'

'Sometimes,' she said and drank the last of her coffee.

Back in the Lodge a pattern had emerged as the candidates came and went, some more confident than others. The interviews were intense and challenging. When Felicity Capstick returned to Temple Studio she looked calm and gave nothing away before walking out to the car park. In contrast Colin Goodenough appeared nervous and apprehensive when he reappeared and made a hasty retreat. Victor Grammaticus merely looked thoughtful after his interview and gave Edna the briefest of glances as he returned to his study. In contrast, Edna Wallop was smiling like a Cheshire cat when she walked out of the Lodge, collected a sandwich from the refectory and climbed the stairs to her study.

In the Lodge, Miss Frensham was using her Pitman's shorthand to great effect as discussion began and Edward turned to each member of the governing body in turn to ask for their feedback.

Walter Penrith, a portly man and a local landowner, was the first to offer his thoughts. 'Well, a mixed bag to be sure, Edward.' There were nods of agreement. 'Sadly, I thought Mr Goodenough was the weakest, particularly when we discussed new funding initiatives. On the other hand he seemed to have a lot of enthusiasm for developing future course structures.' He paused and looked down at the scribbled notes before him. 'Dr Capstick was definitely impressive. I liked her ideas for improving our range of courses. Professor Grammaticus was what we would expect . . . excellent in all matters. He stood out. Dr Wallop put all her eggs into the financial basket and that seemed too one-dimensional for me.'

Cedric Bullock intervened immediately. 'You're entitled to your opinion, Walter, but it's plain to see who stood out as the outstanding candidate. Dr Wallop is the only one who can secure the financial future of the faculty. We can't live in the past any more. We need urgent funding and Dr Wallop can provide it. With this in mind and, as she is clearly head and shoulders above the others, not to mention she has shown she can do the job already, I suggest we move swiftly to a resolution.'

'Not so hasty, please, Cedric,' said Edward, raising a hand in warning. 'We need to have a full discussion.' He turned to Elizabeth Glendenning, a long-standing governor. 'What are your thoughts, Elizabeth?'

The tall, slim, elegant sixty-year-old academic leaned forward and peered over her half-moon spectacles with a gimlet eye. 'Thank you, Edward. I thought we saw four talented but contrasting candidates. However, I agree with Walter that Dr Goodenough was probably the weakest. I was impressed with Dr Capstick, particularly her positive ideas regarding driving forward a wide variety of new masters degree courses. Then, of course, we have Professor Grammaticus, undoubtedly the safe pair of hands at this point in the faculty's development and, in my view, he performed best on the day.'

Edward raised his hand again to prevent an interruption from Cedric. 'Go on, Elizabeth. What about Dr Wallop?'

'Formidable,' said Elizabeth with a cautious smile. 'She is clearly anxious to secure this post and her plans to increase our funding are persuasive. It's whether she can deliver on her promises that I somewhat doubt.'

'Thank you,' said Edward. He turned to his left. 'John, what are your thoughts?'

John Whittingham, a local entrepreneur, glanced at Cedric before responding. 'Edward . . . I have to concur with Cedric. Dr Wallop has provided a blueprint for considerable additional funding and this cannot be ignored. We need rapid expansion.' He turned to the man next to him with a conspiratorial nod.

'I agree,' said Peter Lyons, owner of a chain of shoe stores. 'We shall lag behind other comparable universities if we don't secure a significant number of overseas students. That's where the money lies and Dr Wallop was confident she could make this happen.'

'Exactly,' interjected Cedric. 'Victor Grammaticus simply tries to be everyone's friend. He doesn't have the steel to confront the issues that face this university.' He paused for a moment. 'Having said that, I would have given him my vote if Dr Wallop had not been shortlisted.'

Edward gave him a sceptical glance and nodded to Miss Frensham to make sure she recorded the last comment. The discussion ebbed and flowed and it wasn't until the bell rang for one o'clock that a decision was made. Victor received two votes whereas Edna secured the other three.

'I was hoping for a unanimous vote,' said Edward, 'but I shall go with the majority. I'll contact Dr Wallop first and, assuming she accepts the post, I'll speak with the other candidates.'

It was lunchtime. Owen and Tom were in their study sitting at their desks and marking students' work. Through the leaded window, pale sunlight lit up the room. Tom sat back and looked across at the unshaven Welshman. 'I wonder how it's gone?'

'We'll soon know,' said Owen. 'There's only four of them.' He glanced at the clock. 'Probably forty-five minutes each. Should be close to a finish.'

'I hope they see sense,' said Tom. 'Surely there will be sufficient governors to realize Edna would be a disaster for the faculty.'

Owen shook his head. 'The Wallop has powerful friends. I never underestimate her influence. She's devious.' He scribbled a note on the bottom of an essay and closed the file. 'And to make matters worse it said on the news this morning that Margaret the Milk Snatcher is the first this century to complete ten years as Prime Minister. So I've had enough bad news for today.'

Tom smiled and changed the subject. 'How's Sue?'

There was a flicker of concern before Owen answered. 'Any time now. Everything's packed. Her parents are organized down to the last toothbrush and her dad has practised the route to the hospital half a dozen times. So it should be fine.' He stood up. 'Come on, Englishman, let's get some lunch.'

They walked to the door as the telephone rang. Owen

hurried back to his desk and grabbed the receiver. 'Yes?' There was a mumbled message. 'I'm on my way.' He slammed down the receiver. 'Bloody hell, Tom. The baby's coming. They're taking her to the hospital now.'

'Let's go,' said Tom. 'I'll drive you there,' and they both ran downstairs two at a time. As they dashed through a crowded reception and headed for the car park Tom gave a shouted message to Perkins.

'Good luck,' cried Perkins and then looked around at the crowd of sixth-formers who had just arrived for an introductory visit. 'It's like Piccadilly Circus in here,' he muttered.

In Victor's office the telephone rang. It was the Vice Chancellor.

'Good afternoon, Victor. Is this a convenient moment to have a word?'

'Yes, Edward, my last tutee has just left.' He sat back in his chair and waited, knowing the next few minutes would determine his future.

'Well, Victor, it is with regret I have to inform you that, in spite of your excellent interview, the post of Head of Faculty has been offered to Edna and she has accepted.'

There was silence. Victor tried to gather his thoughts. The enormity of the impact of this decision on his career and that of his colleagues was like a hammer blow.

'Are you there, Victor?'

'Sorry . . . yes . . . I was just thinking.'

'I fully understand.' Again Edward paused. He knew this would be a demanding call. 'You will appreciate that in the end it was a very close decision. I'm also aware this is the second occasion on which you have been unsuccessful.

However, I want to reassure you that you are a valued member of the team and we would not wish to lose you.'

'I see,' said Victor quietly. 'Thank you for saying so.'

'I know this will be difficult for you but it's important we pull together on this one. As it says in Mark, chapter three, verse twenty-five, if a house be divided against itself, that house cannot stand.'

Victor wasn't in the mood for biblical platitudes but remained polite. 'Of course, Edward. I do understand.'

'We shall talk again soon, Victor, and once again I'm sorry to be the bearer of this news.' Again there was silence. 'I have to contact the other candidates so I'll say goodbye for now.'

There was a buzz on the phone as the call ended and Victor slowly replaced the receiver. Then he sat back in his chair and sighed deeply. He knew it was the beginning of the end.

'Congratulations,' said Cedric Bullock. He raised a glass of whisky towards Edna and settled back in his armchair.

Edna was staring out of the window, a triumphant look on her face. 'And so it begins,' she said with a smile. 'Let's celebrate tonight over a meal. My treat.'

'Of course,' said Cedric. 'What did Edward have to say?'

'He bumbled on like he usually does and mentioned it wasn't unanimous, which is disappointing, but clearly the majority saw sense.'

'So what's next?'

'Good question. First of all I need to get that stupid Stratton girl off my back. I heard on the grapevine that the next issue of the *Echo* could be even more revealing than January's.

It might be possible to arrange to fail her. I'm sure there'll be something in her coursework that will work in my favour. Anyway, she's my first priority.'

Cedric put down his drink. 'But Grammaticus rates her highly.'

'That's of no concern to me now. His views are irrelevant.'

'And what of the ponytailed professor? Have you plans for him?'

Edna raised her tumbler and swirled the amber liquid round and round. 'Of course I have but for now I'm going to let him stew. He'll know something will be coming his way but I'll make him wait. Revenge served cold is so much sweeter.' Once again she stared out of the window at the busy scene below her and quaffed the last of her whisky.

Richard Head was in his study when he received an unexpected telephone call.

'Hello again, Richard. It's Felicity Capstick ringing from Cambridgeshire. How are you?'

'Fine, thank you. This is a nice surprise.'

'I'm ringing because I was at my astronomy club last night and we were discussing next week's conjunction of the moon and Saturn.'

'Oh, yes – exciting, isn't it? I'm looking forward to it. Very early in the morning on Wednesday, the twenty-fourth. It's in my diary.'

'Well, I thought of you and our shared interest in the stars and planets and, of course, your kindness when you showed me around Eboracum.'

'It was a pleasure, Felicity.'

'So will you be up early to observe it? Apparently, the moon and Saturn will share the same ascension.'

Richard naturally knew all this. 'Yes, it will be four degrees, twenty-one minutes to the south of Saturn and the moon will be nineteen days old.'

'Correct,' affirmed Felicity. 'That was my reckoning as well.'

'Technically a close approach of two objects like this is called—'

'An appulse,' interjected Felicity.

'Quite right!' exclaimed Richard, recognizing a fellow astrophile. He heard laughter down the line.

'Richard, I was just thinking that I'm visiting my sister in Malton the day before. We could watch this appulse together.'

'That would be wonderful.'

'In that case I'll meet you in York.'

'Yes, just ring and we can arrange it.'

'Perfect,' said Felicity. 'I'm so pleased. It was lovely to meet someone like oneself with a shared hobby.'

'Definitely,' said Richard. 'By the way, I'm sorry the result of the interview didn't go your way.'

'I'm not!'

'Really?'

'Yes, there were a few things not to my liking. I'll tell you when I see you.'

'I shall look forward to it,' said Richard.

The call ended and the excited scientist wrote himself a reminder to buy a tin of Brasso for his telescope.

*

It was mid-afternoon and Tom had returned to his study after dropping off Owen at the hospital; Owen had promised he would ring when there was news. Tom was marking Ellie MacBride's outstanding essay on Jean Piaget's stages of cognitive development when there was a knock on the door and the sombre face of Victor appeared. Tom shook his head. There was no need to ask about the result.

Victor came in and sat down in one of the armchairs. 'I've just called in on Inger and told her the news. I didn't get the job. It's gone to Edna.'

Tom put down his pen. 'I'm so sorry, Victor.' He stood up. 'Would you like a coffee?'

'Thanks. Yes, please.'

Tom switched on the kettle and found two clean mugs in the cupboard. 'So how was your interview?'

'It went well. I answered everything honestly. There were a couple of guys with a different agenda.'

'Such as?'

'Future funding. Cash before quality. I'm pretty sure Edna will have had that tied up.'

'I'm sad for you, Victor, and for the faculty. They've missed a great opportunity.'

'Perhaps,' said Victor. The disappointment was clearly hurting.

'So what will happen next?'

'Edna will fashion the faculty in her style.'

'And will you be here to see it?'

'I doubt it. I'm just waiting for the axe to fall.'

'Won't you stay on? All your colleagues would see you as the voice of reason in the future.' Tom spooned in the coffee and poured the boiling water.

'That may be out of my hands. It's the students I feel sorry for. Eboracum won't be the same again.'

'And the sword of Damocles is waiting for me,' said Tom.

Victor stared into his coffee. 'You're not alone. There will be many staff changes.'

'Have you told Pat?'

Victor gave a wry smile. 'Ever the optimist as usual. He reminded me that when life gives you lemons, make lemonade. Typical of him. Even so, he was sad. He knew how much it meant to me.'

'He's a good man,' said Tom.

They chatted for a few more minutes and then Victor left to pass on the news to Zeb and Richard.

At 9.30 p.m. that night Tom was at home in his cottage, drinking a mug of tea and reflecting on the day. He wondered how Victor was feeling and was pleased that Pat would be there for him. On the television the *Panorama* programme on BBC One had begun with a discussion about the aftermath of the Hillsborough disaster and its effect on football in the future. It was then that the telephone rang. It was Owen.

'Hi, Tom. Guess what . . . I'm a dad!' yelled the excited Welshman.

'Brilliant! How's Sue?'

'Tired but fine. Resting now with our baby son. Eight and a half pounds. Healthy and drinking milk for Wales.'

'Great news, Owen. Congratulations!'

'I'm leaving the hospital now with her mum and dad. He said there's just time to wet the baby's head on the way home. We could knock on your door and call in the pub on your high street.'

'OK. I'll be ready.'

The call ended and Tom realized that Owen had been too excited to ask about the result of the interview. That could wait at least until Owen had decided which position his son would play on the Welsh rugby team.

He switched off the television, sat down to finish his tea and wondered what the future would bring.

Chapter Seventeen

The Quality of Mercy

It was a perfect morning as Tom drove into York. A pink dawn had bathed the land with warmth and light. A riot of bramble, like nature's barbed wire, scoured the hedgerows and butterflies hovered above the buddleia bushes. The bright foam of cuckoo spit in the lavender leaves sparkled in the sunlight and the drone of bees filled the air. As he pulled into the university car park, Zeb's students were unloading props and staging from an old wagon for the dress rehearsal of *The Merchant of Venice.* There was activity everywhere. It was Friday, 9 June, and a day of drama and disaster was about to unfold.

Tom walked into the quad where Ellie MacBride gave him a wave. She was in conversation with Sascha Dupont, a tall, graceful young woman who was to play the part of Portia. Ellie was clutching her prompt script and they were on their way to the refectory and a welcome coffee and croissant.

'Morning, Tom,' she called out. 'Just talking through the "quality of mercy" speech with Sascha. You'll love the play.'

'Yes, looking forward to it.' Tom turned to Sascha. 'Good luck, Sascha. How are you feeling?'

'A little nervous.' With a Swiss mother and a French father, she had a distinct French accent. 'It's my first big part and I've got an agent from Manchester coming to see my performance.'

'That's great, isn't it, Tom?' said Ellie.

'Really special. You must be good.' It also occurred to Tom that Sascha was the perfect choice to play the rich, intelligent and quick witted Portia.

'Catch you later, Tom,' said Ellie and they strode off, full of animation and life.

Tom watched them walk away and was aware they were both outstanding students who were likely to have contrasting destinies.

Meanwhile, in the science block Portia's famous quote 'The quality of mercy is not strained; it droppeth as the gentle rain from heaven' was far from Richard's mind. He was more concerned with 'acid rain'. Richard was discussing World Environmental Day with a group of his fourth-year students including Kimberly. Last week a number of them had marched through the streets of York to demonstrate their support.

Richard was determined to make a difference. 'We have to raise awareness of the destruction of the environment,' he said, 'particularly the so-called "greenhouse effect". I'm encouraged that European leaders have agreed to phase out the use of chlorofluorocarbons in products by the end of the century but we must do more.' The students nodded in agreement. After all, they would be the new custodians of the planet. 'These CFCs are damaging the world's ozone layer so we must be vigilant.' As they dispersed to progress their own dissertations Victor walked in and Richard waved in acknowledgement.

Victor sought out Kimberly and they found a quiet corner.

'How are you?' she asked. He appeared to have aged since the interviews. Over three weeks had passed since that day and now there were deep furrows on his forehead and his whole demeanour was dejected.

He sighed. 'I'm fine but it's you I'm concerned about. I've heard from some of my students that the next issue of the *Echo* will be even more controversial.'

Kimberly leaned back and folded her arms. 'They're right but I can't discuss it with you. It's best that way.'

'My concern is Edna's response. She's even more dangerous now that she's Head of Faculty. Life could be made much more difficult for you.'

Kimberly shook her head. 'I can handle that. It's her who should be worried. I've got statements now from at least a dozen overseas students. The evidence is overwhelming.'

Victor looked concerned. 'Kimberly . . . it might be wise to hold back for a while. I've tried to speak with her on a number of occasions but her responses often make little sense.'

Kimberly frowned. 'Are you saying she's unstable?'

Victor paused to gather his thoughts and glanced around to ensure no one was within earshot. 'I have to be cautious what I say. It's just that when I ask her a logical question she is evasive and she comes back at me with a cluster of meaningless non sequiturs.'

'Victor . . . I'm sorry to hear that but this is important to me and I'm determined to see it through. Dr Wallop is clearly corrupt and I mean to make it front-page news.'

Victor stared at this determined young woman. Like Margaret Thatcher back in 1980, here was another lady who was *not for turning*. 'When do you go to press?'

'Next week.'

'You do realize she will do her utmost to stop it?'

'Perhaps.' There was steel in her words. 'It will make no difference.'

Victor turned to leave. 'Are you going to the performance tonight?'

'No, I'll probably see it tomorrow evening with Gio. I'll be working on the front-page article for the rest of the day.'

'Take care,' said Victor and he left quietly.

Owen was sitting at his desk when Tom walked into their study.

'Hi, stranger,' said Tom.

Owen was working his way through a huge pile of students' files. 'Trying to catch up,' he said and shook his head. 'I'm up umpteen times in the night with Gareth. I'm knackered.'

By all accounts Gareth William Llewellyn was proving to be a handful.

'What about Sue?'

'She seems to be taking it in her stride. Life is definitely different with a baby. Feeding, sleeping, nappies, long walks with the pram. *War and Peace* updates over the phone to her mother.'

'So how is he?'

'Closing in on one month old. Healthy. I've introduced him to his new rugby ball soft toy.'

'No surprise there then.'

'By the way, there was a call for you a few minutes ago.'

'Yes?'

'It was the Wallop. Short and not very sweet. Wants a word.'

'What about?'

'It won't be anything good, that's for certain.'

'When does she want to see me?'

'Soon . . . but make her wait.'

'I'll go at lunchtime. What about you? Are you going to Zeb's play?'

'Love to but can't. Promised Sue I would get straight back. I've spoken to Zeb. She understands. If Sue's up to it we may see the earlier performance tomorrow but nothing's certain.'

'OK. Maybe catch you later. If not, have a good weekend and get some sleep.'

Tom rummaged through the filing cabinet, found his lecture notes on Jane Austen and headed out for the English block.

Cedric Bullock had arrived in Edna's study and sat heavily in one of the armchairs. 'Have you heard?' he said. 'Stratton is going to publish early.'

'What?' Edna looked apoplectic. 'When is she planning?'

'Next week. The word is she's going to point the finger, maybe in your direction.'

Edna stood up and stared out of the window. Below her students were erecting the stage. 'Stupid and misguided,' she muttered.

'What can we do?' asked Cedric. His face was flushed with the exertion of climbing the stairs.

'There are ways in the long term but for now I need to stop publication. Then I can deal with her personally. I know she burns the midnight oil in that study of hers. I may have to pay her a visit. In the meantime, keep your eyes and ears open.'

'What about Victor?'

Edna gave a self-satisfied smile. 'I'm keeping him dangling on a string. The end is near for him.'

'Any more students in the pipeline?'

Edna grinned and rubbed her hands together. 'Four from America coming in next week. So things are looking up.'

'Except for Stratton,' said Cedric.

Edna gave him an icy stare. 'As I said, she will be dealt with.'

At morning break, Tom picked his way through groups of students in the quad. They were working hard on final preparations for the play. Staging blocks were in place along with curtains and some minimalist scenery. It was clear the members of the audience would have to use their imagination. Inger was drinking coffee with Zeb and Richard when Tom walked into the common room.

'Hi, everybody,' said Tom. 'Can I do anything to help?'

'I've got the sound and lights sorted,' said Richard, 'but you can come and see what I've done.'

'Thanks. I shall.' He looked at Zeb. 'What about the staging, Zeb? They looked busy in the quad but I could help. I have a free session now.'

Zeb smiled. 'Thanks, Tom.'

Tom stared with affection at this determined red-haired anarchist. 'You're one of a kind, Zeb. Eboracum wouldn't be the same without you.'

Zeb squeezed his arm. 'And what about you, handsome? Are you going back to your school in Harrogate?'

Tom shook his head. 'Maybe. Not sure. I've been looking at jobs in the *Times Ed*.'

'Good luck, Tom,' said Inger quietly. 'You'll be missed.'

Tom looked into her blue eyes. 'Likewise,' he said softly.

'By the way,' said Richard, 'have you heard? Victor's getting a party together to go to the cinema next week. I think he's trying to raise our spirits. It's the new Bond film.'

'Which one is it?' asked Inger.

'*Licence to Kill* with Timothy Dalton,' said Richard.

'Lovely actor but I preferred Sean Connery,' said Zeb. 'A heavy-smoking tough guy. Roger Moore was a bit too suave for me.'

'They seem to be turning one out almost every year,' said Inger.

'This is the sixteenth,' said Richard with absolute authority. 'I've reserved two tickets for me and Felicity,' he added proudly.

'She seems to be a regular visitor these days,' said Zeb coyly.

'Yes, we get on well but I think it might be my telescope she's interested in.'

'I'm sure it is,' said Zeb.

'Was she disappointed she didn't get the job?' asked Inger.

'Not at all,' said Richard. 'In fact, she said she would probably have turned it down.'

'Really?' said Tom. 'Why would she do that?'

'I'm not sure but she decided to go for another post in Sheffield.'

'You must ask her why,' said Zeb, 'and let us know.'

'I shall,' said Richard. 'I also heard from Victor that Kimberly Stratton is preparing a *reveal-all* article in the next issue of the *Eboracum Echo.*'

'I wonder if she'll name Edna directly this time,' said Zeb.

Inger looked concerned. 'It will be a brave move if she does.'

Richard stood up. 'So what about the cinema?'

'We must go,' said Inger, 'if only to support Victor.'

'And who can blame him with that bitch supposedly running the faculty,' said Zeb in disgust.

'*Supposedly running?*' queried Richard.

'Yes,' said Zeb. 'She couldn't even run a bath. She struts around like a turkey cock issuing orders in that affected American business speak. Anyway, I've got some friends from Leeds University coming to see the play. There's a vacancy there for Drama. I'm giving it serious consideration.' There was silence as everyone took in the import of this statement. Zeb looked through the window. Students were sitting on the grass and studying well-thumbed scripts. 'Must go,' she said with a grin. 'I promised to cheer up Shylock.'

When lunchtime came Tom decided to report to Edna. He climbed the metal staircase to Alcuin corridor and stood outside her door. It had a new prominent brass plaque that read:

Dr E. J. Wallop
Head of Faculty of Education

He knocked on the door, waited for the perfunctory 'Come' and walked in.

Edna was sitting behind her desk smoking a cigarette and staring down at a document. She picked it up and waved it triumphantly. 'I'll keep this short. Your contract will not be renewed. You had your chance and blew it.'

Tom took his time before replying, glancing around the untidy, smoke-filled room. 'It comes as no surprise.'

'I guessed as much,' said Edna with as much sarcasm as she could muster and vigorously stubbed out her cigarette.

Tom walked towards the desk and looked down at Edna. 'In any case, working *for* you and *with* you would be impossible for me. I'll make a career elsewhere.'

She smiled. 'Don't be too confident. After the reference I'll be giving you, employment might be hard to find.'

'Fortunately, any reference from you won't be worth the paper it's written on, which is why you will not be called upon to provide one,' said Tom defiantly.

'Your naivety even now astounds me. Power lies in who you know and you know nobody.'

'Perhaps so,' responded Tom. He paused while he considered a suitable riposte. 'Which is why we're all looking forward to the next issue of the *Echo*.'

Edna gave him a sharp look. 'Why do you say that? The Stratton woman is a muckraker, always looking for subversive stories.'

Tom paused and smiled. 'I was thinking more of *The Merchant of Venice*. There's sure to be a review of the play.'

Edna frowned and looked puzzled for a moment. 'I suppose there will.'

'Will you be watching it?'

'If I choose to, but I have work to do.'

'If you do, take note of Shylock. You have many of his characteristics.'

Edna hooked her thumb towards the door. 'Out . . . now!'

Richard had met Felicity Capstick at York railway station and taken her to the Cross Keys pub on Goodramgate. They were enjoying ham-and-tomato sandwiches, a pot of tea and each other's company.

'I'm looking forward to the play,' she said. She had bought a new dress and had highlights in hair. Sadly, Richard had not noticed.

'I've set up quadrophonic sound,' he said enthusiastically. 'Four speakers on stands front and back of the stage.'

Felicity nodded knowingly. 'So you've utilized an amplifier with four discrete audio channels.'

'And doubled the standard two channels for stereo.' Richard loved talking high technology with his new friend.

They sipped their tea and relaxed together.

'I've got an interview for Sheffield,' said Felicity. 'It looks promising.'

'As I said before, I was sad you didn't get the Head of Faculty post.'

She gave a wry smile. 'It wasn't to be, Richard, and I doubt I would have taken it up. In fact, you ought to think hard about your own position at Eboracum. There are some dreadful rumours flying around that could have criminal implications.'

'Oh dear. That sounds serious.'

'It is, and Dr Wallop's name keeps cropping up.'

'But how does that affect me?'

'By association, Richard. Your faculty could be tarnished.

There are significant amounts of money involved. Overseas students paying for places at our universities. So take my advice. Distance yourself from Dr Wallop. The word is she is directly involved.'

Richard sat back in his seat. 'I see. Thank you for being so frank. It would break my heart to leave here. I've spent years building up the Science courses.'

Felicity leaned forward and rested her hand lightly on his. 'I know that, Richard, and that is why I hold you in the highest regard.'

Richard smiled. 'Shall we have another pot of tea?'

'Let's,' said Felicity with a smile.

It was six o'clock and Tom and Victor found seats in the back row and stared up at the brightly lit stage where Zeb was walking towards the microphone. 'This takes me back,' said Victor. 'I saw Peter O'Toole's Shylock in Stratford back in 1960. He was a force of nature.'

Tom glanced down at his programme. Alexander Poupart, a brilliant young actor from Middlesbrough in his final year at Eboracum, had been given the key role of Shylock, a Venetian Jewish moneylender. He was the play's principal antagonist and his defeat and conversion to Christianity would be the climax of the play. Tom settled back to watch the familiar tale that formed the major conflict, with Shylock seeking revenge on Antonio for lending money without interest.

'Here she is,' said Victor. Zeb looked amazing in a flowing tie-dyed kaftan. She oozed confidence as she surveyed her audience. 'Welcome, everybody, to this evening's dress rehearsal of *The Merchant of Venice* and thank you for your support. We have two performances tomorrow at two p.m. and seven p.m. As usual with our Shakespeare productions, this is an abbreviated version but I know you will enjoy it. The students from my department have worked tirelessly towards today and I'm so pleased we have representatives here today from the local press, York Theatre Royal, Yorkshire Television and a number of agents to assess our talent.' She walked to the side of the stage and gestured towards the wings. 'So sit back and enjoy as the world's greatest playwright transports us to a street in Venice where the merchant, Antonio, is feeling sad.'

In the back row Tom leaned over to Victor and whispered, 'We know how he feels.' Victor smiled gently. At least for a couple of hours an evening of peace awaited him as inspirational young actors displayed their special gifts. Then Inger's string quartet, comprising two violins, a viola and a cello, began to play. It set the scene beautifully. Tom could see her blonde hair in the distance and she was conducting with perfect tempo. They were in a makeshift orchestra pit to the side of the stage and Inger was standing close to her brother and concentrating hard.

Gradually the four plots of the play emerged bound by the threads of love, generosity, friendship and the wise use of money. It was a familiar story but the audience was gripped by the intensity of the action and the excellence of the protagonists.

There was a brief interval and while Tom stretched his legs Victor ambled away to collect two drinks from the makeshift bar. Behind him the reporter from the *York Post* was making notes and on the far side of the quad the tall figure of Gio was walking quickly towards the staging and then disappeared behind the scenery. A few minutes later a warning bell rang and Victor returned with two plastic cups of wine. Everyone settled once again and the play resumed.

When the character Launcelot stated 'truth will come to light' Victor gave a grim smile and wondered if it would come to pass. Tom was intrigued with the high quality of the acting and all was going well until something unusual occurred.

Sascha Dupont as Portia had just uttered the famous lines 'The quality of mercy is not strained; it droppeth as the gentle rain from heaven upon the place beneath' when there was a disturbance. Sascha glanced anxiously to the side of the stage, aware of a distant noise, and paused as she delivered one of Shakespeare's most famous lines.

'It is twice blest,' prompted Ellie MacBride from the wings. Immediately Sascha was back in role and the play proceeded smoothly. The brief interruption was soon forgotten and when the final curtain came down the cast earned a richly deserved standing ovation.

In the balmy light of a midsummer evening, the cast and audience slowly made their way to the common room that had been reserved for the after-show party. Zeb was surrounded by a crowd of well-wishers congratulating her on the success of the performance. Sascha was deep in conversation with a man in a linen suit and expensive brogues. He was inviting her for an audition in London.

Ellie MacBride had sought out Tom. 'So, what did you think?'

'Superb. A wonderful performance. I enjoyed Shylock, a perfect villain.'

'And Portia?'

'The same. She has a great future.' They looked across at the animated young actress. 'From the look of the agent, that future is starting now.'

'I enjoyed being the prompt.' Ellie gave Tom a mischievous grin. 'I may even know this play better than you now.'

'You probably do. By the way, what happened during her "quality of mercy" speech?'

'Don't know. There was a shout offstage from inside the building somewhere. I don't think many noticed.'

Suddenly Shylock appeared out of costume and without make-up. 'Come on, Ellie, there's a free bar,' and he whisked her away towards the drinks table.

Victor had made his way towards Zeb and was congratulating her when Gio suddenly appeared at his side. 'Excuse me, Victor, but I was wondering if you had seen Kimberly? She's not in her room. I thought she might have called in here.'

Victor scanned the crowd. 'Sorry, not seen her.'

Gio looked puzzled. 'I spoke with her around six and she said she was busy with the *Echo*. To be honest she sounded distracted.'

'I'm sure she'll turn up.'

Tom was standing with Inger by the open door that led to the quad. They were enjoying a glass of wine and the success of the evening. 'Great music,' said Tom. 'Really impressive quartet.'

'We're lucky to have such talent in the department.'

'And a tutor who encourages it to its full potential.'

She smiled. 'That's kind, Tom. I love my work, particularly on an evening such as this.'

Tom looked over his glass and admired her. She was wearing a figure-hugging black dress with a blue silk scarf that matched her eyes.

It was then he spotted a swift movement on the other side of the quad. He caught a fleeting glimpse of a short, stocky cleaner in a green overalls running towards reception as if she was being chased by the hounds of hell.

'Wonder what that's about?' said Tom.

Minutes later there was the sound of sirens and an ambulance arrived outside reception. The common room was still full and the noisy celebrations continued.

Tom was curious. 'It looks as though there's been an accident.'

Inger looked concerned. 'I do hope it's not serious.'

At that moment a police siren was heard. A policeman and a policewoman had arrived and they could be seen talking to the cleaner.

'I think I had better have a word with Victor,' said Tom.

He pushed his way through the crowd and extracted Victor and led him to the doorway of the common room. On the other side of the quad bright lights were now visible.

'There seems to be some sort of incident, Victor,' said Tom.

Inger pointed towards Alcuin. 'And now there's a policeman standing outside the door.'

Victor took in the scene. 'Let's check with Perkins.'

Tom and Inger followed him into reception.

'What's happening, Perkins?' asked Victor.

'Good evening, Professor. There's been an accident. Don't know the details. We've got two new temp cleaners, Alvita and Delyse, doing night work. Alvita suddenly ran in to say there was a woman lying at the foot of the stairs in Alcuin. Delyse had stayed with whoever it was. I rang for an ambulance. Then the police turned up. They asked me who was in charge. I told them it was the Vice Chancellor. They said I needed to get him out of the after-show party. They're speaking to him now.'

Tom spotted Edward on the other side of the quad; he was holding his head and looking distraught. Then two men in ordinary clothes – plain-clothes detectives? – arrived and walked swiftly towards the police officers speaking with Edward. The situation was escalating rapidly.

Inger said, 'Perkins, do we know who the woman is?'

'Sorry, no. Only that Alvita said she wasn't moving.'

'My God!' said Victor. He stared out into the night. 'Where's Kimberly?'

Chapter Eighteen

End of Days

'Victor told me they're using my music room as an incident room,' said Inger. 'He rang me first thing this morning.'

Tom, Zeb and Inger were in the university car park and there seemed to be police cars everywhere. It was the morning after the play and a drama was unfolding before them.

'He rang me as well,' said Tom. 'Told me to come in straight away and meet up in the common room. The police are interviewing anyone who was around at the time.'

Zeb lit up a cigarette. 'I spoke to Victor last night. We've postponed today's production. No choice, of course.' She turned her head and blew a plume of smoke towards the university and stared into the distance. 'And we still don't know who the woman is.'

They walked slowly into reception where Perkins was behind the counter. His eyes were red and he looked as if he hadn't slept.

'Morning, Perkins,' said Tom.

'Good morning, all,' he said. 'Grim times.' He nodded

towards the quad. 'Be careful how you go. Police everywhere. They've sealed off Tuke.'

'Any news?' asked Inger.

'Well, sadly, it's a fatality,' said Perkins with a deep sigh. 'The poor woman was removed in an ambulance after the police had done their checks but I've no idea who it might be.'

'What about the women who found her?' asked Zeb.

Perkins shook his head. 'Haven't seen Alvita and Delyse since they were taken home last night in a police car.'

'Who are they?' asked Inger.

'Our new temp cleaners,' said Perkins. 'Sisters from Barbados. Lovely ladies. They do the evening shift. Must have been a terrible shock for them.'

'So what happened exactly?' asked Zeb.

Perkins pondered for a moment, gathering his thoughts. 'Well, I stayed on duty while the play was going on. Then Alvita suddenly appeared and shouted to ring for an ambulance. Said there was a woman collapsed at the foot of the stairs in Tuke and it looked serious – she wasn't moving. Then Alvita ran back to her sister who had stayed with the woman. A few minutes later the ambulance arrived. Then the police turned up and I pointed them towards the quad.'

'There're a lot of female students on that corridor,' said Inger, concern on her face. 'Could be any one of them.'

'I know,' said Perkins. 'It's heartbreaking. They may have informed the parents by now. Anyway, everyone's gathering in the common room. I've been asked to direct you there. The police will be making an announcement.'

'Thanks,' said Zeb and the three of them walked into the quad.

*

Before them was an incongruous sight. The stage was still there and police tape stretched across the scenery to the door that led to Tuke corridor. A policeman was guarding the doorway and another was talking to two students under the far archway that led to the refectory. The Vice Chancellor, looking pale and drawn, was standing on the lawn and talking to two men in plain clothes; one of them was scribbling in a notebook.

When they walked into the common room, they found staff and students huddled in groups while the catering staff served coffee in silence. A young policewoman approached them. She was holding a clipboard. 'Could you give me your names, please?' she asked and then inserted three neat ticks. 'We may have a few questions for you. If you could remain in here until you are called we should be grateful.' She was polite but firm.

'Can you tell us who the student is?' asked Inger. 'All we know is that there has been a serious incident.'

The policewoman shook her head. 'Sorry, I've no information. Just take a seat for now.'

They walked to the serving counter, collected coffee and looked around. There was no sign of Victor.

Ten minutes later the policewoman with the clipboard approached them. 'Which one of you is Dr Frith?'

'I'm here,' said Tom.

'Could you come with me, please? Just routine questions.'

'Of course.' He stood up and followed her into the music room. Tom looked around. The room was very different to normal and you could cut the tension with a knife. Two men and two women sat behind tables interviewing staff and students and making notes. A balding, heavy-set man in a well-worn suit stood up to greet him.

'I'm Inspector Greybourne.' He gestured towards the chair opposite. 'Take a seat, please.'

Tom sat down slowly.

The inspector opened his notebook. 'You're Dr Thomas Frith.'

'Yes,' said Tom simply.

'Could you tell me your movements yesterday evening?'

'I was watching the play.'

'Can anyone verify that?'

'I was sitting next to Professor Grammaticus. There were people around me who could confirm I was there.'

'Did you leave the performance at any time?'

'No. I was in the audience from beginning to end.'

There was a pause while the inspector wrote a few brief notes.

'I'm told there was an interruption to the play. Do you recall that?'

Tom thought hard. 'I remember Ellie MacBride having to prompt at one point. She's one of my students. I think Portia was distracted.'

'Portia?'

'Sascha Dupont. She was playing the part of Portia. I remember she paused for a moment, which was unusual for her. Clearly something had disturbed her but I don't know what.'

'Did you notice anything off-set that might have distracted her?'

'No, I was looking at the stage.'

Once more Greybourne glanced down at his notebook. 'You share a study with Owen Llewellyn.'

'Yes.'

'Where was Mr Llewellyn last night?'

'At home. His wife has just had a baby.'

'When did you last see Mr Llewellyn?'

'Yesterday, briefly.'

The inspector stared at Tom for a long time. Eventually he broke the silence. 'Dr Frith . . . would you say you are an angry man?'

Tom looked surprised. 'No. Why do you ask?'

'You were overheard yesterday lunchtime having an altercation with Dr Wallop. There were raised voices. What was that about?'

'I'm on a temporary lectureship. Dr Wallop made it clear she was not going to extend my contract. She told me so in no uncertain terms.'

'So you were angry.'

'No, just disappointed. I've enjoyed working here.'

Suddenly the inspector changed tack. 'What can you tell me about Kimberly Stratton, the editor of the university newspaper?'

'My understanding is she is an excellent student and an outstanding scientist.'

'Would you describe her as rebellious?'

'She's certainly forthright and determined but perhaps you ought to ask her.'

Again Greybourne scribbled notes.

'Finally, did Professor Grammaticus leave his seat during the performance?'

'No . . . I don't recall . . . apart from buying a couple of drinks during the interval.'

'How long was the interval?'

'Fifteen minutes at most.'

'And how long was Professor Grammaticus away from you?'

'Five . . . maybe ten minutes.'

The inspector stood up. 'Excuse me,' he said and walked to the other side of the room and spoke with a colleague.

Tom looked around. It felt like a surreal experience. He saw Sascha Dupont enter with the young policewoman and sit down opposite an intense man in a grey suit. Inspector Greybourne had a quiet word with him and then returned. 'Thank you, Dr Frith. Please could you wait in the common room in case we need to speak with you again?'

As Tom was leaving he caught sight of Victor in the far corner of the room behind a display screen. He had his head in his hands. The Vice Chancellor was sitting beside him and staring at the wall.

'Miss Dupont, thank you for coming in. Just a few routine questions,' said Inspector Greybourne.

Sascha looked nervous. Last night had been wonderful with glowing praise from the agent who had come to see her performance. Now, this morning, everything was different. 'Yes,' she replied quietly.

'I understand you are a Drama student.'

'That's right, in my final year.'

'And you were in the play last night.'

'Yes, I played the part of Portia.'

'During the play were you aware of a disturbance off-stage?'

'Yes, but only for a moment.'

'Can you describe it?'

'It was a shout. The prompt thought I had forgotten my lines but I hadn't.'

'I see.'

'An agent who had come to see me was in the audience so I wanted to do well.'

The inspector studied the young woman for a long moment. 'Could the noise you heard have been a woman's cry?'

'Maybe, but I was concentrating on my performance so I shut it out immediately.'

'You live in the student accommodation on Tuke corridor. Is that correct?'

'Yes.'

'What is it like up there?'

'OK, I suppose. A bit worn . . . Furniture and floor coverings are not brilliant.'

'Can anyone get into that area?'

'Just us students. There's a locked door between Tuke corridor and Alcuin where the tutors are. So we don't go there.'

'Who has a key?'

'Perkins the porter, I guess, and probably Charlie the caretaker.'

'Anyone else?'

'I don't know.'

'Your room is next door to Kimberly Stratton.'

'Yes, Kimberly is in the first room next to the fire escape and I'm in Room Two.'

'The fire escape?'

'Yes, the metal staircase. We call it the fire escape. It's never used. Don't need to. There's a wide staircase that leads from the ground floor to Tuke and Benedict corridors on the top floor.'

The inspector paused and made a note. Then he looked directly at Sascha. 'What can you tell me about the relationship between Kimberly and Dr Wallop?'

'Relationship? There wasn't one. Dr Wallop doesn't teach Kimberly.'

'Have you ever heard them arguing?'

Again, Sascha looked puzzled. 'No, I haven't.'

The inspector pressed on. 'When did you last see Kimberly?'

Sascha paused and thought hard. 'It must have been some time before the performance. She wished me luck.'

'And where was that?'

'In the corridor outside my study.'

'At what time?'

'Not sure . . . Maybe six.'

'Where did she go then?'

'Back into her study and I came downstairs for the dress rehearsal.'

'Thank you,' said the inspector. 'No more questions for now but please stay in the common room for the time being.'

It was late morning when Inspector Greybourne entered the common room and the quiet chatter ceased.

'Good morning, everyone,' he said in a sonorous voice. 'I have an announcement to make.' There was a scraping of chairs on the woodblock floor as everyone turned to face him. His eyes scanned the room and he waited for absolute silence. 'Thank you all for your cooperation today and for your patience. It was important for us to establish a clear picture of the events of yesterday evening. I'm aware this is devastating news for all of you. Our enquiries will continue but in the interim I am now able to tell you the identity of the female in question as the family of the deceased has been informed.

'So it is with regret I have to inform you that your colleague who sustained fatal injuries is . . . Dr E. Wallop.'

There was a communal gasp followed by a stunned silence. The inspector strode purposefully from the room followed by an ashen-faced Vice Chancellor.

Zeb turned to Victor. 'My God!' she muttered. 'It's Edna!'

For the next few minutes the room was a hubbub of noise. The news had shocked everyone. Slowly the room emptied. Tom returned to Cloisters, sat down in his study and telephoned Owen with the news. Victor spoke with Perkins quietly in reception and used the telephone on the counter to contact Pat before climbing the stairs to Alcuin. In the students' common room, Zeb sought out Sascha and other members of the cast. Richard Head contacted Felicity and they agreed to meet the following day. Inger was about to find her brother to share the news.

'How are you?' asked Andreas.

'Mixed feelings,' she replied but it was for many reasons.

On Saturday evening the streets of York were bustling with theatre-goers, hen parties and locals seeking a riverside drink and companionship. Victor, Zeb, Inger and Tom had met in the Black Swan pub. After a bite to eat they sat there hunched over their drinks, each with their own thoughts.

Finally, Zeb sat back, took a sip of her gin and tonic and lit up a cigarette. She looked at their sombre faces. 'Think about it,' she said. 'Edna was universally disliked . . . but surely no one would have wanted her dead.'

For a moment no one spoke while around them there was the clink of glasses, the chatter of other drinkers and the sound of a far-off jukebox.

'What was she doing on Tuke corridor?' asked Tom.

Victor held his tankard of beer thoughtfully and shook his head. 'Well, we know she had a key for the door at the end of Alcuin and there are strong indications she had been in Kimberly's study in recent weeks.'

'Looking for incriminating evidence, no doubt,' said Zeb.

'Sadly, yes,' agreed Victor. 'We know Kimberly was closing in on Edna's nefarious dealings.'

'So . . . where was Kimberly last night?' asked Inger.

'Initially, that was a worry,' said Victor. 'It was Gio who found her. She had gone to the students' common room to work on her article. Apparently, it was too noisy in her room with the play going on outside her window.'

'A big shock for her,' said Zeb.

'For us all,' said Inger softly.

'The inspector mentioned Edna's family,' said Tom.

'Just an elder sister in Cumbria,' said Victor. 'Never met her. A bit of a recluse, by all accounts. There's no one else.'

'What's the staircase like where she was found?' asked Tom. 'I've never seen it.'

'The students call it a fire escape,' said Victor. 'It's never used. A tall steep metal stairway. All the students on that side of the building use the wide staircase that goes up from the ground floor, past the offices on the first floor and then up to Tuke and Benedict. There must be thirty students that have study bedrooms on those corridors.'

'Come on,' said Zeb insistently. 'I can't be the only one thinking this. Was it an accident or was she pushed?'

'That's what the police will be looking at now,' said Victor.

'We might be suspects,' said Zeb. 'Let's be frank. She did none of us any favours.'

'Well, I was watching the play,' said Tom, 'and Inger was conducting her string quartet.'

'And I was on the front row with Edward,' said Zeb.

Victor looked thoughtful. 'I was out of my seat for ten minutes getting drinks. So not exactly a cast-iron alibi.'

When they finally said goodnight they returned to their homes in a sombre mood. They were coming to terms with the seismic shift in their lives. It was the end of days as they had known them and ahead lay an uncertain future.

The governors had convened an emergency meeting at nine o'clock on Monday morning in the Lodge. It was the same group who had appointed Edna Wallop to be the new Head of Faculty and now she was gone.

'Edward, do we know any more?' asked Walter Penrith.

'Only that the police are still continuing their investigations.'

Walter, local landowner and wealthiest person in the room, leaned forward. 'You mean it may not have been an accident?'

'I presume they are checking all possibilities,' said Edward.

The discerning Elizabeth Glendenning looked thoughtful.

'This is a terrible moment in the history of the university so we must be sure to act wisely now. We owe it to the students. Their courses must continue smoothly.'

'Of course, Elizabeth,' said Edward and glanced at Miss Frensham, who had begun to take minutes in her speedy shorthand. 'So, regardless of the fact this is a difficult time for us, we need to make a decision regarding the Head of Faculty.'

'Well,' said Walter, 'thinking back to the interviews, Professor Grammaticus stood out as the most competent for me.'

Elizabeth nodded in agreement. 'I said at the time that the professor was the safe pair of hands for the faculty.'

Local entrepreneur John Whittingham tapped his fingertips on the table. 'You will recall we voted for Dr Wallop because she had plans to improve our income stream.'

'That's right,' said Peter Lyons, whose shoe shops were now on the high street in York, Harrogate, Leeds and Sheffield. 'Perhaps we need to think about readvertising.'

'That's a lengthy process,' said Walter.

'And we need something in place now,' said Elizabeth.

'What's your opinion, Cedric?' asked Edward.

Cedric Bullock tugged at his collar. He was red in the face and mopped his brow with a handkerchief. He looked distinctly ill at ease.

'Would you like a glass of water?' asked Edward.

He shook his head. 'I'm thinking,' he blurted out.

Edward was surprised at seeing this portly man looking so uncomfortable. He spoke softly. 'Cedric, you will recall you said that but for Dr Wallop's name being on the shortlist you would have voted for Professor Grammaticus.' He turned to Miss Frensham. 'I believe that was minuted.' Miss Frensham gave a brief nod of acknowledgement.

'So I presume that is still the case,' said Edward.

Cedric looked around him, almost in desperation. Edna had gone but he was still involved in her schemes. The future looked bleak. 'On reflection, Edward, I've decided to resign as a governor. It's time for me to move on.'

'Are you sure?' asked Edward. 'This is rather sudden.'

'Yes. I have business matters that are pressing.'

'In that case your decision will be noted,' said Edward. 'However, that does not alter your view that was recorded at the interview.' Before Cedric could respond, Edward pressed on. 'So I thank you for your service to Eboracum.'

Cedric heaved himself out of his chair and stood up. 'Under the circumstances, I'll leave now.'

All eyes followed him to the door.

'Well,' said Edward. 'I think we need to make a decision.'

'I agree,' said Walter. 'There is the immediate matter of the vacant Head of Faculty post. I should like to propose we offer it to Professor Grammaticus.'

'I second that motion,' said Elizabeth.

'Very well,' said Edward, 'I'll put that to the vote. Those in favour . . .'

He turned towards Miss Frensham. 'Unanimous,' he said quietly. 'Thank you. I'll arrange to meet Professor Grammaticus in person after morning lectures and I'll report back to you with his response this afternoon. Any other business?'

Elizabeth Glendenning raised her hand. 'Edward, just a thought . . . the governing body will need to be represented at the funeral. In view of Dr Wallop's personal circumstances it may well fall to us to prepare a eulogy.'

'I agree,' said Edward, 'and I'm happy to give it due cognisance.'

Thirty minutes later Miss Frensham returned from her office and placed the minutes of the meeting on Edward's desk. As always, she took a pride in being efficient and professional. No one would ever be able to read her private thoughts and know that she had heartily disliked Edna Wallop.

It was lunchtime in the Lodge; the telephone rang and Edward picked up the receiver.

'Vice Chancellor, it's Greybourne here. I have some news for you.'

'Yes, Inspector. Thank you for ringing.'

'Our initial inquiries have been completed and we are confident there is no evidence of foul play.'

'I'm relieved to hear that. So you're saying it was an accident.'

'One of Dr Wallop's shoes was found lodged in the loose carpet at the top of the stairway. It would have been dark. We're confident there was no one else involved and that she stumbled.'

'I see,' said Edward. 'The poor woman.'

'It would appear that Dr Wallop died as a result of blunt-force injuries to the head and that is likely to be confirmed at the inquest.'

'Thank you, Inspector. I appreciate your prompt response.'

'I'll be in touch again.'

*

At 12.30 p.m. the Vice Chancellor telephoned Victor and asked if he was free to call into the Lodge. Victor closed the door of his study and walked downstairs and along the winding path. It was a déjà vu moment as Edward welcomed him and asked Miss Frensham to provide a pot of coffee and a plate of biscuits. There was some small talk while she busied herself around the coffee table and the two men settled in the high-backed chairs.

'Thank you for coming in, Victor, particularly in light of these difficult circumstances.'

'It's been a dreadful time,' said Victor.

'You will appreciate the work of the faculty must continue.'

'Of course. My colleagues will always do their best for the students.'

'With that in mind I convened a meeting of the governors this morning.'

'Yes?'

'We all agreed we should offer you the post of Head of Faculty.'

'In the interim?'

'No, Victor, on a permanent contract.' There was silence for a moment, disturbed only by the ticking of the grandfather clock in the hallway. Edward stared intently at Victor's gaunt figure. 'So I have to ask . . . do you accept?'

Chapter Nineteen

New Beginnings

When Tom looked out of his bedroom window a rim of golden light appeared over the distant hills and spread across the eastern sky. It had been a stifling night and an early-morning mist covered the land like a cloak of secrets. After a quick shower he selected a clean shirt and his best suit from his sparse wardrobe. The Vice Chancellor had asked him to call into the Lodge before lectures and he wanted to make a good impression. When he stepped outside and locked the door the air was hot and humid. Wisteria clung to the walls of the cottage. He slung his satchel over his shoulder and walked to his car. As he travelled south, around him the land shimmered in the morning heat haze with a breathless promise. It was Monday, 3 July, and a day of uncertain outcomes awaited him.

He turned on the radio as he drove south. Derek Jameson was on good form with his BBC Radio 2 morning programme and trying to cheer up his listeners by playing Cliff Richard's latest hit, 'The Best Of Me'. Sadly, the news bulletins dampened the spirits in more ways than one. The Employment Secretary, Norman Fowler, was waging war on railmen and threatening to ban all strikes while in North Yorkshire thunder and lightning was forecast.

Tom parked his car, collected his satchel and turned towards the Lodge. As he walked along the winding path he heard the sibilant whisper of stirring branches above his head. He had been summoned and he wondered why. Three weeks had passed since the fatal incident. Edna's funeral had passed peacefully a week ago and apparently Edward had given an appropriate eulogy. Victor had represented the faculty; no one else had attended.

He rang the bell and Miss Frensham ushered him towards the Vice Chancellor's study. There was no offer of morning coffee so Tom guessed it would be a brief meeting. Edward was full of bonhomie as he leaned over his desk and shook Tom's hand. 'I'm so pleased you will be staying with us, Thomas.'

'Thank you, Vice Chancellor, I was delighted with the news. It was also a relief.'

'Victor was most insistent that we kept you on as a member of the faculty.'

'I'm grateful for the opportunity.'

Edward gestured towards a chair. 'Please . . . take a seat. I won't keep you long as I know you have lectures.'

Tom sat down and waited expectantly.

'I asked you to call in because Victor mentioned your positive work with students on teaching practice.'

'I've enjoyed the experience,' said Tom, wondering where this was going.

There was a letter on his desk and he glanced down at it.

'With this in mind I was hoping you would take over sole responsibility for school placements for the new academic year. I'm aware you have already been supporting this work to good effect. However, you will appreciate that now Professor Grammaticus is Head of Faculty he needs to allocate some of his previous responsibilities to his colleagues. It's a demanding role, so how do you feel about it?'

Tom paused for a moment while he assimilated the way the conversation was moving. 'I'm happy to help.'

'That's good to hear,' said Edward. 'Victor mentioned you had made good contact with our local schools. You'll gather this is vital to our work.'

'I agree. Fortunately, Professor Grammaticus has been an excellent mentor. I've learned a lot about establishing good relationships with the headteachers in our area. There's no doubt they are pleased to accept our students so long as they are well prepared and reflect the ethos of the school.'

'Our view entirely,' said Edward. 'I'm aware Victor does most of the preparation during the summer holiday.' He let the import of this statement hover in the air for a moment. 'Letters go out to schools at the outset of the autumn term.'

'Yes, that's my understanding.'

The Vice Chancellor nodded sagely and was keen to summarize. 'So can I take it you are happy to take on this added responsibility for school practice placements during the coming academic year?'

There was a brief pause while Tom realized a lot of work lay ahead. 'Yes, Vice Chancellor. I'll do my best.'

Edward sat back in his seat and nodded. 'And of course, Thomas, we must ensure this extra workload is reflected in your salary.'

Tom smiled. 'Thank you. That would be greatly appreciated.'

'In that case it's settled.' He stood up and shook Tom's hand. 'Set up a meeting this week with Victor.'

'I shall, Vice Chancellor.'

Edward watched the tall figure of the young lecturer walk away and reflected that once he had been a young man with similar energy. In those halcyon days he'd thought life was a never-ending stream of opportunities but now he was older and wiser and ageing had become a capricious companion.

Victor had arrived early and Perkins smiled in acknowledgement as he walked into reception. 'Are you settled in, Professor?'

'Yes, thank you, Perkins. I've kept much of Henry's furniture and I'm adjusting to the new space. I'm certainly not short of bookshelves.'

Following his appointment the Vice Chancellor had given Victor the opportunity to move into a larger study. He had declined to use Edna Wallop's and chose Henry Oakenshott's.

Perkins took from under the counter a large collection of envelopes bound together with thick elastic bands. 'Here's Dr Wallop's mail you requested and I've sorted it as you said. Everything marked "personal" I'll forward to her sister and all the others addressed to the faculty are here for you to deal with.'

'Many thanks,' said Victor and he set off for Alcuin.

*

Owen was packing a sports bag when Tom walked into their study. 'Morning, boyo, you're cutting it fine. Lectures in five minutes.'

'Guess what? I've got a new job.'

'Have you?'

'Yes, just seen the Vice Chancellor.'

Owen nodded. 'Hence the suit. So what did steady Eddie want?'

'I'm taking on sole responsibility for school practice placements.'

Owen gave him a friendly punch on the shoulder. 'Bloody hell! Goodbye, summer holiday . . . and the best of luck.'

'It sounds to be a big job.'

Owen smiled. 'Just see Victor. He'll put you right.'

'And I've got an increase in my salary.'

'Great. How much?'

'I didn't ask.'

Owen picked up his bag, swung it over his shoulder and headed for the door. 'Bloody gormless Yorkshireman! Come on, partner. The bell's about to go.'

It was morning break before Victor was able to sit at his desk and finally sort through the mail addressed to Edna at the faculty. Most of the communications were simply invitations to conferences and matters relating to the introduction of the National Curriculum and the impact on teacher training. But then he opened one with an American postmark and read it with a mixture of astonishment and grave concern.

Dear Dr Wallop

Eboracum University placement for Mae Belle Rivera

Thank you for getting back to me after my initial approach with regard to my daughter Mae Belle joining Eboracum as a first-year student in September 1989. I appreciate your understanding of our situation given that my daughter will not achieve the grades required.

You mentioned that in such circumstances a payment could be made directly to yourself and your colleague on the governing body who would facilitate Mae Belle's unconditional offer of a place. From our conversation, it would seem that this is routine practice. I also understand that this payment is separate to the fees payable for international students.

My daughter is very keen to study in York, given that I was educated in the UK, and, having considered the options open to her, I have decided to proceed. I will therefore transfer the figure you require and would be grateful if you could provide me with your personal bank details and those of your colleague on the governing body to enable the transaction.

Thank you for your help in this matter and I look forward to hearing from you.

Yours sincerely,
Brandon Zachary Rivera

Victor immediately reached for his telephone. 'Good morning, Miss Frensham, Grammaticus here. I need to speak with the Vice Chancellor on an urgent matter.'

'I'll put you straight through, Professor.'

A moment later he heard Edward's familiar voice. 'Yes, Victor.'

'Edward, I have a letter you need to see. It's important.'

The Vice Chancellor recognized the urgency in Victor's voice. 'Let's meet now.'

Minutes later Miss Frensham welcomed Victor and took him through to Edward's study. No words were spoken as he placed the letter in front of Edward. The Vice Chancellor read it, breathed deeply and looked across the desk. 'This is a very serious matter, Victor. Thank you for bringing it to me. It means that everything Kimberly Stratton has written in the *Echo* is vindicated.'

'I'm afraid so,' said Victor, 'and the next issue is imminent. I'll need to speak with her.'

'Yes, please do.' Edward held up the letter. 'Don't mention this, of course. I shall deal with it personally. Also, tell her I'll call a meeting with the students this week before they go down and I'll address all the issues raised in their recent petition.'

Victor nodded. 'I'll speak with her at lunchtime.'

Edward glanced down at the letter again. 'In the meantime, I should be grateful if you could write to the American gentleman and tell him that Dr Wallop has died and his daughter will not be attending Eboracum University.'

'Very well,' said Victor. 'What about the implication regarding the involvement of a member of the governing body?'

Edward's eyes blazed fury. 'I'll deal with that immediately and I shall ask Elizabeth Glendenning to investigate the situation. Any hint of malpractice must stop.'

*

After Victor had left, Edward stood up and opened the door to the adjoining office. Miss Frensham looked up expectantly from her IBM Selectric typewriter with its golf-ball head. 'Miss Frensham,' he said with a frown, 'please put me through to Cedric Bullock.'

Edward waited patiently until he heard Cedric's familiar, slightly breathless voice on the line.

'Good morning, Cedric. It's Edward here. I have an issue of concern that I need to share with you.'

'Oh, have you?'

'A letter has been forwarded to me. It's from a Mr Rivera in America. Does this mean anything to you?'

There was silence.

'Are you there, Cedric?'

'Yes, I am,' he whispered and it was clear he wished he wasn't.

'The letter I have just read includes interesting content. In fact, this could be a police matter.'

The dam burst and a torrent of words flooded down the phone line. 'It was all Edna's idea. Please believe me, Edward. It was her, God rest her soul . . . not me. I was an unwilling accomplice.'

Edward paused and his voice was solemn when he spoke. 'Before I decide how to deal with this matter, I wish to speak to you. I want you here within the hour.' He glanced at the clock. 'If you are not here in the Lodge by midday I shall pass this matter on to the police. Is that clear?'

When Victor arrived back in the quad Richard Head waved and hurried over to join him. 'Victor, you might be able to help me out,' he said anxiously.

'Of course, Richard. What is it?'

'It's the end-of-term ball.'

'Yes,' said Victor, 'in the Assembly Rooms.'

Richard frowned. 'The thing is, it's a black-tie event.'

Victor nodded. 'That's right. It always is.'

Richard looked a little crestfallen and sighed. 'It's just I've never attended before.'

'Oh dear. Of course,' said Victor. 'I'm sorry, my mind was elsewhere. So how can I help?'

'I haven't got a dinner jacket. I wondered if you might have a spare.'

Victor looked at the man before him, who was six inches shorter. 'I'm sure we can come up with something. I'll ring Pat. He has access to the costumes at the theatre. There's sure to be something appropriate there that will fit you.'

'That's wonderful. Many thanks. It struck me after Felicity said she was keen to come and started talking about long dresses that I didn't have anything to wear.'

'I'm so pleased you are going, Richard,' said Victor, recognizing the enthusiasm in his colleague's voice. 'Call into my study later this afternoon.' He walked away thinking that, as Head of Faculty, problems would arrive, literally, in all shapes and sizes.

It was 11.30 a.m. when an ashen-faced Cedric Bullock entered the Lodge. Miss Frensham ushered him into the Vice Chancellor's study but the coffee cups remained in the kitchen. She was aware this would not be a convivial meeting. She took a seat in the far corner of the room and, after opening her shorthand notebook, waited patiently. Edward was sitting behind his desk. He did not rise to greet his visitor. 'Sit down please, Cedric.'

Cedric looked over his shoulder nervously and saw Miss Frensham with pen poised.

Edward fixed Cedric with a cold stare. 'Miss Frensham will be recording minutes of this meeting, which will be brief.'

'Yes, V-Vice Chancellor,' stuttered Cedric. He bowed his head. 'I'm so sorry.'

Edward held up the letter. 'I want you to explain this clearly and concisely from the beginning.'

'It was Edna. She came up with the idea.'

'Go on,' said Edward.

'It was when she went on her American management course. She met a few businessmen. They wanted their sons and daughters to be educated at a university in the UK. Money changed hands and even larger sums were promised.'

'Explain your involvement.'

'Simply to support her on the governing body and try to persuade others to follow her lead.'

'And did you persuade others?'

'No. They made up their own minds on the issue.'

'So, think hard, Cedric. Is this a true recollection of the events relating to yourself and Dr Wallop?'

'Yes, Vice Chancellor.'

'And have you received any money?'

He shook his head. 'No, I haven't.'

'Do you have proof?'

'Yes.'

'This needs to be presented to me within forty-eight hours.'

'Yes, Vice Chancellor.'

Edward stood up. 'You will now wait in Temple Room until summoned.'

Cedric stumbled out like a beaten dog.

Edward looked at Miss Frensham. 'Two copies please.'

Minutes later Cedric had signed both copies with a trembling hand and Miss Frensham placed each in a stiff white envelope.

'Show Mr Bullock out please, Miss Frensham,' said Edward. Side by side they watched him stagger out of the Lodge and up the winding path beneath the gathering clouds.

'I presume this is confidential, Vice Chancellor?' asked Miss Frensham as she unlocked the bottom drawer of her desk.

'Yes . . . for now,' replied Edward. 'Could you call Elizabeth Glendenning, please? Once we are connected I should be grateful if you would ensure that I am not disturbed under any circumstances.'

'Of course, Vice Chancellor,' said Miss Frensham.

Edward returned to his desk and waited. Minutes later the telephone rang. 'Miss Glendenning for you, Vice Chancellor.'

'Hello, Edward, how nice to hear from you. I take it that this call relates to university business and if so how can I help?'

'As ever, Elizabeth, you are absolutely correct,' replied Edward. 'I'll get straight to it, if I may. You may recall that concerns have been raised by students, and in particular by Kimberly Stratton, the editor of the *Echo*, regarding potential financial mismanagement.'

'Yes, I do recall, although there was a suggestion – unfounded, I'm sure – that it was more to do with financial corruption than mismanagement.'

'Quite so, Elizabeth,' said Edward. 'Well, new evidence has come to light that lends weight to the argument.'

'Oh dear! Surely not, Edward.'

'Unfortunately, it appears to be so.'

'In that case, how can I help?'

'I need someone on the governing body to investigate and I can think of no one better suited than yourself to carry out the task.'

There was a pause. 'May I ask, is this likely to result in a criminal investigation?'

'I am hoping not. However, if that is the case, I shall not hesitate to pass on all that you discover to the police.'

'And does it concern our late Head of Faculty?'

Edward gave a grim smile. 'As always, Elizabeth, your deductive reasoning is second to none. So you will appreciate that a meeting to discuss this matter is important.'

'I would agree and the sooner the better by the sound of it.'

'Shall we say six thirty this evening in my office? Is that convenient for you?'

'Yes, I shall be there.'

'Thank you, Elizabeth. I'll ask Miss Frensham to be present also so that everything discussed is carefully minuted.' With that he replaced the receiver.

*

At lunchtime Victor and Kimberly met in a quaint tea room in the Shambles. Both of them shared an affection for this wonderfully preserved medieval landmark with its cobbled street and overhanging buildings. They sat next to a bay window and poured tea through a silver strainer.

Victor sipped his tea while Kimberly nibbled on a fruit scone. 'So where are we now,' he asked, 'in relation to the next issue of the *Echo*?'

'It's out tomorrow,' said Kimberly, 'but significantly revised. There's a brief obituary for Dr Wallop . . . simple and to the point.' She gave Victor a knowing look. 'Nothing contentious.'

'That's wise,' said Victor quietly.

Kimberly glanced left and right, then leaned forward. 'I've decided not to mention her directly in the main article about the links between attracting overseas students and the capacity for fraud. This has been reported in much more general terms. It's certainly created interest in other universities. The mail I've had is considerable.'

'I'm not surprised,' said Victor.

'And don't forget,' added Kimberly with a conspiratorial smile, 'I've still got the tape recording with her making threats against me.'

'Keep it safe,' said Victor. 'In the meantime, you'll be pleased to know the Vice Chancellor will be speaking with the students in the next couple of days and he'll respond to the concerns raised in the recent petition. He may well have a brief word with you privately to reassure you that all will be well in future.'

'That's good to hear,' said Kimberly. 'I'll tell Richard. I

know he was worried that Edna had suddenly taken an interest in my research for my dissertation. Have you any idea what that was all about?'

'Whatever it might have been is of no concern now,' said Victor neutrally. Privately he guessed Edna, being her vindictive self, had had some kind of sabotage in mind.

Shortly afterwards, they made their separate ways back to the university, anonymous in the bustling crowds.

Tom was on his way back from the refectory after enjoying a brief lunch break with Owen. Zeb waved from a bench in the quad as Tom walked by. She was sharing her cigarettes with two of her students who had been arrested at Stonehenge. They had been among the 250 revellers celebrating the summer solstice on 21 June and returning to Yorkshire had proved difficult. Life in the dance and drama department was always eventful.

For Tom it had been a busy morning with English Two and the poetry of Percy Bysshe Shelley before break, followed by tutorials with final-year students up to midday. Suddenly he heard a familiar voice.

'Hi, Tom.'

It was Ellie MacBride in a knee-length floral print dress. She looked sunburned and glowing with health. Her hair had grown again and was held back with a blue ribbon. Tom couldn't help but notice how beautiful she was. 'Hi, Ellie. You look happy.'

'I've just received a copy of my end-of-term assessments. They're better than I could have hoped. Did I really deserve top grades in English and Educational Studies?'

Tom smiled. 'Your essays have been excellent and your

last teaching practice was outstanding. You've definitely chosen the right career path. I'm pleased for you.'

She reached out and laid her hand on the sleeve of his suit. 'It's thanks to you, Tom. You've been a brilliant tutor. I'll be sad to see you leave.'

'There's no need. I'm staying on. Just signed a new contract.'

Ellie stared up at Tom in wonderment. 'But that's brilliant. I'm so pleased.' Her cheeks flushed red and she put her hands to her face. 'Oh, no! I'm about to make a fool of myself and burst into tears. This means so much.'

Tom decided to move the conversation on. 'So . . . what about the holiday. Any plans?'

She paused before answering. 'I'm going to Greece for a couple of weeks in August. The Parthenon, ouzo and . . .' Another pause. '. . . Ricky Broadbent.'

'Ricky? Is he a student?'

'Trying to be. He's a librarian in Barnsley. Nice guy. Well read and gentle. His wife left him last Christmas for a flash businessman from Leeds. We met in the library café. It developed from there.'

'Sounds good, Ellie. You can impress him with your knowledge of the poems of T. S. Eliot.'

'And Jane Austen and Dickens and every bloody Shakespeare tragedy you've thrown at us this year, Tom,' she added with a grin.

'I hope it's right for you,' said Tom quietly.

She shook her head and gave a wry smile. 'It will always be elusive for me, I think.'

Tom saw Victor on the other side of the quad. 'Ellie, I need to catch up with Victor.'

'Damn!' she said. 'I almost forgot. English One are having an end-of-term drink in the Guy Fawkes Inn on Friday lunchtime. Join us if you're free.'

'Thanks for the invitation. I'll do my best to be there,' and he hurried away.

'Like the suit,' she called after him.

Tom caught up with Victor as he approached the door to Alcuin. 'Excuse me, Victor. The Vice Chancellor suggested I meet with you to discuss school placements.'

Victor glanced at his watch. 'Let's have a brief word now and then we'll fix a date at the beginning of the holiday for a more in-depth discussion.'

They climbed the stairs to his study and walked in. The changes to the room were immediately obvious from the day Zeb described it as a place of books and dust. 'Hey, this is different,' said Tom appreciatively.

'Yes but I can't take all the credit. Pat has been in a couple of times with a few artefacts and fabrics. He's good at that sort of thing.' A vase of sweet peas on the coffee table provided a fragrant scent and there were new mint-green curtains at the leaded windows.

Tom sat down in one of the leather armchairs while Victor opened a filing cabinet that had already been carefully indexed and selected a folder. 'For the time being, Tom, just have a glance through this. It's a list of schools we use with names of headteachers. Simply familiarize yourself with their locations as we have to provide transport where necessary, particularly when we need to go as far afield as West Yorkshire and a few schools on the east coast. Then I suggest we meet next week and spend a morning going through the process. Would next Monday at nine be convenient?'

Summer holiday plans for Tom suddenly receded. 'Yes, that's fine.'

'In that case I'll let you get on.'

As Tom left he passed Richard climbing the stairs and heading for Victor's study.

Victor smiled as Richard tapped on the door and walked in. 'Good news, Richard,' he said with a warm smile. 'I've spoken to Pat and he said he would look for something suitable in the costume department and give it to me to pass on tomorrow so all should be fine.'

'I'm really grateful, Victor.' He looked around wistfully. 'Henry would be pleased you have his room.'

'Thank you. I feel at home here.'

Richard paused by the door. 'And while not wishing to speak ill of the dead . . . we can all look forward to a brighter future.'

As the door closed Victor reflected that his professional life had become a series of new beginnings. Then he settled down with the first draft of next year's timetable. There was a potential problem with the use of the music room and he had asked Inger to call in at 3.30 p.m.

During afternoon break Tom and Owen were in the common room enjoying a cup of strong tea and a cream slice.

'So you're back in on the first day of the holiday,' said Owen with a hint of scepticism. 'I hope they're paying you well for this.'

Tom shrugged. 'So what are your plans?'

Owen stroked his stubbly chin thoughtfully. 'Sue sorted it last night. We're going to Skegness on Saturday. Her parents have rented a caravan for a fortnight. They're coming for the first week then leaving us to enjoy ourselves with Gareth for the second. Mixed feelings, to be honest, but as they're paying for it I can't complain.'

'They will love spending time with their grandson,' said Tom, trying to lift the mood. His Welsh friend was looking a little disheartened.

'I guess so.' He stared out of the window. The pressure had been building all day and thunderheads were gathering in the far distance. 'Storm coming,' he said. 'I might make an early start for home.'

'Good idea,' said Tom.

Owen began to pack his sports bag. 'By the way, have you got yourself a dinner suit for Friday?'

'I'm hiring one from a shop in York. Collecting it late Thursday.'

Owen smiled and carried his bag to the door. 'We'll look like a couple of bloody penguins!'

Tom heard him whistling 'Land Of My Fathers' as he disappeared down the corridor. He sat at his desk to scan the file he had received from Victor and the immensity of the task became real. Outside the sultry air lay heavy on the land.

Inger and Victor were looking at Zeb's list of drama events for next year and its impact on the use of the music room. They were sitting in armchairs and drinking Victor's special blend of real coffee served from a beautiful cafetière, a gift from Pat to celebrate Victor's promotion. He studied the graceful Norwegian for a moment as she drank her coffee and guessed there was a lot on her mind apart from the timetable for the next academic year.

'I'll support as much as I can,' said Inger. 'I'll talk to Zeb and I'm sure we'll be able to come to a compromise. I've already got dates in my diary for external music examiners during the autumn term.'

'OK,' said Victor. 'At least we're all aware of the situation. It would be good to follow it up before Freshers' Week so it's in the faculty diary.'

He poured more coffee and saw Inger visibly relax. 'Are you looking forward to the ball?'

'Yes,' she said simply.

'Tom will be a good partner.'

Inger nodded but as ever kept her thoughts to herself.

Victor was effusive. 'I was so pleased he accepted a permanent position. He's taking on school practice placements for me.'

'That's good. He will be good at that.'

'He's also a hard worker. I hope he will be with us for many years to come.'

Inger smiled. 'Yes, it's good to have loyal friends.'

'I agree,' said Victor.

The clock on the mantelpiece ticked on and her silence told him there were secrets she was unwilling to share. It seemed to Victor that she was burdened by a millstone of memories.

At that moment in the far distance there was a flash of lightning followed by a boom of thunder. Heaven's marching army was about to descend on York and Victor counted quietly. 'Ten seconds,' he said. 'Light travels faster than sound. A five-second gap means it's a mile away.' He stood up and looked out of the window. 'So it's two miles away and heading for us. You'd best get home as soon as you can.'

Tom had closed his study door and was walking up the Cloisters corridor when Inger appeared. 'There's a storm coming, Inger. You need to get home quickly.'

Inger looked concerned. 'I walked in this morning. It was fine then.'

'In that case get your bag and I'll give you a lift.'

Inger gave a relieved smile. 'Thanks, Tom.' She picked up her shoulder bag and they hurried down the stairs.

As they reached the quad the stifling electric atmosphere reached its moment of release and Tom and Inger looked up. The world suddenly darkened and ragged streaks of lightning split the sky, followed immediately by the boom of thunder. Inger instinctively grabbed Tom's arm as a torrent of rain bounced on the cobbles. The storm was directly overhead and the car park was slick with running water.

'Run!' shouted Tom as they skidded towards his car. He opened the passenger door and Inger jumped in. Her hair was wet and her shoulders soaked. Tom looked like a drowned rat as he started the ignition and the car moved slowly towards Gillygate and the road out of York. The queue of traffic was almost at a standstill as they reached the Knavesmire. It was then, in the eerie darkness, that a cloudburst like an iron fist crushed the shattered earth. This was a thunderstorm of massive ferocity: above them the heavens were being ripped apart.

Inger shouted above the drumbeat of rain on the windscreen, 'We're here, Tom. Pull off the road now!' Her driveway was a river of running water as Tom parked beneath the deluge. 'Come on,' she said. 'Run for it!' They sheltered under the tiny porch as Inger searched for her key and then finally tumbled into the hallway.

They both looked at each other and laughed out loud. The relief was palpable. Tom looked at Inger. 'You need to dry your hair. You're soaked.'

'You too, Tom. There're towels in the bathroom. Help yourself. I'll get changed.'

Twenty minutes later they were sitting at her kitchen table enjoying a quick snack of beans on toast and a glass of wine as the storm passed by overhead. Then Tom relaxed with a coffee while Inger played a few tunes on her Challen baby grand piano. Finally, the sun came out again and Tom stood up to leave.

'I'm looking forward to the ball on Friday,' he said.

'So am I,' she said and kissed him lightly on the cheek.

As Tom drove home he turned on the car radio. The Bangles were singing 'Be With You' and he smiled.

Chapter Twenty

The Shape of Love

When Tom awoke on the morning of Friday, 7 July, the first soft kiss of ambient sunlight was casting shadows on his bedroom wall. He climbed out of bed and peered through the curtains at the distant glow of a new dawn. A band of golden fire had appeared above the distant hills to herald a new day and Tom smiled. He had finally made it. The academic year was about to end and tonight he would celebrate with Inger at the annual ball. A day he was destined to never forget stretched out before him. Hanging from the handle of his wardrobe drawer was his double-breasted dinner suit with its barathea jacket and silk peaked lapels. *Owen was right,* he thought . . . *We will look like bloody penguins!*

After a quick shower he dressed in jeans and a denim shirt and ate a bowl of Kellogg's Crunchy Nut cereal while listening to the radio. Jason Donovan was singing 'Sealed With A Kiss' and he thought of Inger's farewell in the doorway of her apartment after the thunderstorm. He was full of expectation as he drove out of the village. There was honeysuckle in the hedgerows and the promise of summer heat as he wound down the window. The warm breeze ruffled his hair as the miles raced by. Beyond the hedgerows the fields were alive and golden barley swayed in a random sinuous rhythm. It was as if whole fields had a life of their own, rippling with swirling shadows, and he was content as he drove into the university car park on this last day of term. He picked up his satchel and walked into reception.

'Good morning, Dr Frith,' said a smiling Perkins. 'Congratulations on completing your first year.'

'Thank you, Perkins.'

The head porter looked with affection at the young man. 'It's been eventful, hasn't it?'

'I've appreciated your support,' said Tom and opened his satchel. 'Here's a little something for you and your wife.' He placed a bottle of red wine and a small box of Dairy Milk chocolates on the counter.

Perkins beamed. 'That's very kind,' and he slipped them out of sight. 'You'll see my Pauline tonight. Professor Grammaticus always makes sure we get an invitation. She looks a picture in her new dress.'

Tom could see the pride in the head porter's face. 'I'll look forward to meeting her.'

Perkins gave an enigmatic smile. 'Word has it *your* partner is Dr Larson. She's a fine lady and a rare beauty. You're a lucky man.'

Tom leaned forward. 'We both are,' he said and they shook hands.

*

As Tom set off towards the quad Perkins watched him walk away and reflected on the past year. So much had happened. He was pleased the young man had survived and there seemed to be a new confidence about him. It was just a pity he never ironed his shirts.

At midday, after morning lectures, Tom returned to his study and emptied the books from his satchel on to his desk. He added them to the bookcase and smiled. Once the shelves had been bare and now they were full. He wandered over to the window and saw the familiar sight of groups of students in the quad. Zeb was sitting on a bench in conversation with some of her drama students. As usual, she was sharing her cigarettes. Then he stood by the mantelpiece and stared once again at the photograph of Owen's fierce rugby team. The Welshman had become a good friend and, on occasions, sharing a study with him had proved a salve to his soul.

The door opened and he walked in. 'Fancy some lunch, *anwylyd*?'

Tom looked puzzled. '*Anwylyd?*'

'It means *darling*,' said Owen with a grin. 'You were staring at my photo like a tart in a trance.'

Tom ignored the oblique innuendo. 'It's a great picture,' he said. 'Must bring back some memories.'

It was Owen's turn to stare wistfully at the image of the rugby team. 'I'll be going back to Tumble later in the holiday to see my ma and pa. Sue wants them to see Gareth. He's growing up fast.' He looked up at Tom. 'Why don't you come? You would enjoy Wales for a few days.'

'Sounds good. Let me think about it. I've not made any definite plans yet.'

Owen threw his sports bag under his desk. 'So, what about lunch? I'm starving.'

'I'm going into York. English One invited me to join them for a drink . . . so I'll catch you later.'

Tom strolled out of the university and walked under Monk Bar towards the Guy Fawkes Inn. Standing in the shadow of York Minster, he stared at this famous meeting place. The usual cluster of American tourists were outside snapping photographs. Way back in 1570 it had been the birthplace of the notorious Guido Fawkes and across the road was the church of St Michael le Belfry where he was baptized.

Ellie MacBride was the first to welcome him when he walked in. 'Thanks for coming, Tom,' she said with a warm smile.

'Let me buy a round,' he said and headed for the bar.

'Thanks,' said Ellie. 'That's very generous. It's just beer and lemonade.'

The English One students were gathered at the far end of the pub sitting around a large table. On it was a tray of sandwiches, bowls of crisps and nuts plus four almost empty jugs. Everyone looked relaxed. It had been a busy year and as Tom looked around him he felt that at last he belonged. He carried two more jugs to the table.

'Cheers, Dr Frith,' shouted two of the men and they raised their half-pint glasses in salute.

Tom waved in acknowledgement of the happy group. A long holiday awaited them and they looked relaxed. He sat on a nearby bar stool and ordered a half of bitter. Ellie came to sit beside him. She was wearing a summer dress and her hair had bleached in the sun. 'I appreciate you calling in,' she said.

'Good to be here but I can't stay long. I'm meeting Owen for lunch.'

'That's OK. Everyone knows you're busy.'

Tom smiled. 'So how are you? Any news?'

'We had a positive meeting with the Vice Chancellor yesterday.'

'That's good to hear.'

'Yes, he responded really well to our petition and put our minds at rest regarding all the rumours of possible corruption. Then he invited Kimberly to speak and congratulated her on her journalism. Dr Wallop's name wasn't mentioned, which was probably just as well.'

'I'm pleased he spoke up. I know he wants the best for Eboracum.'

Ellie looked down into her glass of lemonade. 'It's good you're staying on, Tom.'

'I'm looking forward to it. Busy times, though. I've got school placements to plan so there's a mountain of admin facing me in the holiday.'

Ellie looked concerned. 'Will you be taking a break somewhere?'

'Probably. Not decided yet. I saw some cheap package deals advertised in York. There's a gîte in the Dordogne that looked great, plus I spotted a writers' retreat in Ireland. So maybe next week I'll get round to it. What about your holiday? Greece, isn't it?'

Ellie twiddled her fingers around a lock of hair and looked thoughtful. 'Problem is, Tom, Ricky's keen on me but it's not reciprocated.'

'Ah, I see . . . I'm sorry to hear that.'

'Don't be. It's just the way it is. He's good company and

a kind man. I'm safe with him and I've always fancied going to Greece.'

'Well, enjoy it.' He picked up his glass. 'I had better circulate for a few minutes.'

She touched the sleeve of his denim shirt. 'Tom . . . I want to do a special study in my second year on Jane Austen. I wondered if you might supervise.'

'Good choice,' said Tom, 'and glad to help.'

For the next few minutes he chatted with members of the group before heading back. When he left, Ellie watched with conflicting emotions as he walked away.

Back in the refectory, Owen was sitting with Zeb and Inger when Tom joined them, a plate of quiche and salad in one hand and a fruit juice in the other.

'Hi, Tom,' said Zeb. 'All set for tonight?'

'Yes, I collected my suit. Looks OK . . . well, almost.'

'Word on the grapevine is that Zeb's got a hot date,' said Owen with a mischievous grin.

Zeb pressed a forefinger into the centre of Owen's polo shirt. 'I live life to the full, Welshman. You ought to try it some time.'

Owen shook his head. 'Wish I could but life seems to be just nappies and night feeds at present. I know Sue is looking forward to a night off.' He sighed. 'Her parents are with us again.'

'What about you, Inger?' said Zeb. 'At least you've got Tom for company. You could do worse. He might be a big tall hunk but his students say he dances like a broken deckchair.'

'Don't knock my partner,' said Owen. 'He's got some decent moves. I've seen him practising in our study.'

'Don't tease,' said Inger with a sympathetic smile. 'I'm sure Tom will be fine.'

Tom looked up from his quiche. 'I'm still here, you lot. Pick on someone else.'

The repartee continued until one by one they departed. Finally, Inger returned to the table with two herbal teas and sat opposite Tom. 'So what time shall I see you?' she asked.

'I'll pick you up at six thirty if that's OK?'

Inger gave a gentle smile. 'I'll be ready.' She glanced at her wristwatch. 'We've got a gathering now in the music room for final-year students so I'll see you later at the faculty meeting.'

'Until then,' said Tom and he watched with appreciation the poised way she swept out of the room.

It was four o'clock and everyone in the Faculty of Education had gathered in the common room. Victor was standing behind a table on which he'd placed a simple agenda. Surprisingly, Zeb was sitting alongside him. She took out her packet of cigarettes from the shoulder bag hung over the back of her chair, then thought better of it and replaced them. She sat there attentively and Tom wondered why she had chosen to sit next to Victor.

When the conversation died down Victor stood up and surveyed his audience. In spite of the hot weather he was wearing a crisp long-sleeved white shirt, a yellow bow tie and a mustard waistcoat. His new blue jeans had been neatly pressed and the toecaps of his brown leather shoes shone in the sunlight that filtered through the high arched windows.

'Thanks for your time, everyone. I won't keep you long.

I know you all need to get home before we meet up in the Assembly Rooms from seven onwards.'

Tom looked around at his colleagues and recalled his first meeting in this room when Edna Wallop had addressed the faculty. This was different. Everyone looked supportive and attentive.

'We've experienced difficult times during this past academic year,' said Victor, 'and I'm grateful to you all for rallying round when it was most needed.' He turned to his left. 'I'm happy to announce that Zeb has been offered the post of Deputy Head of Faculty and I'm delighted to say she has accepted.' There was a spontaneous cheer followed by a round of applause. Victor smiled down at Zeb. 'Having made that appointment, I'm realistic enough to know I won't be getting things all my own way.' There was laughter as Zeb pointed a warning finger. 'Even so, you know we shall do our best to enable you to teach effective courses and provide our students with high-quality experiences.'

There were appreciative smiles from everyone.

Victor glanced down at the notes in front of him. 'There are two important messages I wish to pass on. First of all, I've set up a Students' Council to join us for future meetings. There will be one student from each year group. It's important from now on to have an open forum.'

There were a few cries of 'Hear, hear'.

'Also, we shall have one new member of staff in September. Dr Rosie Tremaine from Cornwall will be joining the faculty in the English department. Rosie specializes in Victorian literature and has also written a paper on school leadership. I've no doubt she will be an asset to the faculty.'

Tom was interested. This meant he would be working alongside a new colleague.

'Finally,' said Victor, 'let's meet on Monday, the fourth of September, at ten o'clock just before Freshers' Week so we can plan for the new academic year.'

There was no other business and Owen and Richard were the first to congratulate Zeb, with Tom close behind. 'Sorry, guys,' said Zeb. 'I couldn't mention it at lunchtime.'

'Perfect,' said Richard, 'and richly deserved.'

Owen gave her a kiss on the cheek. 'Great news, sex goddess,' he whispered.

'Congratulations,' said Tom and shook her hand.

Zeb looked moved by the attention and finally reached for her cigarettes.

By six o'clock preparations were well under way for the Annual Ball. Tom was in his cottage standing in front of the hall mirror.

'Wish I'd hired a clip-on,' he muttered. It was his third attempt with his bow tie. He stared at his reflection. His stiff white shirt had a wing collar that made him look like an Edwardian bank clerk and his black trousers had a single row of braid down each leg. The jacket with its shiny lapels was tight across his broad shoulders. Finally, he rubbed the toecaps of his black shoes on his trouser legs and stood back. The image that looked back at him wasn't too bad. He had even added a more than liberal application of Old Spice aftershave – one that could have stopped a clock at ten paces. Ten minutes later he grabbed his car keys from the hall table and drove into York.

When Inger opened the door, Tom could barely speak.

She was wearing a classic off-the-shoulder black dress, her long blonde hair hung free over her shoulders and she had on only the merest hint of make-up. She looked stunning.

'Inger . . . you look wonderful.'

'Thank you. I'm afraid this is just an old dress that I save for important concerts.'

'It's simply perfect,' said Tom and they walked out to the car.

He parked in the university car park and Inger stepped out with a shawl around her shoulders. They followed other couples heading in the same direction towards the Assembly Rooms on Blake Street.

At seven o'clock they walked under the huge entrance porch beside the soaring colonnade that supported the portico of grey stone. One of the earliest neo-classical buildings in Europe, it was like walking into a Roman forum.

The doorman accepted their tickets and they stepped into the Great Assembly Room with its polished dance floor bordered by Corinthian columns. Above them hung sparkling chandeliers. Tom noticed that every head turned to look at Inger. It was like a scene from Audrey Hepburn's *Breakfast at Tiffany's*.

Owen and Sue were standing at the bar with Zeb. Owen was enjoying a pint of bitter and Sue and Zeb were sipping cocktails.

Sue smiled. 'Hi, Inger. What a lovely dress.'

'Thanks, Sue.' She glanced around. 'Excuse me while I go to the cloakroom.'

'I'll lead the way,' said Sue and they wandered off with a click of high-heeled shoes. Tom and Owen looked at them with admiring eyes.

'So,' said Owen, 'what's it to be, partner?' he asked, raising his glass.

'Same as you,' said Tom. His eyes widened. 'Hi, Zeb, you look great.'

Zeb was wearing a twenties-style dress and her flaming red hair was held in place with a black Gatsby flapper headband. She placed her cigarette in the ashtray and stretched up to adjust his bow tie. 'You're not so bad yourself, handsome.'

Owen leaned towards Tom and twitched his nostrils. 'Bloody hell! What's that you've got on? You smell like a poof's parlour.'

'It's Old Spice.'

Zeb smiled at Tom. 'Don't take any notice. Political correctness doesn't come naturally to our Welsh reprobate.'

'Bugger correctness,' retorted Owen and stood back to survey Zeb's shapely figure. 'In that frock you look as though you're on the pull in Tiger Bay.'

Zeb rolled her eyes and took another drag of her cigarette. 'Tom, I'm so glad you're staying on with us. You can work on Owen's chat-up lines. They need a little refining.' Then she looked towards the door as a tall, lithe man with dreadlocks and a white dinner suit strode towards them. Zeb stubbed out her cigarette and smoothed her dress over her hips. 'Sorry, guys, my date is here.'

'Who's that then?' asked Owen.

'Jonny Baglioni, an Italian crooner,' said Zeb. 'His singing is crap but he has the body of a Greek god.'

Tom and Owen watched her skip towards her newfound friend. 'Let's put it this way,' muttered Owen. 'She'll be doing more than *cwtch*ing on the sofa tonight, boyo.'

Just then Sue and Inger returned and the four of them sat at a nearby table. Owen ordered another cocktail and gave it to Inger. 'You look fantastic, Inger,' he said, 'and if you need a decent dance partner don't be afraid to ask.'

Owen gestured towards Victor and Pat, who were sipping cocktails at the far end of the bar, deep in conversation. 'They do that every year,' he said.

'It's a shame they can never dance together in public,' said Inger.

'That will never happen,' said Owen, shaking his head. 'Look around you. They couldn't do that at an event like this. The manager would ask them to leave.'

'A great pity,' said Inger, 'because they clearly love each other.'

'Quite right,' said Sue. 'It's obvious and, one day, when they can come here and dance together, I shall cheer.'

'I agree,' said Tom. He looked at Owen. 'Society is changing, my friend. We need to move with the times.'

Owen looked puzzled. 'Maybe . . . It's just hard to keep up.'

Sue gave Owen a kiss on the cheek. 'Come on, you Welsh dinosaur, show me some of your moves,' and she dragged him on to the dance floor as Belinda Carlisle's 'Heaven Is A Place On Earth' was put on the turntable.

Tom and Inger looked across the room at Victor and Pat. The two men both looked immaculate in their dinner suits. The only difference between them was that Pat had chosen a crimson bow tie.

Richard Head arrived arm in arm with Felicity Capstick. They made an interesting couple. Felicity was wearing a voluminous purple dress with a matching string of beads while Richard looked as if he had stepped out of an eighteenth-century French novel. Pat had secured for him from the theatre's costume store a tailcoat evening suit and a shirt with frilly cuffs. 'It's from the recent production of *Beauty and the Beast*,' Pat explained. Richard had been delighted and Felicity thought he looked very dashing.

The disc jockey was Groovy Kevin from Whitby. He had a fish stall in York market and the Faculty of Education Annual Ball was one of his regular gigs. The fact his turntable and speakers always smelled of fresh cod didn't put off the punters as he had a suitcase of vinyl records for every age group.

On arrival he had made a gentle start with Linda Ronstadt and James Ingram's 'Somewhere Out There' and a few couples stepped out on to the floor. As the evening progressed more couples joined in.

'Just watch Richard,' said Inger. 'I've never seen him looking so happy.'

The confident Felicity was guiding the hesitant Richard around the dance floor. Groovy Kevin had put on 'I Knew You Were Waiting (For Me)' sung by George Michael and Aretha Franklin, and Richard and Felicity were enjoying every word.

'Another round?' asked Tom and he set off for the bar. Zeb was sitting on a stool smoking a cigarette while her partner was talking to Victor and Pat at a nearby table. Tom ordered the drinks and turned to the flame-haired beauty beside him. 'I'm really pleased for you, Zeb. Great news about your appointment. When was the interview?'

'A couple of weeks ago. I'm guessing you were out that week on teaching practice. It was short and sweet with the

Vice Chancellor and then Victor simply rubber-stamped it. So quite quick really.'

'And who's the new tutor? I seem to recall seeing an advert a long time ago but I'm guessing the appointment's just happened.'

'Yes, confirmed yesterday. Rosie will be an ideal addition to the team. You'll get on well, I'm sure. I heard she's some kind of chess champion, a real brainbox apparently.'

'Intriguing,' said Tom. 'I'll look forward to meeting her.'

Jonny Baglioni reappeared with two large cocktails, put them down and took Zeb's hand. 'Come on, babe,' he said. 'It's our record.' Chris de Burgh was singing 'The Lady In Red' and the floor filled up with amorous couples.

It was when the hot food was being served that Victor found an opportunity to speak with Edward in confidence. Pat was chatting with Zeb and her partner about future performances at the Joseph Rowntree Theatre so Victor walked to where Edward was standing in the shadow of one of the Corinthian columns.

'Ah, Victor,' said Edward, 'a wonderful evening. Good to see all our colleagues relaxing together with such convivial spirit.'

'Quite right, Edward, without doubt a successful evening.'

Edward lowered his voice. 'You will be interested to hear of our deliberations regarding the investigation.'

'Of course. I would appreciate knowing what has happened in the interim.'

'Well, thanks to your quick action regarding the letter

from America I put Elizabeth Glendenning on to the case and, as you would expect, she left no stone unturned. There was significant evidence of money changing hands involving Dr Wallop but thankfully no other member of staff. Cedric Bullock, as you are aware, resigned immediately and has since revealed all he knew. Dr Wallop's demise clearly affected our subsequent actions as a governing body. Suffice to say it has been dealt with in such a way that there is no stain on the reputation of the university and we can move on with confidence.'

Victor was wise enough to appreciate that he had been taken into Edward's confidence and not to press for further details. 'Thank you for that reassuring news, Edward.'

'Always a pleasure, and next time you're passing the Lodge I have procured an excellent sherry.'

'An inviting prospect,' said Victor and he smiled. Trust always began with the truth and Edward was the most honest of men.

Later the lights began to dim and the dancers were gradually slowing, but as midnight approached many remained on the dance floor. Groovy Kevin was playing Whitney Houston's 'So Emotional'. When it had finished, Tom and Inger took a break and sat down. Tom watched the various couples. The contrasts were striking.

Perkins was holding his wife in his arms and Pauline was looking lovingly up into his eyes. They swayed gently from side to side, two fifty-year-olds whispering sweet nothings. In their private space no one else existed and Tom recognized the image of unconditional love.

On the far side of the hall Owen had stripped off his

jacket and undone the buttons of his waistcoat as he held Sue in a muscular grip. They moved slowly around the floor and it was clear from the way Sue rested her head on his shoulder that she loved this fiery Welshman.

Predictably, Zeb was the best dancer. Even at this late stage of the evening she moved with sensuous rhythm and there was no doubt what she had in mind for her man of the moment. She had her fingers entwined behind his neck and their bodies seemed glued together.

Richard and Felicity were clearly enjoying their evening. Felicity, once a teenage ballroom champion, was still taking a slightly wooden Richard through his paces and he was clearly loving it. The OCD scientist who only walked in straight lines had discovered a diagonal pathway across the dance floor. For Richard, love had always existed in the constellations of Alpha Centauri and Ursa Major but now it appeared he had found it on terra firma.

The scene proved to Tom that love comes in many shapes and sizes.

Finally, Groovy Kevin announced the last dance and Tom held Inger close. They moved slowly around the floor while ABBA's Agnetha Fältskog sang 'The Winner Takes It All'. In the darkness at the far side of the dance floor Victor looked at Inger and smiled.

At midnight there were gentle farewells and a heartfelt camaraderie as each couple walked away into the darkness. Tom and Inger wandered back to the university car park under the vast purple sky that spread over the Vale of York. Beneath a blizzard of stars there was silence between them as they drove slowly away.

When they pulled up outside her apartment, Inger spoke quietly. 'I've really enjoyed tonight.'

'So have I,' said Tom. 'Good to relax.'

She looked at him for a long time. 'You look happy.'

Tom sat back in his seat and stared out of the windscreen. 'I am. I feel as though I actually belong here now. There are so many good friends and colleagues around me.'

'I'm glad you're staying on.'

'So am I.' He turned to look at her as she pushed a strand of hair from her face. 'What are your plans for the holiday?'

'I travel to Norway next week to spend time with my parents. What about you?'

'Not sure. Possibly a writing break in Ireland or exploring churches in France. What's Norway like?'

Inger was suddenly animated. 'I love it. Mountains, glaciers and deep fjords. Oslo is my favourite. My city of green spaces, music and museums.'

'I've never been to Norway,' mused Tom.

'You would love it. I was brought up fishing with my father, skiing with my mother and making music with my brother. It was a wonderful childhood.'

'You were fortunate,' said Tom quietly.

Inger looked at this gentle yet eager man in his ill-fitting dinner suit. There was kindness in his eyes and goodness in his heart. 'Perhaps you should come,' she said softly.

'I'd like that,' he said.

A crescent moon lit up the distant moonstone hills and the vast sky was changing from red to purple.

'Let me walk you to the door.'

They strolled hand in hand in the twig-combing breeze towards her door and paused as they reached it. On this perfect summer evening they stood beneath stars shining down like cosmic guardians, a million watchtowers in the vast firmament.

Inger unlocked the door and paused again, waiting.

All that remained now was silence, except for the distant sounds of the night: a hooting owl and the cry of a solitary fox. They stood there hand in hand and stared up at a view painted in heaven.

Tom lowered his gaze to the blue eyes of this beautiful woman and reflected that life was complicated. There were too many loose ends and unfulfilled promises.

Then it happened. Inger gently drew him close. 'Tom . . . I don't want to be alone tonight.'

He looked down at her smiling face and took her into his arms. In that moment it was as if she had shaken the thunder from the skies. Above them the stars continued to shine like celestial fireflies and scatter the sky with stardust.

Then she leaned forward and kissed him lightly, the touch of her lips gossamer soft.

Hand in hand they walked inside.